"My name is Matthew Sloan, Jr., and I'd like to speak with you, Miss Doe. About your...inheritance."

"What can I do for you, Mr. Sloan, Jr.?" She said his name slowly, drawing out each syllable in a mocking sort of way. She was baiting him, trying to throw him off guard. C. J. Doe wanted the upper hand. As he watched her toss her hair over her shoulder and felt a warmth curl through his stomach, he had to admit she probably already *had* the upper hand.

"The Townsends would like to make an offer. As you know, they're eager to get back the land Victoria left you."

She didn't respond, just stared at him with unwavering eyes.

Matthew came right to the point. "They're willing to offer you a million dollars."

"The land is not for sale."

"A million dollars, Miss Doe. Think what you could do with all that money. You can travel, leave Coberville, make a new...

"And what...Mr. Sloan, Jr.?"

He was tal...nce words failed him.

"Money can't buy my true identity," she told him. "I would still be Christmas Jane Doe."

Dear Reader,

Have you ever thought you might be adopted? Have you ever wished you *were* adopted? Okay, I won't go there. But have you ever wondered from whom you got certain traits? I guess we all have. In my case, I don't have to do much wondering. I look like my mother and act like my father, or so I've been told. My brothers and I all have brown eyes and brown hair. We're all different but share a number of characteristics. That's being part of a family; it's in our genes.

But what if your background was a blank sheet? No parents, no one to tell you who you looked or acted like...

I thought about this when I read an article in the paper about a baby girl being found on someone's doorstep. She had no past, no identity; no one knew who she was or where she came from. I sincerely hope she was adopted by a loving family and has a wonderful life. But I couldn't stop thinking about her. How would she deal with life, especially once she was old enough to understand? How would people treat her? Would she feel driven to find her biological parents?

That's how Christmas Jane Doe came to me. You'll read C.J.'s story in the following pages—complete with a handsome hero and a twenty-first-century fairy-tale ending! After such a beginning, she deserved no less.

Hope you enjoy learning *The Truth About Jane Doe*.

Linda Warren

THE TRUTH ABOUT
JANE DOE
Linda
Warren

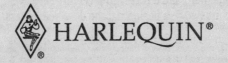

TORONTO • NEW YORK • LONDON
AMSTERDAM • PARIS • SYDNEY • HAMBURG
STOCKHOLM • ATHENS • TOKYO • MILAN • MADRID
PRAGUE • WARSAW • BUDAPEST • AUCKLAND

ISBN 0-373-70893-9

THE TRUTH ABOUT JANE DOE

Visit us at www.romance.net

Printed in U.S.A.

To the hero in my life,
my husband, Billy, my Sonny.

CHAPTER ONE

A CRISP MARCH WIND tugged at the tall stately cedars that stood guard over the Coberville cemetery. Their fanlike branches swayed with faint sighs, befitting the arrival of another funeral procession.

A long black hearse rolled through the gates. An endless stream of cars and trucks followed, lining the graveled entrance and highway. The whole town had turned out to pay its last respects to Matthew Sloan, Sr.—neighbor, friend, confidant and judge to the small Texas town for more than forty years.

Family and close friends gathered beneath a green canopy. Others huddled together on the lawn. Words of love and praise rang out and blended with the wind.

The service over, Matthew Sloan, Jr., escorted his mother to their car. Soft sobs and sad whispers rippled through the crowd. Belle Sloan trembled and Matthew's arms tightened around her. He hoped he could get her home before she broke down. His parents had been so close, and he worried that his father's death was going to be too much for her.

He helped his mother into the passenger seat. "Are you all right, Mom?"

Watery blue eyes focused blankly on him. "I'll be fine, son," she answered, her voice shaky.

She touched his face in a loving gesture. Matthew tried to smile, tried to reassure her, but smiles and words were hard to come by today. His father's passing had left a tremendous void.

On his way to the driver's side, he paused a moment to look back at the grave. People were getting into their cars, the wind catching at their clothes. Time to leave, time to get on with living. A sick feeling churned his stomach. He wondered if that was possible. Just then he noticed a solitary figure standing to one side of the cemetery—a young woman dressed completely in black. Wind whipped long black hair around her like a shield. People rushed by her. No one spoke or acknowledged her presence. She held her back straight and her head high. Her beauty touched something inside him, and for a moment Matthew couldn't drag his eyes away. Who was she? What was she doing at his father's funeral?

AFTER THE LAST CAR had driven off, Christmas Jane Doe walked to the grave and knelt in the fresh dirt, laying a single white rose among the array of flowers already there.

She folded her hands and said a silent prayer, then stared at the casket and asked, ''What did you know about my birth? Why couldn't you share your secret with me?'' She swallowed hard, trying to accept the finality. ''I guess you had your reasons. Thank you for being so nice to me. Goodbye, my friend. Rest in peace.'' Getting to her feet, she walked to her truck, face devoid of emotion.

C.J. TOOK THE CORNER on two wheels, tires screeching. The Watsons' entrance loomed ahead and she didn't slow down. She was thankful the gate was open. Dust swirled behind her like a thunderstorm, matching the anger inside her.

So many emotions fueled her anger: grief, frustration, despair. She would never see or talk to Matt Sloan again.

He would never tell her what he knew about her birth. She'd been certain that he knew *something*. Now everything seemed so hopeless. But she couldn't give up. She had to keep searching. Finding the truth was the most powerful driving force in her life.

She would uncover the secret of her birth and...and what? Would that change things? Would people treat her differently? She didn't think so.

She had been the subject of backroom gossip in Coberville ever since her mother abandoned her as an infant on Pete and Maggie Watson's doorstep on Christmas Day twenty-six years ago. No one knew who she was or where she came from. People called her simply C.J. and treated her with an indifference that always got to her, as it had today. Their behavior hurt deeply, but she would never let them see her tears.

About a hundred yards from the house, she slammed on the brakes. Dust blanketed the truck like fog. She needed a few minutes to curb her emotions before she saw Pete and Harry.

When Maggie had died years ago, Harry, Pete's older brother, had moved in with them from his place on the creek to help them deal with the loss. Harry had an intensely protective streak toward C.J. He didn't like anyone upsetting her. He was known to have a short fuse and she didn't want him fighting her battles. She could look after herself. Taking a calming breath, she counted to ten—a trick she'd learned as a kid when children taunted her.

She slowly relaxed and gazed at the small house she shared with Pete and Harry. Her favorite place. Her home, or the closest she would ever get to a real home. The cabin, built in the 1800s by Harrison Watson, Pete and Harry's great-grandfather, was made of sturdy logs and stone and stood high on a hill nestled among large oak trees.

Halfway down the hill a small lake shimmered in the welcoming rays of sunlight. Some of the best horseflesh in Texas grazed contentedly in a green coastal meadow between the house and the lake. Rosebushes with blooms of red and white climbed a barbed-wire fence that separated the house from the corral and barn to the south. Maggie's flowers. C.J. smiled wistfully. How she longed for Maggie's presence.

With a soft sigh she pressed the gas pedal. She drove to the garage and got out.

Pete Watson stepped onto the long wooden porch that covered the front of the house. The screen door banged shut behind him. He stood over six feet, his skin weathered by sun and hard work. In his seventies, he was still a striking figure, with his handlebar mustache, cowboy hat and spurs that jangled when he walked. An Old West hero, standing toe-to-toe with Wyatt Earp and Matt Dillon. That was how C.J. saw him—her hero, her protector, giving her a home when her parents—whoever they were—hadn't wanted her.

Pete and Maggie had tried to adopt her, but the authorities said they were too old to adopt a baby. They had waited and waited for Social Services to find her a permanent home. Over the years numerous couples had applied, but at the last minute each was turned down for some reason or other. The Watsons couldn't understand it, but it had all worked out for the best. She'd stayed on with the people who'd wanted her.

Noticing her black outfit, Pete frowned, his shaggy eyebrows knotted together in disapproval. One finger curled the end of his gray mustache. He always did that when he was upset.

C.J. chewed her lower lip and walked up the stone path.

Then she sat on the top step, tucked her dress beneath her and waited for the inevitable.

Pete sat down beside her, his spurs spinning with a familiar melodious sound. "You went to his funeral, didn't you?"

She swung her hair over her shoulder and turned to look at him. "Yes."

Pete removed his hat and scratched his head. He had long gray hair, thinning on top. "Girl, why do you put yourself through such misery?"

She swallowed past the constriction in her throat. "He was a friend. I had to say goodbye."

"Friend?" he bellowed, jamming his hat back on his head. "He was the Townsends' lawyer, hired to take away from you what was given out of kindness."

She raised her chin a fraction. "He wasn't trying very hard. He wanted the Townsends to dismiss the case, to accept their mother's will. That's why it's been months and nothing has been done."

He shook his head. "Matt Sloan was a good man, I'll give you that. He had a soft spot for you, no doubt about it, but he was the enemy, girl. You have to remember that."

C.J. knotted her fingers together and gazed off to the hilly landscape in the distance. Miles and miles of Cober land, but a small part of the enormous tract now belonged to her. Who would have thought that Victoria Cober Townsend, matriarch of the wealthiest family in Cober County, would leave a thousand acres and a hundred thousand dollars to Christmas Jane Doe? Victoria's family was outraged and determined to break the will at any cost. Their lawyer, Matthew Sloan, Sr., had been C.J.'s ally in a sea of enemies. Now that he was dead, she wondered what the Townsends' next move would be.

"Pete."

"Hmm?" He leaned back on his elbows, his eyes following hers to the Cober landscape.

"Why do you think she did it? I mean, really? She knew it would upset her family, but she still did it. Why?"

He didn't have to ask who she was talking about. He knew. The whole town knew the story. He shook his head again. "Got no idea. She was just a good lady always trying to help people, and like Matt Sloan, she had a soft spot for you."

"Yes," C.J. murmured, remembering the old lady's white hair and beautiful blue eyes. "Whenever she saw me, she'd always stop and chat for a few minutes. She'd ask about you and Harry, and she never failed to tell me how pretty I was becoming." C.J. gave a troubled sigh and pushed her long hair away from her face with both hands. "Do you think she knew my parents?"

Pete leaned forward and rested his elbows on his knees, his eyes thoughtful. "You know the rumors as well as I do, girl."

"That Rob or John Townsend is my father." The words left a bitter taste in her mouth. John Townsend, a retired U.S. senator, had paraded his women in front of his wife. Throughout his political career, he'd brought home his so-called secretaries and aides for lengthy weekends. Why Victoria put up with such behavior had been a mystery to everyone. Their son, Rob, was equally known for his many affairs, chasing women in five counties and several states, even after his marriage. The thought of being the offspring of one of their meaningless affairs was repugnant. Her need to know, though, was greater than any revulsion she felt toward the Townsends.

She frowned. "I can't see her being so generous to a bastard child of her husband's, but if she'd learned something about Rob and one of his girlfriends, it might be the answer to all my questions.''

''We'll never find out now, will we? She's gone.''

''That's what's so frustrating. Why couldn't she tell me what she knew?''

''Presuming she knew something.''

''Oh, Pete!'' she snapped. ''She knew *something,* or all this—'' she gestured toward the thousand acres ''—wouldn't be mine.''

His brown eyes grew pensive and for a moment he was silent. ''Victoria Cober Townsend was a very kind lady,'' he mumbled.

C.J. stuck a hand in front of his face. ''Have you got blinders on or something? No one's that kind.''

''Maybe,'' he admitted absently, then asked, ''did you see Sloan's boy at the funeral?''

The soft curve of her mouth tightened a fraction. ''Yes, he was with his mother.'' Matthew Sloan, Jr., was a man no woman would overlook. Even with her limited experience she realized that. A vivid picture surfaced in her mind. A tall dark-haired man, with prominent features that held a certain sensuality. She detected a slight arrogance in his step and his manner, except when he'd helped his mother. Loving and caring, she'd immediately thought— but she knew better. Rumor had it that the famed New York attorney ripped people apart in the courtroom. She'd do well to remember that.

''Heard in town he's gonna clear up all his father's open cases before he heads back to New York.''

Her lips compressed into a thin line. ''Yes,'' she murmured. Matthew Sloan, Jr., would not be a friend the way his father had been.

Pete voiced her thoughts. ''He ain't like Matt Sloan. He

ain't gonna care about you. He's gonna care about winning. That boy always liked to win.''

C.J. had heard Matt say the same thing about his son. Matthew Sloan, Jr., didn't like to lose and he rarely did. In her heart she knew the Townsends would eventually hire big guns to bring her down. Going down wasn't in her plans, though. If she'd learned anything in her life, it was how to survive. The land and money would give her independence and security, and they showed her that Victoria had thought of her as a person in her own right. Matthew Sloan, Jr., would not snatch it away from her without the biggest fight of his life.

A gunshot echoed in the distance. C.J. and Pete exchanged a knowing look, both aware that Harry was out hunting. ''I'm not eating whatever he's killed this time,'' C.J. said with a grin. ''Armadillos and rattlesnakes aren't exactly to my taste. I prefer the food at the supermarket.''

''Whoever your parents are, they have highfalutin' taste,'' Pete grumbled.

Did they? she wondered. What were they like, these mysterious people who'd left her on a stranger's doorstep? Over the years she'd run through a range of emotions— sadness, anger, rage, confusion. Now she just had a burning desire to know the truth. To know why her mother had abandoned her and left her to face an unforgiving world alone. *Why didn't she want me?* That question taunted her dreams and tormented her waking hours, but the answer always eluded her.

She flexed her fingers, feeling the answer was now within her grasp. Victoria Townsend's will had stirred things up. People were talking, asking questions. That was fine. She wanted them to talk, to remember. Then, and only then, would the truth emerge.

MATTHEW POURED ANOTHER CUP of coffee and glanced at the clock. Almost midnight. He wasn't used to going to bed this early. In New York his head rarely hit the pillow before two in the morning, but here life was different. No crowds, noise or bright lights. Just a simple way of living he remembered well.

Growing up in Coberville, he had always yearned for something more. Excitement. Adventure. After graduating from Harvard, he knew his parents had secretly wanted him to come back to Coberville and practice law with his father. But his dreams were bigger than Coberville. Although he admired his father, he hadn't wanted to be a small-town lawyer. He'd been lured by New York—facing interesting legal challenges, big courtroom drama and, of course, the big bucks had something to do with it, too. Sometimes, though, he wondered what he was trying to prove.

He sighed, knowing it made little difference. Whatever his choices, his parents had always loved and supported him. Now it was time to return some of that support. His mother needed him. But how long could he stay here?

Matthew's thoughts shifted to his dad. Thank God he'd gotten home in time to see him before his death. Emphysema from years of smoking had finally taken its toll on his lungs. He could barely breathe or speak, but he had gripped Matthew's hand with fierce determination, uttering, "Case." Matthew assured him he would take care of all his clients, and the stress on his face had eased.

Glancing up now, he saw his mother standing in the doorway. Belle Sloan, a petite woman with curly salt-and-pepper hair, wore a sad expression on her usually serene face.

Matthew was instantly on his feet. "What is it, Mom?"

"Oh, nothing." She dismissed his concern with a wave

of her hand as she walked to the refrigerator and removed a carton of milk. "I just couldn't sleep. I can't get used to that empty space beside me." Her voice cracked on the last word.

Matthew hugged her. "It's going to take time."

"I know." She pushed out of his arms and poured milk into a pan. "A glass of warm milk, and I'll be fine."

Matthew had his doubts about that. He wished he could soothe her pain and take the sadness from her eyes, but there was nothing he could do and that hurt him the most.

They sat at the kitchen table, Matthew sipping his coffee and his mother her milk. He glanced around, realizing this big warm kitchen hadn't changed since he was a kid. White cabinets trimmed in blue, a darker blue counter, stove and a large oak table where all their problems had been solved.

"Your dad had a beautiful funeral, didn't he?" his mom asked, breaking through the comfortable silence.

His father had been buried more than a week ago, and every day she asked him the same thing. Tonight, for some reason, the question triggered thoughts of the young woman in black. He had been meaning to ask about her.

"Yes, it was a very special funeral. The whole town turned out." He smiled reassuringly, then said, "Mom, there was a young woman at the funeral. I didn't recognize her. She was completely dressed in black. Even her hair was black and hung below her waist."

Belle took a nervous swallow of her milk. "That has to be the Doe girl."

"Doe? You mean the baby who was left on Pete Watson's doorstep?"

"Yes."

The Doe girl. How could he have forgotten the little girl who'd paralyzed a town? Until she mysteriously appeared on the Watsons' doorstep, the people in Coberville had been close and friendly. The abandoned baby changed things. People began to look at each other a little differently, and they distanced themselves from the child. She represented a dark side of the community and they didn't know how to deal with her. So they left her alone.

Christmas Jane Doe. God, how she'd changed. He remembered a small thin girl with thick black braids and a face that never smiled. The last time he'd seen her she was about six, sitting on a bench, waiting for the bus. The other children were teasing her, calling her names. She held her back rigid and stared straight ahead, never reacting to their words. Much as she had at the funeral, he thought. Some things never change. But C. J. Doe certainly had. The little waif had turned into a beautiful woman.

"That must have been twenty-five or more years ago." His mother's words interrupted his reflections. "You know, I don't think Pete or Harry was at the funeral. But I guess that's understandable under the circumstances. It's so sad the way we all grew apart. So sad."

His mother was rambling. She did that a lot these days. He tried to make sense of her words and failed.

"What circumstances?"

She glanced up, her face puzzled, as if she'd forgotten he was in the room. "Oh," she said, and blinked, obviously collecting her composure. "The Townsend case. Your dad was their lawyer."

He still wasn't following her. "Dad did a lot of work for the Townsends."

With a nervous hand she set the glass of milk on the table. "I don't like talking about that girl and the mystery that surrounds her. It's depressing, and your dad and I never saw eye to eye about her."

His eyes narrowed. "You and Dad argued about this

girl?'' In all the years he'd been growing up, he couldn't ever remember his parents arguing. They had a unique way of talking things out.

''We didn't actually argue. I just felt he knew something about the girl he wasn't telling me.''

''Like what?''

''I don't know.'' She shook her head and got to her feet. ''I think I'll go to bed now.''

Matthew kissed her cheek and watched her leave the room, his curiosity running riot. He would've sworn his father had never kept anything from his mother. What did he know about the Doe girl that was so confidential he couldn't talk about it? Matthew ran a hand through his hair. While he was here, he intended to meet Christmas Jane Doe and find out for himself.

CHAPTER TWO

COBERVILLE WAS A QUIET community of fewer than five thousand people. A three-story limestone courthouse in the Second Empire style sat in the middle of a town square. Main and Cober streets ran parallel, and just about every business in town was located on one of those two streets, except for larger stores like Wal-Mart and H.E.B., which were located on the outskirts of town. Matt Sloan's office was across from the courthouse in a nineteenth-century building typical of the business district.

Matthew stood in the middle of his father's office, soaking up the atmosphere. Shelves filled with law books lined one wall and filing cabinets were up against another. On the third wall, beside the large window, hung family pictures. Files cluttered the desk and in the single ashtray was a half-smoked cigar. This big cluttered office was the essence of his dad. He remembered visiting here after school, and the way his dad had always smiled and said, "Come on in, son. I could use a second opinion."

He had spent many afternoons here, reading, watching his dad labor over the letter of the law. He could almost hear his voice. "Never forget that people are human and never take their opinions or feelings lightly." Had he lost those finer aspects his father had taught him? He ran his finger along the edge of the large oak desk, hoping he hadn't.

Even after his dad had retired as judge, he never forgot

about people and their emotions, their needs. People kept calling him, wanting his advice. So he'd come out of retirement and reopened his old office and practiced law part-time.

Matthew took a deep breath and glanced around at the general chaos of the office. Before he could decide what to do next, the front door opened and Miss Emma, his dad's secretary of forty years, walked in.

A short plump woman, Miss Emma Stevens had a mound of dyed red hair curled atop her head. As a boy he used to wonder how it stayed there so neatly. She frowned at him from behind thick glasses with cat's-eye frames and rhinestones at the corners. They must have been made in the 1950s.

"You didn't tell me you were coming in today," she accused in her irritating high-pitched voice.

He didn't like having to explain his actions, but remembering the manners his parents had instilled in him, he replied, "Mom's visiting with the reverend and I thought I'd get acquainted with Dad's files."

"You should've called me."

"It's no big deal, Miss Emma. I only plan to stay for a little while, and I really don't need any help."

"How will you find anything?" She waved an impatient hand. "I have a special filing system, and I don't like anyone messing it up."

He forced himself to take a calming breath and wondered how his father had put up with this woman for so many years. Diplomacy, that was it. His dad knew how to handle people. He hoped he'd inherited some of his father's tact.

He looked around at the dust and clutter. "Can you get someone to clean the office?"

"Clean?" she shrilled, her eyes darting around. "What's wrong with this office?"

"Everything needs to be cleaned, from the floors to the windows. The place has been closed up for weeks."

"I don't see anything wrong with it."

Yeah, he thought, she probably had cataracts the size of doorknobs. He smiled his best smile. "Humor me, Miss Emma. Find someone."

She hesitated, then his smile won her over. "Okay, I could get Bertha. She cleans the bank."

"Fine, get Bertha." His smile broadened at the small victory.

She took a step, then turned back, pointing a finger at him. "She'll cost you. She won't do it for free."

His smile immediately vanished. "I didn't expect her to," he answered, a slight edge to his voice.

Miss Emma turned on her heel and headed for the door, muttering, "His father never had any complaints. City ways gone to his head. Nonsense, just nonsense."

As the last word died away, Matthew grinned and sank into his father's chair. He marveled at the comfort and the way the contours seemed to fit his body. Maybe he and his dad were more alike than he'd imagined.

Reaching for a file, he heard the door open again. Now what? Surely Miss Emma wasn't going to argue some more.

To his surprise, a tall blond man with a veneer that bespoke money and power entered the room. John Robert William Townsend. Even though Rob, as he was called, was eleven years older than he was, Matthew knew him and his family well. The Cobers, Rob's mother's family, had settled Coberville in the 1800s and they stilled owned almost everything in and around the town.

Matthew got to his feet and shook Rob's hand.

"It's good to have you back in Coberville, Matthew." Rob's smile showed off his perfect white teeth and angular features. Rob Townsend was known for his charm and virility, which were apparently lethal to any and all women. At forty-nine the man still hadn't lost those qualities.

"Thank you," Matthew replied.

"I'm sorry about your dad. He was a good man."

"Thank you," Matthew said again. "Have a seat."

Rob hiked up his tailored slacks and sat in one of the leather chairs opposite the desk. Matthew resumed his own seat, wondering what Rob Townsend had on his mind.

"How long has it been?" Rob mused. "A long time, I'd say, but I remember you as the young hero that led the Coberville Tigers to the state championship. Quite a victory for this town."

Matthew smiled at the memory.

"I wished my parents had let me finish high school in Coberville, instead of sending me to school back East. All that togetherness and bonding sure could've helped me in this election."

At Matthew's puzzled look, Rob explained, "I'm running for Dad's senate seat in the fall."

Matt raised one dark eyebrow in amusement. "Are you here to ask for my support?"

Rob chuckled. "No, not really." Then his expression grew serious. "I was glad to hear you're staying in town, taking over your father's cases."

"I promised Dad I would."

"I didn't realize you had a Texas license or practiced anything but criminal law."

"I got the Texas license mostly for my dad's sake," he said. "I hadn't planned on practicing here this soon, but I assure you I can handle most cases."

"How long do you plan on staying in Coberville?"

"I'm due for a long vacation. So I plan to stay as long as Mom needs me and until I get all of Dad's cases closed. At least a month."

"That's good to hear. I presume you're familiar with the case your dad was handling for the Townsend family?"

"No," Matthew said, "can't say that I am." He figured this had something to do with the case his mother had mentioned last night. He wished she'd told him more.

"Then you haven't got a clue about what's going on around here." The statement held an accusing tone, similar to Miss Emma's earlier. It had the same effect on him. But Rob was a client and deserved his patience.

"No," Matthew repeated. He picked up a pencil and, searching for a pad, came across the Townsend file. "Dad must have been working on it because the file's right here."

"Hmm," Rob murmured. "Sad to say, your dad didn't give it a lot of attention."

"Oh?"

"He was dragging his heels so long I was thinking of hiring an attorney from Austin."

"Doesn't sound like Dad. He always believed in taking care of business."

"My mother had a lot of faith in him, but I guess he just wasn't feeling up to par."

"Maybe," Matthew admitted reluctantly, knowing his dad would never let a client down. He touched the thick file. "I'll review this tonight, but generally what's the case about?"

Rob crossed his legs and began to talk. "After a lengthy illness my mother passed away about six months ago. Her will was pretty straightforward, leaving everything to her three children. She also stipulated that Aunt Martha could live at Seven Trees until her death with all expenses paid, and she left her a trust fund, as well.''

"You don't have a problem with any of that, do you?''

"No, it was what we expected. Mother was the sole owner of the Cober estate. She bought out Aunt Martha a long time ago. Dad and my mother had been having marital difficulties for years, and they had separate estates. So we all knew the bulk would go to her children, but what we didn't expect was an outside party being named in the will.''

"An outside party?''

"Christmas Jane Doe.''

Surprise darted along Matthew's nerves, but he made sure that nothing showed on his face. "The girl who was left on the Watsons' doorstep?''

"Yes. Mother left her a hundred thousand dollars and a thousand acres of Cober land.''

"What?'' Matthew's surprise turned to shock.

"You heard me right. My mother had to be insane if she thought we'd accept this. As I said, she was ill for a long time and she wasn't thinking straight. I want this will broken and I want it done as soon as possible.''

"Was your mother making business decisions up until her death?''

"Yes, although Dad and I advised her. She would never relinquish her power.''

"Let me see if I can find the will,'' Matthew said. He opened the file and quickly sorted through the contents. "Here it is.'' He pulled out the legal document and glanced through it briefly. "There's a personal letter from your mother.''

"Oh, yes, about how she wants us to accept her decision.''

"It's very heartwarming." Matthew scanned the letter and wondered at Rob's coldheartedness.

"Mother thought we took our inheritance for granted, and she wanted to give something to someone who'd appreciate it. It's all crap. Mother just felt sorry for the girl. We will not accept an outsider inheriting Cober land."

"I see," Matthew replied, continuing to read through the papers. One small detail caught his eye. He glanced at Rob. "Did anyone mention the date on this document?"

"No, I don't believe so. I just assumed she'd made it recently."

"This document is dated twenty years ago." Matthew turned the will around so Rob could read the date.

"What?" he choked out. In one swift movement Rob was on his feet, grabbing the document from Matthew's hand. "Damn, how could this have slipped by us? By your father? Surely he knew the date and he never said a word! I only saw this letter briefly. It's been in your father's custody ever since. How could this have happened?"

Their eyes locked. Matthew didn't miss the slur on his dad's capabilities as a lawyer—and he didn't like it. But he also knew his dad had been ill. "I have no idea," Matthew said slowly, "but did anyone check for a recent will?"

"That was the only will at the bank where she kept all her important papers. I'm sure there isn't another one."

Matthew nodded at the document in Rob's hand. "That's going to make it much harder to break."

"Dammit, I'm so tired of dealing with this." Rob tossed the papers on the desk. "We only plan to spend the spring months in Coberville, so I want to get this settled. I need to concentrate on campaigning, instead of this bizarre mess." He turned away. "Why the hell would Mother do this to me? To her family?"

Matthew folded his hands across the file. If he was going to represent the Townsends, he had to be completely honest. "I was only a kid when the baby was found, but I still remember the rumors."

Rob swung around, his blue eyes dark with resentment. "My father and I have nothing to do with that girl's existence!"

Matthew stared at Rob. His eyes didn't waver as they challenged that statement.

"Okay." Rob threw up his hands. "I've had my share of women and so has my dad. I'm not denying that, but if either of us had gotten some girl pregnant, she would have bled us for every penny. Instead, she leaves the baby five miles from our house. That doesn't make any sense. Anyway, just look at C. J. Doe with all that black hair and those green eyes. She looks nothing like us, and no one's going to make me believe that Mother knew anything about her birth. It's all just rumors. The truth is, some teenager probably got pregnant and, being scared and alone, decided to leave the baby on the Watsons' doorstep. Everyone knew how desperately Maggie Watson wanted a baby. That makes more sense than those ridiculous rumors about us."

Matthew could see the fear in his eyes. Rob wasn't sure the girl wasn't a Townsend, but he was never going to admit any doubts. He was a Cober and a Townsend. He didn't have to.

Suddenly Rob's eyes narrowed. "Offer the girl a million dollars."

Matthew frowned. "Pardon me?"

"I'll pay her a million dollars to keep from dragging this through the courts. I'm sure the greedy little witch will take it."

"I strongly advise against this. Let me—"

Rob cut him short. "I'm not asking for your advice. I'm ordering you to make her an offer. If you have a problem with it, I can find another attorney."

Matt's first impulse was to tell him to do exactly that, but he'd made a promise to his dad and he wouldn't go back on his word. Besides, there was something going on that made him very curious—his dad's reluctance to move on the case and the date on the document, among other things. He had to find the answers for his own peace of mind.

Giving in to Rob's highhandedness wasn't in his nature, though. He'd been an attorney, and a successful one, for a long time and he didn't like being talked to like some hack for hire.

He got slowly to his feet, his eyes narrowed with a warning his colleagues knew well. "It's my job to advise you."

By the glint in Rob's eyes, Matthew could see that he was debating whether to tell him to go to hell or to see if the New York lawyer could live up to his reputation. As the blue eyes darted away, Matthew knew the latter impulse had won.

Rob ran a quick hand through his expertly groomed hair. "Hell, man, I know you're a good lawyer and I trust your judgment, but this whole situation has my family in turmoil. I just want it settled, and I'd rather spend the money than put the family through a long court battle."

"If your mind is set on this, I'll make the offer," Matthew conceded. He knew it was useless to try to persuade him otherwise.

"Fine," Rob muttered. "You'll find her at the Watson place. I'll be waiting for her answer." With that he turned abruptly and headed for the door. Suddenly he turned back.

"A note of caution. Don't let her wrap you around her finger like she did your father."

Matthew frowned. What was Rob talking about? His father wouldn't be involved with C. J. Doe; he was the Townsends' lawyer. He shook his head. There was so much he didn't understand. The confusion made him more determined than ever to solve the mystery between his father and C. J. Doe.

LATE AT NIGHT, a light burned in the law offices of Dylan, Kent and Reed in Austin, Texas. Attorney Stephen Reed was hard at work. He had a lot to catch up on after six months in France. He heard a noise and glanced up. A big man with a mask over his face stood framed in the doorway. The gun in his hand pointed at Stephen.

"What do you want?" Stephen asked in a barely audible voice.

"Victoria Townsend's will," came the shocking reply.

"That's confidential and—"

"Are you willing to die for it?" the man asked.

"No." Stephen headed for the safe, which was installed behind a painting. With a shaky hand, he pulled back the picture. He quickly turned the dial to the correct numbers and the safe swung open.

He saw the gun kept there, on top of the papers. It was his only chance. His hand closed over the cold steel and he turned swiftly around. Before he could pull the trigger the man fired and Stephen fell to the floor.

The man jerked the mask from his face and stepped over the body. Pulling several documents out of the safe, the man searched until he found what he wanted. "Bingo." The will of Victoria Cober Townsend, dated one year ago. Hastily he put the other documents back and closed the safe.

As he turned to leave, a rattle of keys sounded and a security guard entered the office. Another gunshot echoed in the room. The guard toppled to the carpet.

DALE WEEKS HELD the will in his hand and dialed a number. "I've got it," he said.

"Good," the voice on the other end answered. "Is it what I expected?"

"Yeah, she tells everything she knew or suspected and changed her will accordingly. It's very interesting. You really should read it."

"I have no interest in reading that garbage. Destroy it. Do you understand me?"

"Sure, that's what you're paying for. There's just one small problem."

"What?"

"Reed was in the office and I had to shoot him...and the security guard."

"Why?"

"It was unavoidable. Besides, no one'll ever know the safe was broken into. They'll think the guard interrupted a routine robbery. Your secret is safe. Trust me."

"I don't trust anyone, Weeks, especially you. Just make sure your tracks are covered."

Dale Weeks hung up the phone, then stared at the document in his hand. A smile twisted his lips. So many secrets. A shame no one would ever know. Except him.

CHAPTER THREE

THE NEXT DAY Matthew headed out to the Watsons' place
with mixed emotions. He knew he could break the will.
The task would require a little finesse, but he could do it.
He should have made that clearer to Rob, but somehow he
hadn't. The memory of a little girl with a face that never
smiled swam before his eyes. Maybe it was time that girl
got a break in this world.

God, what was he thinking? He was the Townsends'
attorney!

Had the same thing happened to his father? The will
should have been broken weeks ago. What had kept his
dad from doing his job? Then there was the date on the
will; he wouldn't keep something like that from a client,
would he? And if he had, it must've been for a very good
reason. At times, his dad had cared about people so much
that he'd become involved in their lives, as friend, confidant and advisor more than lawyer. Was that what had
happened with C. J. Doe? Well, it was time to meet the
lady and answer some of his questions.

The Watsons' place was on a country road not far from
Seven Trees, the Cober mansion and ranch. He drove to
the entrance. The gate was firmly locked and the signs that
greeted him were hardly welcoming. Posted. Keep Out. No
Trespassing. The Watsons weren't the most hospitable
people in Coberville. *Now what?* he thought.

He could see the house on a hill through the trees and

two trucks parked by the garage. Someone had to be home. He slipped out of his suit coat, loosened his tie, got out of the truck and climbed over the gate. He'd come here to see C. J. Doe, and he intended to do so.

Brushing dust from his dark slacks, he reminded himself that he needed to change his wardrobe. Coberville didn't call for expensive suits and custom-made boots.

As he walked, he sucked air into his lungs, enjoying the outdoors. He had forgotten the freedom and freshness of country life. The place was almost magical with the smell of spring, towering oak trees, green grasses; the small lake in the distance triggered memories of lazy Sunday afternoons spent fishing with his dad. Had he changed so much from that country boy? With a regretful sigh, he knew he had.

Now most of his days were spent in his office or in a courtroom. At first he'd thrived on the long days and hard consuming work, but lately he'd been feeling restless. Something was missing in his life and he didn't know what.

He had everything he'd worked so hard to achieve: fame and wealth. His fame had started with his first big case— a movie actress who'd killed her husband because he'd been pimping her to his rich clientele for years. Everyone knew the actress was going to be put away for a long time. Everyone except him. He knew that if he could put twelve jurors in her shoes, make them live her life, feel her pain, her degradation, he could get her off. And he did. Many more trials followed, most of the clients wealthy, each one making the news. It wasn't the course he'd set for himself; it just happened that way.

He only accepted clients he believed in. If he didn't, he couldn't do his job. Matthew considered the Townsends. Did he believe in their quest to reclaim Cober land? If he was honest with himself, he had to admit he had no real drive for this case. His only wish was to get it over with and get back to New York. The Peterman case was waiting for him, and the sooner he got back, the better. He felt sure C. J. Doe wasn't going to turn down a million dollars. Who would? Now if—

Several gunshots pierced the peaceful silence, kicking up dirt at his feet and dusting his boots. He jumped back and then froze. Someone was shooting at him! It happened so fast he didn't have time to think, to react, to do anything but stand there like a target.

A man appeared from the side of the house. Big and menacing, he had long gray hair and a beard that hung to his chest. A dark hat was pulled low over his forehead, covering his eyes. He wore overalls and a khaki shirt. Two big dogs hovered at his heels. Harry Watson.

Every kid in Coberville grew up fearing Harry Watson. Mothers used him as a disciplinary tactic. "If you don't behave, the Hairy Man will get you." Those words struck fear in the heart of every child, including him. All these things went through Matthew's mind, but only one held his attention. The shotgun pointed at him. Harry was known for shooting first and leaving the questions for someone else.

"You're trespassing," Harry growled. The rough voice would have sent the young Matthew running, but the adult Matthew stood his ground, facing the Hairy Man.

Courage was only a breath away. Matthew took that breath, very deeply. "I'm here to speak with Miss Doe."

"She don't want to speak to no one. Now git, before I fill you full of buckshot."

At the threat in Harry's voice, Matthew's heart jumped wildly in his chest, but he had no intention of letting Harry intimidate him. "My name is Matthew Sloan and I have news for C. J. Doe." His message rang out, clear and crisp.

"Matthew Sloan is dead." The gun was raised a little higher. "'In delay there lies no peace.' Now git."

Matthew blinked, not understanding what the hell Harry was saying. "I'm Matthew Sloan, Jr., his son." Matthew had the feeling Harry knew who he was. He was playing a cat-and-mouse game, trying to scare him.

Harry studied him down the barrel of his shotgun, but before Harry could reply, a black horse and rider came flying over the fence into Matthew's vision. It was the girl. C. J. Doe. She reined the horse in next to Harry. No saddle, Matthew saw; she was riding bareback. Dust swirled around the stallion's dancing feet. Sleek and spirited, the big horse had the look of being wild and untamed—much like the girl on his back. Tossed by the wind, her long black hair hung in disarray all around her, like a silken web. Her slim legs, clad in jeans and moccasins, gripped the horse's sides with ease.

The horse reared up on his hind legs, but C.J. clung to him effortlessly and patted the rippling muscles in his neck, murmuring in soothing tones. Immediately the horse quieted. Then she turned her head, her eyes settling on Matthew.

"What have you got here, Harry?" she asked in a soft husky voice.

"A trespasser," Harry muttered.

Continuing to stroke the horse's neck, C.J. took in the trespasser from his expensive boots to his dark hair. So Matthew Sloan, Jr., had come calling. He stood with a commanding air of confidence. Here was a man who didn't bend easily, she thought. Not many men would react so calmly to someone shooting at them. He was certainly different from his father, who would have been cursing at

Harry by now. Yet the laugh lines around Matthew Sloan, Jr.'s mouth indicated he laughed as easily as his father. But he wasn't laughing now.

A swath of hair fell across his forehead and his dark eyes gazed at her with undisguised interest. Under that intense gaze, her heart started to pounded rapidly.

Wrong reaction, her mind told her. *Be on guard.* Matthew Sloan, Jr., was here for a reason.

Matthew watched her long slender fingers stroke the horse. For a crazy moment he envied the animal. If she touched *him* like that, he'd do what she wanted, too. Rob Townsend's words echoed dimly through his mind. *Don't let her wrap you around her finger.* He knew now what Rob had been talking about. C. J. Doe had the power to distract any man, even him. Annoyed, he shook his head; the gunfire had just impeded the blood flow to his brain, he told himself. He was here to make her an offer, that was all, and he had to do it soon.

"My name is Matthew Sloan, Jr., and I'd like to speak with you, Miss Doe."

C.J. slid from the horse in a graceful movement and handed the reins to Harry. "Would you rub Midnight down while I talk to Mr. Sloan, Jr.?"

"You don't have to talk—"

"It's okay, Harry."

"You sure?"

She regarded Matthew speculatively. "I'm sure, but if he gets out of line, I'll let you shoot him. How's that?"

Matthew didn't find that amusing, but Harry did. A grin cracked his worn face as he led the horse away, the dogs obediently at his heels.

The only reaction C.J. noticed was a tightening of Matthew's lips. The New York lawyer—the Townsends' new representative—was tough, and she wondered how to handle him. She knew without a doubt that Matthew Sloan, Jr., was here on the Townsends' behalf. Her eyes narrowed to green slits. "What can I do for you, Mr. Sloan, Jr.?"

She said his name slowly, drawing out each syllable in a mocking sort of way. She was baiting him, trying to throw him off guard, Matthew realized. C. J. Doe wanted the upper hand. As he watched her toss her black hair over her shoulder and felt a warmth curl through his stomach, he had to admit she probably already had the upper hand.

The thought made him stiffen his backbone. "I've taken over the Townsend case from my father and I'd like to talk to you about it."

She shrugged. "What's to talk about?"

"The Townsends would like to make an offer."

"An offer?"

The sun was hot and he ran a finger around the collar of his white shirt. "Could we talk someplace where it's more comfortable?"

C.J. eyed him for a moment, wondering if it was wise to extend hospitality to Townsends' new attorney. But it wouldn't hurt to hear him out.

"Sure," she finally replied, and led him toward the long porch at the front of the cabin.

Her back was straight as an arrow and her shoulders appeared slightly tensed, as if she was bracing herself for the worst. He could almost see the wall she'd built around herself, a wall strengthened by years of hurt and disillusionment. What would it take to breach that wall, to make her smile, hear her laugh?

He closed his eyes for a second, forcing away such thoughts. He wasn't here to wonder about C. J. Doe. As he opened his eyes, he caught sight of long black hair swaying against her jean-clad bottom—shapely and rounded just enough to seriously distract a man. A jolt of sheer pleasure shot through him, which he quickly curbed.

Matthew followed her up the steps and tried to focus his attention on the surroundings. Everything was clean and orderly; not a weed grew in the flower beds, and logs were stacked neatly by the door for firewood. Not exactly what he'd expected from the Watson men. The scent of honeysuckle floated to his nostrils.

At one end of the porch hung a wooden swing, which squeaked as she sat on it. Matthew took the chair that was propped against the wall.

She stared at him with a direct gaze and he found himself staring back. He'd met a lot of lovely women, but he'd never met anyone as striking as her. Creamy skin sun-kissed to a warm gold, delicately carved facial bones, a pert nose and bow-shaped mouth. Thick dark lashes framed emerald-green eyes. And all that black hair, silken tresses that flowed around her, magnified the beauty of her eyes.

''You're staring.'' Her quiet voice stopped his avid inspection, and he was about to apologize for his gauche behavior when she asked, ''Do I remind you of someone?''

Her eyes sparkled with anticipation and her mouth softened into a hint of a smile. While his senses absorbed the pleasure of that near smile, he understood what she meant. She thought she reminded him of someone—someone who could be related to her.

Matthew cleared his throat. ''No, you don't remind me of anyone.'' That was true. He'd never seen anyone like her.

The sparkle died in her eyes, and Matthew wished he could tell her what she wanted to hear. But like everyone else in this town, he hadn't a clue who had left her on the

Watsons' doorstep. All he knew was that he liked looking at her—too much.

Swallowing hard, he returned to business. "As you know, the Townsends are eager to get their land back."

She didn't respond, just stared at him with unwavering eyes.

Matthew came right to the point. "They're willing to offer you a million dollars."

A million dollars! The trump card, she thought. Mercy, the Townsends knew how to get a girl's attention. But that was all they got. This only increased her belief that the Townsends had something to hide.

With a slow hand she tucked her hair behind her ear. "The land is not for sale."

He expected surprise, jubilation, something besides that stubborn expression.

"It's a very generous offer."

"The land is not for sale," she repeated.

He leaned forward, realizing this wasn't going to be as easy as he or the Townsends had anticipated. "A million dollars, Miss Doe. Think what you can do with all that money."

She didn't say a word, just kept her green eyes focused on him.

"You can travel, leave Coberville, make a new life for yourself."

One eyebrow rose slightly. "And what would I be called in this new life, Mr. Sloan, Jr.?"

He was taken aback by the question, and for once words failed him.

"Money can't buy me my true identity," she told him.

"But it could change a lot of things."

"It would change nothing for me, Mr. Sloan, Jr. I would still be C. J. Doe."

His eyes held hers and he knew C. J. Doe was fighting her own inner struggle, a struggle she'd fought all her life, because of not knowing who she was. He searched for a way to reach her. "You should talk it over with someone. Your lawyer."

"I don't have a lawyer" was the startling reply.

Matthew frowned. "But the lawsuit was filed six months ago. Surely someone has advised you."

Her eyes darkened. "Your father said to let things ride, and eventually they'd work out."

"Wait a minute." He held up one hand to ward off the nagging feeling building inside him. "My *father* advised you?"

She nodded.

Matthew's body went rigid with shock. He couldn't believe his dad would advise both sides. Something was wrong.

He took a cautious breath. "My dad was the Townsends' attorney. He had no right to advise you."

"He was only trying to help me."

"Still…"

"I'm sorry, I forgot to tell you how sad I was at his passing. He was one of the nicest men I've ever known."

There was such sincerity in her voice. Her condolences were nothing like the perfunctory gesture Rob Townsend had made. God, that shouldn't matter. What mattered was getting this case resolved. But nothing was going as he'd planned—or expected. She was beginning to make him feel like a bumbling first-year law student.

The thought sent all his legal instincts into action. "Miss Doe, if you don't take the money, do you know what that'll mean?"

She tilted her head slightly. "That I'll be meeting you in a courtroom."

"Yes," he replied. "I'll have to break the will and, believe me, Miss Doe, I *can* break it."

Her eyes met the challenge in his. "Mr. Sloan, Jr., if you can break the will so easily, I don't think the Townsends would be offering me a million dollars."

He sighed heavily. "The offer is just a matter of expediency, Miss Doe. With the election coming in the fall, the Townsends want to get this over with as quickly as possible."

"I bet they do."

Hearing the mocking tone in her voice, he rested his elbows on his knees and folded his hands, eyes trained on her. "Miss Doe, don't take this lightly. I'm very good at what I do."

"I'm sure you are, but to break the will you'll have to prove Mrs. Townsend wasn't in her right mind or that I influenced her in some way."

"There are other approaches I can take. All I have to do is prove Mrs. Townsend felt sorry for you and had a momentary lapse in judgment."

From the look in her eyes, he knew he was finally getting through to her. Time to go for the jugular—tell her everyone felt sorry for her, call her a nobody, make her cry, watch the tears roll down her face and reinforce that she didn't have a chance in hell against him and the Townsends. Then tell her to take the money and build a new life. But when he looked at her throat, all he saw was gorgeous creamy skin… He couldn't do it. He couldn't break her down. The thought rocked him to the core. What was happening to him? Had Coberville made him soft? Or was it her?

Matthew was so caught up in these troubling thoughts that he didn't notice a rider had come into the yard until he heard the dogs bark.

He glanced toward the corrals to see a tall rangy man dismount. Pete Watson. With handlebar mustache and spurs jingling, he wasn't hard to recognize. As a kid Matthew remembered him coming to the school with his horse and ropes, giving the kids rides and teaching them to rope. He was right out of a Western movie. The kids adored him.

Matthew had forgotten that small aspect of his childhood. He used to dote on Pete, wanted to be a cowboy just like him. He guessed every little boy had that dream, but he'd outgrown it, as most of them had.

Harry said something to Pete, who looked toward the house. Swiftly, his long strides brought him closer. He was still an impressive figure, and Matthew felt a stirring of admiration, just like that little boy of long ago.

Matthew got to his feet and shook Pete's outstretched hand. He felt the calluses and the strength that epitomized Pete Watson. After explaining his reason for being there, he added, "Maybe you can help me encourage Miss Doe to take the offer."

Pete removed his worn hat and studied it a moment before answering in the deep baritone Matthew remembered. "C.J. makes up her own mind."

Matthew glanced from one to the other, realizing Pete wasn't going to be much help. "Look at this as a godsend. It's the best solution for both parties."

"The land is not for sale," C.J. said again in that stubborn voice.

Matthew knew nothing he said was going to change her mind. But still, he had to try.

"Miss Doe, let me make this very clear. To keep the land and the money, you're going to have to face a court battle, and I can guarantee that you will lose. On the other hand, the million dollars is there for you free and clear, without strings. All you have to do is sign your name to a legal document.''

"This isn't about money or land, Mr. Sloan, Jr.,'' she said, her eyes blazing with purpose. "It's about an old lady who showed me a kindness no one except the Watsons ever offered me before. Until I know the reason behind her generous act, the land stays with me.''

"You have your answer, Mr. Sloan,'' Pete said.

Matthew knew it was time to leave.

"I'll give you a couple of days to think it over. It's a lot of money, and I don't think you should turn it down without consideration.''

"It's not going to make any difference,'' was her sharp response.

"Son, I'm sorry about your dad,'' Pete said. "Even though we were on opposite sides of the fence, I respected him.''

Another sincere condolence. Matthew began to wonder if *he* was on the right side of the fence.

"Thank you.'' He nodded at C.J., "Like I said, it's a good offer.'' With those words he headed down the steps and back to his truck.

C.J. GOT UP FROM THE SWING and stood by the railing. Her eyes followed Matthew's lean figure. Beneath those expensive clothes was a superb well-muscled body. Some women might be attracted to that, but she wasn't. Then why had she felt a weakness in her stomach when he'd looked at her? It was the uncanny resemblance to his father that made her so aware of him, she told herself. Yet he wasn't like his father, not really. She had a feeling Mr. Sloan, Jr., could be quite ruthless when provoked. She'd do well to remember he was the enemy with a capital *E*.

Pete sat down and took out his pipe and tobacco. He

watched C.J. with a curious eye. "Mighty handsome young man," he commented.

C.J. whirled around. "I hadn't noticed," she said. The lie falling so easily from her lips startled her. She resumed her seat on the swing with a frown.

"Really?" He lit his pipe with amusement and puffed on it a couple of times to get it started. "From the way you were staring at him, I'd say you noticed plenty."

The swing creaked at her agitated movements. "I was just thinking how much he looks like his father."

"Strong resemblance," Pete conceded dryly. Smoke swirled around his face.

"Yes, he's handsome and I noticed," she snapped, unable to lie to Pete for any length of time. "But he's too citified," she added. "I bet he couldn't wait to get out of our sight to wipe the dust off those fancy boots."

Her words were flippant, but her emotions weren't. She *had* stared at Matthew Sloan, Jr., and for the very reason Pete was insinuating. She was attracted to him. Okay, she admitted it. But she couldn't allow herself to be attracted to any man, especially Matthew Sloan, Jr.

He wanted her to take the money. She could see it in his eyes and hear it in his voice. The message was there— take the money and be happy. But happiness, for her, lay in finding the truth about her birth. That was the only thing that mattered to her. Having had loving parents, Matthew Sloan, Jr., wouldn't understand that.

"So, what do you think about the offer?" Pete asked.

C.J. slung her dark hair over her shoulder. "The Townsends think I'll take the money, but they don't know me very well if they think it's money I want."

THE NIGHT WRAPPED C.J. in a warm cocoon. She sat in the swing, her legs curled beneath her. Crickets chirped a deafening song. A wolf howled in the distance; several horses whinnied. Familiar sounds, but they were lost on C.J. Her thoughts were inward.

She had expected various different responses from the Townsends, but a million dollars wasn't among them. The offer still shook her. What would she do with all that money? She had no idea. There was only one thing she wanted: to find her parents. If Matthew Sloan, Jr., had said, "Release your claim on the land and money, and the Townsends will tell you about your parents," she would have taken the offer in a heartbeat. She sat perfectly still as something occurred to her. "That's it," she said aloud.

She stood up and walked to the railing, her face embracing the coolness of the night. "That's it," she said again. "That's it." A smile tugged at her lips. It was so simple. She intended to fight Matthew Sloan, Jr., every step of the way. The land and money gave her prestige, but it wasn't prestige she wanted. It wasn't money, either. She wanted an identity.

C.J. had racked her brain so many times trying to find the reason behind Victoria's gift. Now she thought she knew. The land gave her the power to force the truth. Victoria had known that the Townsends wouldn't stand for an outsider owning Cober land; she'd known that eventually they'd find a way to break the will. But C.J. held claim to the land now and had power over the Townsends. A plan had formed in her mind, and she knew what she had to do. Matthew Sloan, Jr., was in for a big surprise.

CHAPTER FOUR

MATTHEW ARRIVED at the office early because his mother had gone over to the church to help the reverend work on his books. She'd been the church secretary since he was a small boy. Little by little she was putting her life back together. She just needed time, as he did.

He stopped short as he came through the front door. Miss Emma was there, as usual, but what caught his attention was the big birdcage sitting on the corner of her desk and the colorful parrot inside.

"Pretty boy. Pretty boy," the parrot shrieked.

The squawking voice irritated Matthew, and he gritted his teeth. "Miss Emma, what's that bird doing here?"

Miss Emma raised her eyebrows. "Now don't go getting your nose out of joint. Herman's not feeling well and I'm taking him to the vet."

"Herman bad. Herman bad," the parrot said.

Matthew eyed the green bird, his plumage shot here and there with yellow and orange, and said the first thing that entered his head. "The phrase *chicken-fried* comes to mind."

"Matthew Sloan, Jr., bite your tongue," Miss Emma scolded, and grabbed her purse. "I'll take him to Doc Lowe's right now."

"And take him home afterward, because I don't want to listen to him babbling all day."

Miss Emma flashed him a sharp glance, then picked up

the cage. "You know, young Matthew, you're too wound up. You should let go and have some fun. Find yourself a girl, get married and have some kids. Don't let life pass you by like I did."

"Herman bad. Herman bad. Pretty boy. Pretty boy."

The parrot's words followed him into his office. He wasn't wound up. And his life wasn't anything like Miss Emma's. She had taken care of her sick mother until the old woman died, and after that she'd begun to work for his father. By then all the eligible bachelors were gone, and Miss Emma had become an old maid before she knew it.

Wound up. Dammit, he had to admit he was. He was coiled so tightly inside he felt as if he was going to explode. The past month had been horrendous—his dad's illness, then death, and taking care of his mom. Now he had to deal with his dad's caseload while worrying about his own. Everything seemed to be crowding in on him.

With a deep sigh he rubbed both hands over his face and sank into his chair. He had lived with pressure all his life, so he should be used to it. Living in his father's shadow hadn't been easy; the very best had always been expected of him. That was probably the main reason he'd chosen New York to practice law. He had wanted to live his own life, and to do that he'd had to leave Coberville, Texas.

He groaned. Had he been trying to prove something to his dad all these years—that he was a better lawyer, had a more exciting life and made more money? Matthew raked his hands through his hair. If he had been, he'd fallen short somewhere along the road, because his dad had been happy and content while those feelings still eluded him. Maybe his dad was right, and a person could never shake his roots.

That thought reminded him of C. J. Doe. All her life, she'd been searching for her roots, while he… Had he been running from his? He didn't like to think so because he loved his father, and Coberville had a way of getting into his blood.

God, this soul-searching was driving him insane. Something about coming home always had him questioning his motives and the reasons for everything he'd done in his life. But he was doing what he wanted to do—practicing criminal law. And he was doing it where he wanted to do it—in New York. Happiness and all the rest would follow. Wouldn't it?

Scooting his chair forward, he decided it was time to get his mind back on business. The Townsend case could be a problem and keep him in Coberville longer than he wanted to stay. He stared at the telephone. Should he call the Townsends? No, he'd told C. J. Doe he'd give her a couple of days. Maybe she'd realize how foolish she was being. But he knew that hope was in vain. Her pride, the same pride he'd witnessed in her as a child, wouldn't let her. She was going to hold on to the land, making his life miserable. He'd be forced to take it away from her. The mere prospect knotted his stomach. Why couldn't she just accept the damn money and get on with her life?

He leaned forward and picked up a pencil, tapping it against the desk. Suddenly all his frustrations welled up inside him and he threw the pencil. It bounced off the phone and landed on the carpet near the door.

Matthew stared at the pencil, then slowly raised his eyes to see C. J. Doe standing in his doorway. For a moment he was sure he'd imagined her, conjured her up. Last night she'd flitted in and out of his dreams with her long black hair cascading around her and green eyes beckoning.

Now her long black hair fell in a heavy braid down her

back. Tight jeans molded her legs and hips. A green shirt intensified the color of her eyes—liquid green eyes that weren't beckoning. They were somber and staring at him.

Slowly he got to his feet. "Miss Doe, come in."

C.J. stepped farther into the room, then stopped. "Miss Emma wasn't at her desk so I—"

"It's okay," he interrupted. He couldn't resist a grin. "Just be grateful she's gone or she'd be making you sit there for a while."

"Miss Emma's a stickler for procedure, all right. Your dad used to tease her about it," she said, enjoying the grin on his face. The New York lawyer had a devastating smile.

How did she know so much about his dad? Matthew wondered. As he shook that thought from his mind, he gestured toward a chair. "Have a seat."

"No, thank you, I won't be staying that long."

He waited, but she didn't say anything else. The offer had to be the reason she'd come here. He could have sworn she'd never change her mind, but money was always a good persuader. Disappointment ran through him, and he didn't understand why. Because if C. J. Doe took the offer, it was going to make his life a whole lot easier.

"I assume you're here about the offer," he prompted.

Her eyes narrowed. "Have you seen the Townsends?"

"No. I told you I'd give you a couple of days."

"Good." The lovely lines of her face relaxed. "I have a counteroffer."

He stared at her. "I beg your pardon?"

"I want to make a counteroffer," she repeated.

He shook his head. "I don't understand. I thought you were here to accept the money."

Fine eyebrows darted up in surprise. "Afraid not. Money doesn't mean that much to me."

"Then...why are you here?"

"I just told you." Her voice became strained. "I have an offer of my own."

"What?" he asked. What did she have to offer the Townsends?

She took a deep breath. "I will release my claim on the land and money on one condition."

He tried not to let the shock show on his face. After all, he was a professional and good at hiding his emotions. He massaged his temple with a forefinger. "What condition?"

Looking him straight in the eye, she said, "That Rob and John Townsend take paternity tests."

"I see," he said quietly. His mind racing, he picked up a pen and studied it as if it was twenty-four-carat gold.

"The land and money would have been nice, but since I've never had either, it doesn't matter that much. What matters most to me is finding my parents. I feel Mrs. Townsend wanted that for me, too."

C.J. had a one-track mind—finding her parents. That goal could be very costly to her, and Matthew wondered if she really understood what she was giving up.

His dark gaze searched her face. All he saw was a spirited woman who warmed his blood. That wasn't good; he was too aware of her, her beauty and her emotions. He had to get back to New York and to the kind of women he knew how to handle. Because he had no idea how to deal with C. J. Doe and her country-girl charm.

Matthew moved around his desk, hoping for a way to reach her. "Everyone knows Mrs. Townsend had a big heart. Don't you think that what she wanted was to give you some security? And in that case, it had nothing to do with your parentage."

She was thoughtful for a moment. "You're good. For a second there I almost believed that."

Sitting on the edge of the desk, Matthew folded his arms

across his chest. "Obviously you believe the rumors that have been circulating around this town for years."

"Rumors start somewhere."

One rumor stood out in Matthew's mind, and he knew it stood out in hers, too. "As I recall, the rumors started with Joe Bob Schaffer. He claimed a beautiful dark-haired woman drove into his gas station around eleven o'clock on Christmas Eve asking directions to the Townsend ranch. As he was putting gas in her car, he noticed a baby in a basket on the back seat."

"Yes," she murmured. That rumor had haunted her for years. Maybe because it had always seemed credible to her.

"Evidently you've forgotten that Joe Bob stayed drunk ninety-nine percent of the time and didn't remember the incident until two weeks after you'd been found. That is, after the Townsends refused to renew his lease on the gas station. Sounds to me like the man just had an ax to grind."

"Sounds like the truth to me," she replied, refusing to dismiss the rumor so lightly. She took another step toward him. "I have to know who I am. I have to know why I was left on a doorstep on a cold December morning. It's been burning inside me for years, and Mrs. Townsend has given me the power to force some answers. I believe that's what she intended all along."

The sincerity of her words touched him, but he felt he needed to be practical, to make her aware of the futility of her decision. "You're willing to give up a million dollars to find out if Rob or John Townsend is your father?"

"Yes," she answered without hesitation.

He didn't understand her reasoning, but he wasn't going to belabor the point. This was what he wanted, an easy solution. But was it easy? For her? And how were his clients going to react?

"You seem to feel sure the Townsends will agree to this."

"There are two things the Townsends understand—greed and power. But when it comes to a choice, greed will win every time."

He couldn't argue that point, but he had to remind her. "You could be the big loser in all this."

"Just knowing one way or the other will be a big victory for me. And I wouldn't consider that a loss."

There was great determination and confidence in her voice, but still he felt a need to warn her. "I strongly advise you to get an attorney."

A look of implacable resolve lit her eyes. "There are a lot of things I'm not sure of in this world, but of this decision I am very sure. I don't need a lawyer to fill my head with irrelevant nonsense." She took another step closer to him, so close he could see the fire in her eyes. "Let me make this easy for you and the Townsends. If one of the tests turns out to be positive, I'll relinquish any hold the Townsends fear I might have on their estate. Plus, whether the tests are positive or negative, I will release my claim on the land and the money."

He whistled between his teeth. "That's a powerful offer."

"Yes," she agreed, and turned toward the door. "When you have an answer, let me know," she tossed over her shoulder. With her hand on the doorknob, she turned back, green eyes twinkling. "Oh, Mr. Sloan, Jr., even though the Watsons are country people, we do have a telephone. So if you plan on coming out to the house, call first and I'll open the gate. A bullet hole could really ruin a suit like that." With those words she disappeared out the door.

A grin spread across Matthew's face. Through all this, she could maintain a sense of humor. He admired that and he couldn't help but admire her.

Unable to stop himself, he followed her to the front door. Through the window, he saw a four-wheel-drive truck pulling a long cattle trailer. Three horses occupied the trailer, and two dogs rested in the bed of the truck. Pete Watson sat on the passenger side of the cab, puffing on a pipe. It was actually a cab and a half, and he could see someone sitting in the back. Harry.

As he watched, C.J. climbed into the driver's side and the truck roared to life. Within seconds it pulled out into the main street of Coberville, the trailer clanging behind it.

"SO HOW'D IT GO?" Pete asked.

"It's going to take the city lawyer a while to recover from the shock. He tried to hide it, but I could see he thought I was crazy for throwing away all that money."

"I hope you get the answers you're looking for, girl," Pete said, and added tobacco to his pipe.

"Oh, I'll get something," she said. "The Townsends will be huddled over this for days, but in the end they won't be able to resist the offer. Then I'll know if I'm a Townsend or not."

"Don't like this," Harry muttered from the backseat.

In the rearview mirror, she caught Harry's bearded face. To some he was a scary figure, but to her he was a lovable old man and she adored him.

"'What's in a name? That which we call a rose by any other name would smell as sweet,'" Harry quoted.

C.J. appreciated his meaning in choosing this Shakespearean quote, but she had to ask, "Don't you want me to know the truth?"

"Truth." He snorted. "'Ye shall know the truth, and the truth shall make you mad.'"

C.J.'s smooth brow furrowed into a frown. Mad? Would the truth make her mad? Mad as in angry? Or deranged? What had Harry meant? She knew better than to ask.

Most of the time Harry quoted Shakespeare, but he often changed the words to suit his purpose. Few people remembered he had studied literature at the University of Texas in his younger days. He wasn't as ignorant as the majority of Coberville residents believed.

She shifted into third and anticipation ran through her. The Townsends *had* to accept her offer. The deal was too good to refuse, and she was counting on Matthew Sloan, Jr., to tell them that. While she'd been talking to him, she got the distinct impression that he was concerned for her welfare. That was ludicrous. Why would he care about her? He was the Townsends' lawyer. But she could still feel those dark eyes touching her skin, warming her in a way that had nothing to do with business. Careful, she warned herself. She had only one goal, and that precluded an emotional involvement with anyone, especially the Townsends' new lawyer.

MATTHEW WAS SO ABSORBED in watching the truck and trailer he didn't hear Miss Emma come in until she asked, "Wasn't that the Doe girl?"

He swung around and tried not to appear guilty at being caught staring. "Yes, it was."

She plopped her big purse on the desk. "I don't know how many times I've told that girl not to park that truck and trailer in front of this office. It takes up five or six parking spaces. Young folk never listen."

"She was only here a minute, and there's no traffic or clients at this hour."

"Still, it's the principle of the thing," she complained, and sank into her chair. "I guess she was here about the Townsend case."

"Yes, we discussed a few things," he replied, not wanting to get into particulars with Miss Emma.

He started to ask about Herman, but decided to let that subject rest. He headed back to his office, then stopped. The last thing he wanted to do was gossip, but his curiosity about C. J. Doe overrode his aversion to cheap talk.

"Exactly what does C. J. Doe do for a living?"

Miss Emma glanced up from going through the mail and gazed at him through those ridiculous glasses. "She works cattle with the Watsons."

"Works cattle?" he echoed blankly.

"Have you been gone from here so long you've forgotten what that is?"

"No," he assured her in a crisp voice. "It's just hard for me to imagine such a…small woman herding, branding and vaccinating cattle."

"They say she's the best," Miss Emma said, ripping open a letter. "She can ride and rope better than anyone around here. Has a way with animals, too. The Watsons are getting older and C.J. does most of the work now." She shook her head. "Never understood it. Why would a young girl give up a good job at the bank to work with those two old fools?"

"She worked at the bank?"

"Right after she graduated from college."

"She went to college?"

Miss Emma frowned at his startled face. "What did you think? That they kept her locked up on the ranch?"

"No, I just didn't see her as someone who could afford something like that."

The sharp letter opener sliced through another letter. "An anonymous benefactor, that's what it was."

"Someone paid for her college education?" He felt like Herman repeating everything she said, but he couldn't help himself.

"Sure did. An envelope of cash started coming to this office every month, and your dad deposited it in her account."

"Unbelievable," he said, then his eyes narrowed. "Did Dad know who was sending the money?"

"I don't think so. The first envelope had a letter of instruction about how the money was to be used. C.J. asked all kinds of questions, but she never found out anything. She even staked out the office. Finally, to put an end to her snooping, a large sum was deposited in your dad's name for her education. Money that couldn't be traced, 'cause believe me, C.J. tried."

Matthew tried to assimilate this bit of information. It was so unreal he had to find out more. "Why did she leave the job at the bank?"

Miss Emma shrugged. "Don't know. I guess she didn't like getting the cold shoulder from people who worked there. Your dad tried to talk her into staying there."

"Seems she and my dad were quite close."

"Your father helped a lot of people. C. J. Doe was just one of them."

That didn't explain anything, but he sensed Miss Emma was on the defensive, so he let it drop—for now.

Back at his desk his head was spinning. The money— that was how his dad had become involved with C. J. Doe. The pieces were starting to fall into place. He'd bet his dad had figured out who was sending the cash and confronted him or her. He'd also bet that person was one of C.J.'s parents, a parent who didn't want to be known to

C.J. or anyone else. So his dad had kept that person's secret, not even telling his own wife. Who was it? And why so much mystery?

He didn't have time to dwell on it now. He still had to deal with C.J.'s bombshell. "Miss Emma, call Rob Townsend and ask if I can see him this morning," he said through the open door.

Acceding to C.J.'s request went against his every legal instinct, but then, nothing about this case was going according to form. He felt she was guaranteed to be the loser and would definitely get hurt in the process. But that was no concern of his. So why did he feel it was?

CHAPTER FIVE

TODAY'S DRIVE WAS THE SAME as yesterday's, except that Matthew traveled about five miles farther down the road to the Cober ranch. Beyond the stone entrance were seven huge live oaks, hence the name Seven Trees. A towering Southern mansion with enormous white pillars stood proudly facing the trees, with a long drive circling in front of it. The scene was like something out of *Gone with the Wind* and it created the same impression of ante-bellum days. Bygone days.

The house had been built in the 1800s by Jeremiah Cober. His descendents had occupied it and Coberville ever since, a powerful family that time had not diminished.

Stopping on the circular drive, he got out and walked up the wide steps to the double front doors. He banged the brass door knocker and waited. A short man in a dark suit, white shirt and bow tie opened the door. The butler.

"Matthew Sloan to see Rob Townsend," he said.

"Yes, sir," the butler replied, stepping aside. "Come this way."

In the entrance, Matthew stared at the magnificent dual spiraling staircases, expecting Scarlett O'Hara to gracefully descend one of them any minute. The place was breathtaking, from the marble floors to the velvet drapes and antique furniture.

He followed the man into a large room that resembled

a library. "He will be right with you, sir," the butler said, and closed the door.

"Thank you." He scanned the room. Bookshelves covered two walls, and an antique desk and chair stood slightly to the right. Velvet chairs and sofa were grouped around a stone fireplace. On the opposite side of the room portraits of Cobers took pride of place, from Jeremiah Cober to William Cober and his two surviving children, Martha and Victoria, as well as his son, Will, who had died in early adulthood.

"Matthew," Rob said, coming through the door dressed in casual slacks and a knit shirt. "Dad and Aunt Martha will be along in a minute. I would like the whole family to be in on this meeting. But my sister Joyce and her husband, Thurman Brown, the congressman, live in Austin and they're busy with some political event. Clare, my other sister, also lives there. She's the editor of one of our newspapers. I'll have to fill them in later. Have a seat." He gestured toward a velvet chair.

Before Matthew could move, the door opened and an elderly lady came in. Martha Cober was tall and big-boned, with cropped gray hair and a rather plain face. Matthew couldn't help but be reminded of the difference between the two sisters. Victoria Cober had been a beauty, small and regal with flowing white hair.

"Matthew, I'm sure you remember my aunt Martha." Rob made the introduction just as a nurse brought a man in a wheelchair into the room. John Townsend. With white hair and drawn features, he was a shadow of the forceful senator Matthew remembered. "And, of course, you know Dad."

Matthew shook hands with the older man and was amazed at his strength. As Matthew glanced up, he noticed the nurse staring at him. Tall with bleached-blond hair and heavy makeup, she looked vaguely familiar.

"That will be all, Stephanie," Rob said before Matthew could make the connection. She immediately left the room.

"Okay, Matthew, tell us the good news," Rob said with a slight smile. "I'm sure the Doe girl has agreed to take the money."

Matthew had barely opened his mouth to speak when another woman strolled into the room in worn jeans and an oversize silk blouse. The clothes were water stained. She held a white poodle under one arm, while a second hovered at her feet. Her brown hair was pulled back into a ponytail, emphasizing her honey-colored eyes and austere features.

Francine Gordon Townsend wasn't the raving beauty everyone had expected Rob to marry. But years ago, when John Townsend's political clout had began to wane, Rob had married the only daughter of a powerful political figure in Texas, forging the two families together and solidifying John Townsend's bid for reelection. Politics did indeed make for strange bedfellows, Matthew thought.

"Darling." Francine's gaze settled on Rob. "You weren't going to have this meeting without me, were you?"

"I didn't think you'd be interested," Rob replied, and walked over to her, giving her a withering glance. "What have you been doing? You look like hell."

An expression of pain crossed Francine's face. "I was grooming the dogs," she answered tightly.

"You pay people to do that," Rob snapped. "Why do you insist on doing menial chores?"

Francine ignored her husband's words and crossed to Matthew. She introduced herself and shook his hand. As Matthew gazed into her eyes, he saw pain. For years she had competed for Rob's attention, and Matthew could see from the defeated look in her eyes that she was wondering if the struggle had been worth it.

She patted the poodle's head and said, "So you're the New York attorney. I heard you're very good in a courtroom."

"Thank you," Matthew said, not sure how to respond to her. He had a feeling Francine Townsend was close to the edge.

"Are you going to make the Townsends' little problem go away?" She leaned in close and whispered, "Makes you wonder, doesn't it? Why would Mother Townsend be so generous to C. J. Doe? Could it be she was trying to bail her son's ass out of a jam one more time?"

Francine knew how to be a proper lady. Having attended the best schools, she could walk, talk and choose which fork to use at the dinner table with the best of them. But evidently she had learned some language in less reputable places, too.

"Rob, your wife's making a fool of herself," Martha said.

Francine swung around and fixed her eyes on the older woman. "Well, Aunt Martha, dear, if anyone can recognize a fool, you can. Look at the way you fawn over your sister's husband."

"That's enough, Francine," Rob ordered.

Francine turned to face him. "I want my children home for the summer, Rob."

"The kids are staying in boarding school," he replied. "You're making a sissy out of Robbie, and our daughter's becoming so wild no one can do anything with her. They need discipline, not a free rein like you give them."

"Rob," she pleaded, a note of desperation entering her voice.

Rob ignored her plea. "Go get cleaned up, for God's sake. You look like the hired help."

At Rob's criticism Matthew saw a flash of unmistakable pain on her face again, but she quickly masked it. "I want my children home," she stated angrily.

"They're staying in school."

"We'll see about that," she replied, and turned toward the door. "Nice to have met you, Mr. Sloan," she called over her shoulder.

As the door closed, Rob apologized. "My wife's been having a rough time since the kids went away to school."

"Ha," Martha retorted.

Rob shot her a quelling glance and then focused his attention on Matthew. "Now, Matthew, I hope you have some good news for us."

Matthew shoved his hands into his pockets. How could Rob treat his wife so heartlessly? Couldn't he see she was hurting? Dealing with the Townsends was going to be harder than he'd imagined—for more than one reason. He brought his thoughts back to Rob's question. "No, I don't."

Rob's eyes narrowed. "Why not? Surely she didn't turn down a million dollars."

"Afraid so."

Rob walked around the desk and sat down, a patently false smile on his face. "Damn, she's smarter than I figured."

Matthew frowned. "What do you mean?"

"She's holding out for more money," Rob replied. "Okay, we can play that game. Offer her two million."

Matthew held up his hands. "Wait a minute. She's not after more money."

Rob spared him a dark glance. "Then what the hell *does* she want from us?"

"She's made a counteroffer."

"A counteroffer," Rob said with a laugh. "What does she have to offer us?"

Matthew took in the skeptical faces. Slowly he answered, "She will release her claim on both the land and the money on one condition."

A tense pause followed his words, and Matthew could almost hear the frantic heartbeats in the room. They had a right to be anxious, he thought. C. J. Doe was about to rock their world.

Finally Rob asked, "And what would this condition be?"

Matthew glanced from Rob to John Townsend. In his best courtroom voice he said, "That you and your father take paternity tests."

Martha gasped and Rob brought his fist down hard on the desk. "No way, Matthew. No way in hell is that ever going to happen."

"She has agreed that if it does, if you both get tested, she will relinquish any claim on the Townsend estate."

"She's thought of everything, hasn't she?" Rob muttered. "But we refuse to give credence to those stupid rumors she obviously believes."

"Well, it's the only way you're going to get the land back without going to court."

"Everybody has a price. Offer her three million."

Matthew gave a frustrated sigh. "Money means nothing to her, I've told you that. You can offer her ten million and she'd still turn it down. She only wants to know who she is."

"She is not a Townsend." Fists clenched, Rob got angrily to his feet. "She—"

"The girl must be crazy," Martha broke in. "John is in no condition to go through such stress. He's recovering from a stroke.'' She sat next to John Townsend's wheelchair and rubbed his arm affectionately.

Matthew shrugged. ''It's a simple blood test. As your lawyer I have to say it's a good offer.''

''You're not suggesting we do this?'' Rob bellowed.

''No, it's your decision, but it's the only offer you'll get from C. J. Doe.''

Rob tapped long fingers against the desk for a moment, then said, ''Offer her three million. Money has a way of changing people's minds.''

''No!'' John Townsend shouted.

Everyone looked at him. The single word was the first he'd spoken during the whole meeting. His blue eyes blazed with a strength of old, and he looked like the powerful John Townsend who could melt a man in his boots with just one word. Even though his legs were weak, Matthew had a feeling John's mind was as sharp as ever.

''Dad, what are you saying?''

''I'm saying we're going to take the blood tests.''

''What?''

''Use your head, son. What's the use of throwing money away when we can end this with a simple test?''

''But, Dad…''

Matthew could see the doubt in Rob's eyes and there was doubt in John's eyes, too, but unlike his son he was willing to gamble that C. J. wasn't a Townsend.

John gazed up at Matthew, his expression fierce. ''Let's get one thing straight, Sloan,'' he said. ''I want this done discreetly. I don't want any publicity—in the newspapers, TV or magazines—anywhere.''

''I don't think she'll have a problem with that.''

''And even if one of the tests is positive, she will not expect anything from this family.''

Matthew watched the fire in the man's eyes and had to

ask. "If she *is* a Townsend, can you turn your back on her?"

"In a heartbeat, sir," he said without hesitation.

Matthew got a glimpse of the ruthlessness that had made this man so powerful. "I see. Okay. I'll set everything up."

Martha clutched John's arm. "You don't have to do this."

He shrugged off her hand. "Shut up, Martha."

For a moment Matthew studied the three people in the room. They had to be the unhappiest people he'd ever met. Just as the old saying had it, money and power really didn't guarantee happiness. But he wondered why they didn't seem to have an ounce of feeling for another human being. Victoria Townsend had felt differently. Why? Why was she so generous to C.J.? But it wasn't his job to solve the mystery between the Townsends and C. J. Doe, he told himself. He was here only to do this job as a courtesy to his dad, then he'd go back to New York and his own world. But the more involved he became with the case, the more it intrigued him.

Clearing his throat, he said, "I'll get back to you on the place and time."

"You do that," Rob said with a curt nod.

Matthew hurried from the room. When he reached the hall, he took a deep breath, trying to dispel the stifling oppressive feeling he'd felt in the Townsend family's presence.

"DAD, WHY ARE YOU DOING this?" Rob asked a moment after the door closed on Matthew.

"Son, haven't I taught you anything? When things get rough, play into your opponent's hand, but always keep an ace up your sleeve."

Rob shook his head. "What the hell does that mean?"

A wicked smile curved John's thin lips. "It means we take the tests, but we make sure they come out negative."

Realization dawned, and a smile spread across Rob's face.

"Being in high places pays off. You meet people who can help you out in a situation like this," John told him, a gleam in his old eyes.

Rob watched his father. "Then you're not sure she's not yours?"

"Just like *you're* not sure she's not yours."

The silence grew heavy with tension. John cleared his throat. "You take your love of women after me, son, but we're not going to let it cost you this election. Understand?"

"Understand." Rob smiled a secret smile.

John nodded his approval, but he wasn't through. "Don't you think it's time you got your kids home?"

The smile vanished from Rob's face. "Don't start," he warned.

"Your wife's falling apart."

"She'll adjust."

"The kids have been gone since the fall. She's not adjusting. She dresses shabbily, uses foul language and spends all her time with those dogs. She's not the lady you married."

"Stay out of this," Rob warned again. "This doesn't concern you. Besides, you sent *me* away to school."

"It didn't help your rebellious streak, did it?"

"No," Rob admitted.

"Then learn from my mistakes, son," he said. "It took Francine so long to get pregnant. Those kids are extra-special to her."

"That's the damn problem," Rob snapped. "She spoils them. No, they're staying in school."

John raised his eyebrows. "Do you want to win this election?" he asked in a low voice.

"Of course I do!"

"Then use your damn head. We need her and her family's support. The minute the semester is over, get the kids home and spend some time together. Go places—and make sure there's a photographer along. Plaster those pictures all over Texas. Let everyone see y'all as a loving family."

At Rob's hesitation John pointed a shaking finger at him. "If you lose this election, I'll never forgive you."

Rob gritted his teeth, then said, "I've never done anything to please the great John Townsend. But I'll win the election and I'll win in a big way."

"You'd better," John told him. "And you'd better get your kids home first."

Rob inhaled audibly. "I'll give it some thought," he promised.

"Good," John replied, victory in his tone. "Now hand me the phone. It's time to get rid of the Doe problem." He laughed harshly. "Never thought the little idiot would make it so easy."

MATTHEW WALKED QUICKLY down the hall to the foyer and the front door, eager to get back to the office. With any luck this case could be wrapped up in a couple of weeks and he could resume his life in New York. He worried about his mom, though. He couldn't leave until she was better.

Quietly closing the door, he started down the steps.

"Hello, Matthew." A silky smooth voice stopped him. He swung around to find the nurse smiling at him. The white uniform clung to her shapely body, and a ready smile indicated she'd been waiting for him.

"You don't remember me, do you?" she asked, moving closer to him.

His eyes swept over the blond hair, brown eyes and red red lips. Something about her was familiar but he still couldn't place her. "Sorry. No, I don't."

"Stephanie Cox, the frumpy brown-haired girl you used to let copy your homework."

"Stephanie Cox," he echoed in disbelief. Suddenly he recalled the shy overweight girl he'd always felt sorry for. The memory didn't jibe with the woman standing before him.

"Isn't it amazing what diet, exercise and makeup can do for a girl?"

He studied her new appearance again. "Yes, it is," he replied slowly, thinking that peroxide and plastic surgery also had something to do with the changed look. He couldn't help feeling that he liked the shy plain young girl much better. There was a hardness in this one's eyes that made him instinctively draw back.

She stepped even closer. Long artificial red nails fingered the lapel of his jacket. Expensive perfume filled his nostrils. "You were always so nice," she whispered, and batted her long fake eyelashes at him. "Are you still a nice man, Matthew Sloan?"

"I try to be."

She batted the eyelashes again. "Why don't we meet for dinner and discuss old times…and our mutual employer?"

So that was it. She was after information. "Sorry, Stephanie, but I'm really busy. I'm trying to wrap up my dad's cases before I go back to New York. Besides, I don't discuss my clients with anyone."

She was so close now he could feel the heat emanating from her body. "Was that a put-down?" she asked.

"Just the truth," he answered with a decided effort not to move away from her. Did she really think that cheap look and act appealed to a man? he wondered. Well, maybe a desperate man, he conceded. But it didn't do a thing for him.

One fingernail traced a blue triangle in his tie, then she smiled suggestively. "I could turn your very busy day into a night you won't forget."

"I'll bet you could, and believe me, I'll keep it in mind." He removed her hand from his lapel, returned her smile with a careful one of his own, then headed down the steps.

"Goodbye, Matthew Sloan," she called after him.

As he climbed into his truck, the air whooshed from his lungs and he realized he'd been holding his breath. What was that all about? Stephanie Cox sure wanted something from him, and it was more than his body. How did she fit into the puzzle of C. J. Doe and the Townsends?

CHAPTER SIX

WHEN MATTHEW GOT BACK to the office, he dialed C.J.'s number, but there was no answer.

Miss Emma poked her head around the door. "You're due at the courthouse at one o'clock."

He looked at his watch. "No time for lunch."

"I'll get Frank to send over a sandwich from the café."

"Thanks, Miss Emma." He smiled. He was beginning to see why his dad had put up with her for so many years. He could use someone like her in New York, he thought fleetingly. Miss Emma in New York. He shuddered at the image.

Later that evening when he opened the door of his parents' house, the most delicious aroma enticed him. His mom was cooking and he recognized the smell of his favorite—pot roast.

He stood in the kitchen doorway and watched her for a moment. An apron with a happy face on it covered her dress. She set plates on the table with a quick hand, but her eyes were cloudy.

She turned and saw him. "Hi," she said in a wobbly voice.

She had to deal with her grief in her own way, but he hated to see her like this. It made him feel so helpless. Putting his arms around her, he said, "Mom, you don't have to cook. I can eat anything."

"It keeps me busy," she sniffed into his shoulder.

Brushing away a tear, she added, "I'm so glad you're here."

"Me, too."

"How was your day?"

"Exhausting," he replied with a teasing note in his voice.

She glanced at the stove, a smile touching her face. "Supper's almost ready, so go wash up."

He left the kitchen without saying a word, feeling like that ten-year-old boy who used to love coming home to the smell of his mother's cooking. Were there women like his mom left in this world? he wondered. Women who cared about home and hearth and family? Most of the women he met were like Stephanie Cox; they wanted something from him he wasn't willing to give. Then there was C. J. Doe....

At the thought of her, he went into his dad's study and dialed her number.

"Hello." Her soft husky voice came down the line.

He felt a swift familiar sensation of desire. Her voice alone had more power over him than Stephanie Cox's entire body. Shaking that reaction from his mind, he said, "Miss Doe, this is Matthew Sloan."

"Yes?"

"The Townsends have agreed to your offer."

A long pause. "Miss Doe, did you hear me?"

"Yes, I heard you. I'm just stunned. I didn't expect them to accept so quickly."

"They want it done discreetly, no publicity."

"I don't have a problem with that."

"I didn't think you would."

"I would like to choose the lab, though."

Startled, he asked, "Any reason for that?"

"Yes. I don't trust the Townsends. They have too much

power in this state. I want a reputable lab that won't be tempted by bribery.''

"I see. And you know of such a lab?''

"I'll make some phone calls and let you know in the morning.''

"That'll be fine,'' he replied, a little surprised by her shrewdness. "You do realize the Townsends have to agree to the lab?''

"Yes.''

"Then I won't do anything further until I hear from you.''

"Thank you, Mr. Sloan, Jr.''

"For what?''

"I'm not sure. I guess for getting things done so quickly.''

"You don't make it easy, especially since you haven't retained an attorney. I wish I could make you understand how important it is for you to have a lawyer, someone to protect your interests.''

"Well, then, that's why I should thank you—for not taking advantage of me.''

"With those trigger-happy protectors around you, a man would have to be a fool to take advantage of you, Miss Doe.''

"Pete and Harry are harmless.''

"If you say so.''

He could feel her smiling and wished he could see her face. The sight had to be magical. His own lips curved into an answering smile. "I'll talk to you tomorrow.''

As he hung up the phone, the smile left his face. He hoped it would all turn out the way she wanted. Then he felt a moment's shock. What was wrong with him? He wasn't her lawyer, so he shouldn't care about her interests, but—God help him—he did.

Had his father experienced these same feelings? Was that the reason he'd done nothing about the case? Or maybe there was something about C.J. that caused men to lose their sense of reason.

C.J. WALKED ONTO THE PORCH and sat on the swing. Dusk had settled in and the earth seemed to sigh, accepting the darkness and peace of nightfall. Pete puffed on his pipe and Harry whittled one of his many horse figures.

As she curled her feet beneath her, thoughts of Matthew Sloan, Jr., soon eclipsed the evening song of crickets and a faraway whippoorwill. Every time she heard his serious voice she got a fluttering in her stomach. Why was she so aware of him? He was the enemy, and a city man to boot. She knew the answer, but it really didn't matter, she told herself. In a little while, he'd be gone and out of her life.

The Townsends had agreed to the tests. It was unbelievable, but it was the best news she'd heard in a long time.

Pete watched her thoughtfully. "Who was on the phone?"

"Matthew Sloan, Jr. The Townsends said yes to the blood tests."

A shaggy eyebrow shot up in surprise. "You don't say."

She clasped her hands together. "Now I'll have some answers. I'll find out if I'm a Townsend."

Pete rested his elbows on his knees, his brown eyes skeptical. "Girl, don't go gettin' your hopes up."

"I'm trying not to, but it's hard."

"'The devil hath power to assume a pleasing shape,'" Harry interjected.

C.J. sighed with exasperation. "Harry, that makes no sense."

His knife slipped through a piece of wood with ease, leaving wood shavings at his feet. "Beware of the devil in men, my girl," he told her.

She chewed on her lower lip and decided to give up trying to understand Harry and his quotes. But sometimes there was logic hidden in his words. Tonight, though, she didn't want to search for logic. She wanted to savor this moment.

Pete took a puff on his pipe, his eyes narrowed, as the aromatic scent of tobacco drifted toward her. "Just be sure this is what you want, girl," he said. "Because when it's all over, you're not gonna have anything Victoria Townsend left you. All you'll have are the results of a couple of blood tests."

"I'll have the truth," she said fiercely. "I have to know who I am."

Why couldn't anyone accept how badly she needed that? Pete and Harry, in their practical wisdom and their deep concern for her, saw only that the land and money would give her a secure future. But without a past she *had* no future. She would only be existing in a world where she didn't belong. This was her last chance to find her identity. In her heart she knew it was what Victoria had wanted for her.

What if the results are negative? a voice inside whispered. She'd simply start over, she decided resolutely. She knew the risks and she was willing to take them. Negative or positive, she could handle the results.

Getting up, she headed into the house. "I've got some phone calls to make." She stopped by Pete's chair; her hand touched his shoulder in a hesitant gesture.

He patted her hand. "I understand, girl."

She knew he did. He'd watched her suffer over the years, and if the blood tests were going to give her some peace, then he'd support this. She realized he had nagging doubts, but for her, he'd pushed them aside.

She bent and quickly kissed his rough cheek, knowing that whatever she had to go through in this world, Pete and Harry would be behind her one hundred percent.

THE NEXT MORNING C.J. walked into Matthew's office and laid a piece of paper on his desk.

At the sight of her his pulse quickened. Her long hair was pulled back and held in place by a single red ribbon. Snug Wrangler's hugged her long slim legs, and a red sleeveless shirt set off her slender tanned arms. A pink hue tinted her cheeks, either from the flush of excitement or just the reflection of her shirt. He couldn't be sure. Whatever the reason, the effect was stunning.

He tore his eyes away and picked up the paper, scanning it.

"That's a lab in Austin. Ryder Laboratories. Cliff Ryder is the director," C.J. said.

Matthew fingered the paper. "Exactly how are you acquainted with this lab?"

She slanted him a cool look. "Why are you asking?"

"Because a lab shouldn't be chosen if it has an association with one of the involved parties."

She sighed in annoyance. "I met Cliff Ryder at a party in college. I haven't seen him since. He's a reputable man, and he wouldn't jeopardize his career for me or anyone." Taking a deep breath, she added, "I have nothing to gain from any fabrication."

"I have to guard the Townsends' interests."

She shrugged impatiently. "By all means."

He called the Townsends and explained the situation. When he'd hung up, he said, "I have to check out the lab. Make some inquiries. You understand?"

"Sure, no problem." She sat down and with one hand gathered her hair over her shoulder in a quick smooth movement.

He'd expected her to leave, but then she never did what he expected. Picking up the phone, he called his law firm in New York and set the wheels of inquiry in motion.

They waited in silence. Matthew twisted in his chair, watching her. She sat perfectly still, her eyes unblinking, unwavering. All that intensity focused on him made him edgy. He almost felt seventeen again, a confusing condition he hadn't liked then and liked even less now.

He cleared his throat. "This could take a while."

"I have all the time in the world, Mr. Sloan, Jr." Her tone was faintly mocking, as if she knew something he didn't.

"We're going to have to do something about that."

"About what?"

"My name. Mr. Sloan, Jr., is getting a little tiresome."

"It is your name, isn't it?"

He knew she was teasing him, baiting him just a little. "Yes, but I prefer Matthew."

"Matthew." She said his name with a warm sweetness. He could almost taste the sound. "Okay, I'll call you Matthew." She smiled a tantalizing smile that charged his senses. That smile was everything he'd known it would be—dazzling, beguiling, mysterious. Her face relaxed and the curve of her mouth softened. Softened so temptingly that all he could think about was touching it with his own and...

He moved restlessly in his chair. "And if it's okay, I'll call you C.J."

"Sure," she replied, a look of faint amusement on her face.

Was she flirting with him? God, he was in big trouble

if he had to ask himself that. He had experienced flirting many times, but with C.J. it was different. She had a naïveté about her that threw him completely off guard.

Suddenly her eyes darkened. "You think I'm crazy for turning down a million dollars and offering to give back the land, don't you?"

He blinked, hardly able to believe she'd sunk her pride enough to ask the question. It was the first chink in that wall he had noticed the first day he'd met her. He wanted to give her an honest answer, but couldn't. He wasn't her attorney. "I really can't say."

Her brow furrowed. "Knowing who I am is much more important to me. You've had loving parents all your life. You don't know that…that emptiness. Wondering if the lady at the grocer's is your mother or the man sitting next to you in church is your father. There's no worse feeling than not knowing."

The despair in her voice tied his stomach in knots. "I can only imagine."

She threw up her hands. "This whole thing is bizarre. It doesn't make sense."

"What do you mean?"

"It doesn't make sense that Victoria Townsend would leave me a thousand acres of Cober land. That one-hundred-acre tract Pete and Harry own in the middle of Cober property has been a thorn in their side for years."

Matthew leaned back in his chair. "Exactly how did the Watsons end up with that land?" Growing up in Coberville, he had heard the story, but he wondered how much he'd heard was true.

"It goes back over a hundred years. Daniel Watson helped Jeremiah Cober settle Coberville. They built the town together, but Jeremiah was the one with money and power. Daniel had skills and brawn, but he liked to drink and gamble and he lost everything he'd acquired.''

She paused, winding a strand of hair around her finger. ''Down on his luck and with only a pair of mules to his name, Daniel invited Jeremiah to a poker game. Jeremiah agreed because he wanted those mules. As the night went on, so did the drinking. It was finally Daniel's night. Jeremiah was losing big and eventually he had to deed over a hundred acres to settle his debt. When Jeremiah sobered up, he was furious and wanted the land back, but Daniel refused. He knew it was his last chance to have anything. He changed his way of life, got married and settled on the land. The Cobers tried for years to buy back those hundred acres, but the Watsons were there to stay. That's what doesn't make sense. Why would Victoria add to the tract? Cobers must be turning over in their graves.''

''It does seem odd,'' he mused, hearing the pride in her voice when she talked about Daniel Watson. She might not be a Watson by birth, but her loyalty was with them. He wondered if the story had any relevance to the present situation between C.J. and the Townsends.

''So you see, I feel Victoria had something else in mind.''

At his confused look she explained. ''The land and money give me the power to force the truth. Victoria knew the Townsends would do anything to get the land back— even take a blood test.''

So that was how she'd come to her decision, he thought. She was betting everything to discover her identity. Nothing else was important to her, not land or money.

The phone rang, and he picked up the receiver immediately. ''Yes? Oh, Fred... When can you get it fixed? Not till Friday? I need my truck.... Yes, I know I can walk to the office, but I do go other places. Just fix it.

"That was Fred at the garage," he told her. "He's working on my dad's truck. It's like dealing with Goober of Mayberry."

An understanding flash of humor crossed her face.

The phone rang again and Matthew wished Miss Emma would answer it, but this was her beauty-shop morning and she wasn't in yet.

"Excuse me," he said, and picked up the receiver again. "Hello. Yes. Okay, Tom. Fax me what you have. Yes, we have a fax machine in this one-horse town. The number is the same as the office phone, and mind your p's and q's. You're talking about my hometown."

He was smiling as he hung up, and she thought the smile changed his whole appearance. It softened the lines around his mouth and brought out the warmth in his dark eyes. She felt the flutter in her stomach again.

"My firm didn't find out a whole lot, but the lab seems reputable and Dr. Ryder has a stellar reputation."

"I told you that."

His smile broadened. "So you did."

They stared at each other for a long moment. Matthew's smile lingered as his gaze traveled over her lovely features, dark hair, smooth skin, full inviting lips. The smile left his face as a feeling of desire stirred deep in his belly. A desire that had nothing to do with labs or blood tests. A desire he shouldn't feel for a woman who was on the opposing side.

At his lazy stare the flutter in C.J.'s stomach became almost unbearable. His eyes were so dark and warm, and when he looked at her like that, his gaze sliding over her features so slowly, so thoroughly, it made her skin ache for his touch. C.J. was shocked by the direction her mind had taken. He was working for the Townsends, she had to remind herself—not to mention her own suspicions about him. She had to get her emotions under control.

Matthew was the first to look away. "When do you want to do this?" he asked, his voice all business now.

Realizing he was waiting for an answer, she said quickly, "As soon as possible."

"I knew you were going to say that."

He called the lab and spoke to someone, obviously a receptionist. Dr. Ryder was out of town and wouldn't be back until Thursday. Matthew scheduled the appointments and hung up.

"Your blood test is at ten on Thursday and the Townsends' are at one," he told her. "I've made an appointment to see Dr. Ryder at nine-thirty to make sure he's aware of the situation and what we want done."

"Fine," she said, getting to her feet. "Since your truck is out of commission," she said hesitantly, "and we have to be there about the same time, would it be unethical if we rode together?"

Matthew frowned, complete surprise on his face. "Are you offering me a ride?"

Was she? C.J. didn't know what she was doing. One minute the thought crossed her mind; the next she heard the words coming out of her mouth. It was dangerous, her head told her, but her heart was saying something else.

Her eyes caught his. "Yes," she heard herself say.

An invitation was the last thing he'd expected, but spending time with her was too tempting to refuse. Besides, he didn't see anything unethical about it.

As he opened his mouth to speak, she added, "That is, if you don't mind riding in a four-wheel-drive truck."

He moved around his desk and toward her. "I think I can handle it," he murmured. "Thanks for asking."

"You're welcome," she said, his nearness causing her

pulse to pound in her ears. "I'll pick you up at eight. We'll take the shortcut on 1292. That should give us enough time."

"Sounds great. See you Thursday."

She nodded and left the office.

Matthew rubbed his temples. He should have thought this over a little more. The Townsends weren't going to be pleased about his riding into Austin with C. J. Doe. But when he was with her, he couldn't seem to remember which side he was supposed to be on. He wondered, not for the first time, if she had that effect on all men—his dad, too. This had definitely never happened to him before. Nothing ever got in the way of his cases. He'd call later and cancel, he decided. He'd borrow his mother's car for the day.

C.J. SAT IN HER TRUCK. Two women walked by, whispered, pointed at her. C.J. barely noticed. What had made her do such a stupid thing, offering him a ride like that? He was the Townsends' lawyer. But he was also Matt's son.

One hand hit the steering wheel in anger. *Admit it,* she told herself. *Admit what you're really feeling.* She was attracted to Matthew, and it frightened her to death. When he'd come out to the house that first day, Pete had teased her about staring at him. She had stared for obvious reasons, but she'd also been looking for a resemblance to herself. There, it was out in the open, playing havoc with her mind—forcing her to face the possibility. *They could be related.* She closed her eyes, feeling utterly miserable.

C.J. had faced the same fear ever since she'd found out the difference between boys and girls. She didn't know who she was, so there could be no involvement with any man in Coberville. Why *had* she offered Matthew a ride?

It was insane. When she looked at him, though, she saw no resemblance, no familiar characteristics. Something inside her was driving her on. She had to get rid of the doubts, and the only way to do that was to spend time with him, to ask questions.

Deep down she sensed that they weren't related, but she had to *know*. Just as she had to know if she was a Townsend. With both hands she gripped her throbbing head. Would she ever learn the truth? Would the doubts ever end?

THE PHONE RANG in a seedy apartment on the south side of Austin. "Yeah?" Dale Weeks bellowed into the receiver.

"I've got a job for you."

"Already?"

"Yes. C. J. Doe will be traveling to Austin for a ten-o'clock appointment on Thursday. I want you to ensure that she doesn't make it."

"Are you saying you want me to kill her?"

"Make it look like an accident."

"This'll cost you fifty big ones."

"I'll get twenty-five to you tonight. You'll get the other half when the job's done."

"What is it about this girl that's got you so scared? There's nothing she—"

"I want her dead, Weeks," an impatient voice interrupted. "That's all you need to know."

"Sure thing. Consider it done."

PROMPTLY AT EIGHT O'CLOCK Thursday morning, C.J. drove up to the front of Matthew's house. She studied the white board house with its long porch, white columns and black shutters. Perfect. The picture-perfect yard with neat flower beds and white picket fence. Like a scene out of a Norman Rockwell painting. What did it feel like to be raised in a perfect home with two loving parents? She could only imagine.

Matthew emerged from the front door in a dark suit and crisp white shirt. As his long confident strides brought him closer, her heart thudded noisily, despite her attempts to suppress any awareness of him.

She glanced down at the black slacks, vest and emerald-green blouse she'd chosen to wear. Damn. She should have worn her usual jeans. He was going to get the wrong impression. She was flirting with the enemy and that meant danger. Danger to her heart.

On his way to the truck Matthew scolded himself for not calling her to cancel. He'd been so busy and somehow it had slipped his mind. Or maybe it had slipped his mind on purpose, a little voice whispered. Now there was nothing he could do but enjoy the ride. He noted she was driving a different truck from the one he'd seen her in the other day. This one was also white, but newer.

He climbed into the cab and gave her a nod. Buckling his seat belt, he noticed her clothes, saw that there was even a green ribbon entwined in the French braid hanging down her back. Her fresh radiance reached out to him.

He shifted uncomfortably and took in the blue interior and leather seats. "Nice truck," he commented.

"Thanks," she answered, pulling away from the curb. "This is my truck. We use Pete's to haul the big trailer."

They stopped for a blinking red light at the intersection. Little traffic was on the road at this hour, so she drove on.

"This is a big day," Matthew said, attempting conversation.

She turned onto County Road 1292. "It'll be an even bigger day when the test results are in."

"I suppose," he murmured, and they didn't speak again for several minutes.

A soft melody on the radio filled the silence. He watched her hands on the steering wheel. She looked so fragile, yet he knew she was strong. That was evident from the way she'd controlled her horse the other day. Fragility and strength wrapped in a charming package. A very potent combination.

"I'm sure you'll be glad to close this case and get back to New York."

He blinked in momentary confusion. "Uh, yes, I can't stay away too much longer."

"Your dad was so proud of you. He talked about your cases all the time."

He stared at her, his eyebrows drawing together. "Dad talked to you about me?"

She met his startled gaze for a second. "Yes, he enjoyed your big victories. Like that eighty-four-year-old man you got off for killing his cancer-ridden wife."

"I didn't exactly get him off. He received a ten-year probated sentence and is under psychiatric care."

"But he's not in prison with hardened criminals."

"No," Matthew answered absently, feeling an ache in his chest. Why had his father shared so much with C.J.? He now knew about the money for her education and his dad's involvement. But their association went beyond that. They'd obviously shared everyday events. Yet, despite the many conversations he'd had with his father, C.J.'s name had never been mentioned. Why?

CHAPTER SEVEN

THEY RODE FOR A WHILE in silence. The road, an old blacktop, led straight into Austin, shortening the trip by at least fifteen minutes. The ride was relatively smooth, except for the occasional pothole.

Matthew turned slightly, resting his arm along the back of the seat, his fingertips about three inches from C.J.'s shoulder. He wanted to find out more about the relationship between her and his father. The only way to do that was to ask questions. He was good at asking questions.

"Tell me about yourself," he invited, knowing the best place to start was at the beginning. "About your childhood."

She shot him a glance. "Are you curious about me?"

"Enormously," he admitted. "I know you were left on the Watsons' doorstep as a baby and they couldn't adopt you because of their age, but why didn't Social Services find you a home?"

Her green eyes held a distant faraway look. "Maggie said that when I was an infant, they were approached by several couples who wanted a baby, but later they were told each one was found unsuitable. Social Services kept looking. When I was old enough to understand, Maggie told me that one day a beautiful woman and a handsome man would come for me. They would be my new parents. I used to watch the road waiting for them. But then I'd hope they'd never come because I didn't want to leave

Pete and Maggie." The fingers gripping the steering wheel had whitened. "No one ever came. Finally we decided I'd just gotten lost in the system. Pete and Maggie considered it a blessing."

His heart ached for that little girl waiting for someone to claim her. At least she'd had the Watsons. Clearing his throat, he asked, "What happened to Maggie?" He knew Maggie had died some years ago, but didn't recall the details.

A shadow of pain darkened her eyes. "She died of cancer when I was twelve."

"You must have loved her a great deal."

"Yes, she was the only mother I ever knew." Her voice and her face held a certain sadness. After a moment she added, "When she died, I was afraid Social Services was going to come and get me and put me in a girls' home. I told Pete, but he said no one was ever going to take me away. I believed him 'cause Pete never lies to me." She paused, then said, "When we finally realized Social Services wasn't interested in me anymore, Pete said we should go down to the courthouse and change my name to Watson. I thought about it, but I decided I didn't want just a name—not even his. I wanted my *real* name. I wanted to know whose blood ran through my veins. That was the beginning of my quest to find my parents. I started asking questions. I talked to everyone from the sheriff to every person who had green eyes or black hair. Everything brings me back to the rumors and the Townsends."

She spoke with a quiet firmness and he had to ask, "How does Pete feel about your decision?"

"Pete always supports me. He and Maggie taught me never to make a decision unless I had the strength to handle the consequences."

Did she have that much strength? She could lose everything. Why did that bother him so much? He shook his head, reminding himself that he was getting sidetracked.

"How did you find out you were left on their doorstep?"

She shrugged while negotiating a turn. "Seems like I've always known. I can remember as a small child people pointing at me and whispering."

He remembered that, too, and had often wondered how people could be so cruel. "That must have been hard for you."

"Yes." She managed a laugh. "I never could understand why people didn't seem to like me. Maggie said they were afraid of me. They didn't know who I was or where I came from. I could be a sister, daughter, cousin or related in some way, and people don't like skeletons in their closets. So instead of dealing with it, they chose to ignore me."

"That probably changed when you went to college."

"Yes, people were friendlier there."

"And I bet those college boys buzzed around you like bees around honey," he said.

"I didn't notice. I was too busy concentrating on my studies."

"You don't expect me to believe that, do you?"

She spared him a quick glance. "Okay, I had lots of invitations for dates, but I didn't get serious with anyone until my senior year. When his parents found out I didn't even know who my parents were, Shawn's interest cooled. I promised never to let myself in for that type of pain again." She took an aching breath, hardly able to believe she was telling him her innermost secrets. Secrets she never shared with anyone.

Figuring turnaround was fair play, she said, "I suppose you've had lots of serious relationships?"

"A few," he admitted.

She noticed his forefinger rubbing his temple. He did that whenever he was uncomfortable, she decided. Obviously Matthew didn't like to talk about the women in his life.

Throwing caution aside, she pressed on. "So why haven't you ever married?"

A long pause followed her question. She could feel those dark eyes boring into her, but she kept her own eyes steadily on the road.

Finally he said, "I don't know, but I guess after witnessing the perfect marriage, I find it hard to settle for anything less."

Perfect marriage. He was talking about his parents. Those old fears clamored in the back of her head.

"So you're looking for someone like your mother," she said to block out doubts she didn't want to feel.

"Not exactly. It's that special feeling my parents shared. They were partners, friends, lovers and so much more. They just enjoyed being together and still held hands and kissed right up until the end. My parents were truly in love and that never changed—like it does with so many these days."

Matthew thought of Gail back in New York, one of the lawyers in his firm. He never liked to get involved with a colleague, but through many long hours and late nights, they were drawn together. They'd been seeing each other about a year. He knew Gail was getting serious, so he'd decided to slow things down because he didn't want her to be hurt. This time away was what he needed, to sort through his feelings. He hated to admit he hadn't missed Gail at all and thought about her very little. It was the trauma of his dad's death, he told himself, but he knew it was more. That special feeling just wasn't there.

C.J. heard the love in his voice when he talked about his parents. There was no way she'd ever want to change that. She noticed his distant look and knew he wasn't thinking of his parents now. It was someone else. A special woman probably. Whoever she was, she was very lucky, C.J. mused. She didn't want to analyze that feeling much further.

Matthew watched hypnotically as C.J.'s hands maneuvered the steering wheel. She was so different from Gail and the other women he dated. She was real, like a red rose among a bouquet of silk flowers—no facade or superficial decoration, just a genuine beauty, inside and out. He wondered what it would feel like to spend every day with her. He turned the conversation resolutely in a different direction.

"Other than the Townsends, you don't have any clues to your parentage?"

She was startled at the quick change of subject, but promptly marshaled her thoughts. After all, this was what she wanted to talk about. She had to choose her words carefully. "No," she answered. "When the money started coming for college, I figured that was it, now I'd find out. But nothing happened. It was so frustrating and I thought…" Her voice trailed away.

"What?" he prompted.

She turned and looked him straight in the eye. "That your dad was giving me the money."

Matthew met that look. A flicker of apprehension coursed through him. Her face was saying much more than her words, but he couldn't figure out exactly what. His eyes narrowed. "Did you ask him?"

"Yes, and he denied it."

"You didn't believe him?"

She shrugged. "At times I did, others I didn't. But I

always felt he knew something about my birth he wasn't telling me.''

"Like what?"

"If I could answer that, we wouldn't be making this trip.''

He took a deep breath and decided to confront her. "Listen, C.J., you're trying to tell me something, so why don't you just come out and say it, and we can discuss it like two adults?''

How could she tell him her doubts? She had a hard enough time telling herself, but the words were there. She had to say them.

Matthew watched her struggle. Something was creating a great deal of turmoil. Was she thinking about his father? The money? What was causing her such distress?

"I really…" she started, then stopped, frowning into the rearview mirror.

"What is it?"

"That eighteen-wheeler truck's been following us for some time, and now he's right on my tail.'' As the last word left her mouth, the truck hit the bumper, jarring them.

"Damn,'' Matthew cursed. He turned to look out the rear window as the big truck loomed over them. It hit them again and C.J. swerved to keep from being pushed off the road. "What the hell does he think he's doing?''

"I don't know.'' C.J. kept her eyes on the road, hands tight on the wheel. "But if he's in such a hurry, I'm going to ease over and let him pass.''

The road was narrow and C.J. pulled onto the uneven grassy verge. The truck bounced up and down and the big cab roared alongside them, but didn't pass. Instead, it veered, hitting the driver's side with a crashing sound of metal against metal. The blow knocked them almost into the ditch. C.J. managed to steady her truck.

"The damn fool," Matthew said just as the cab crashed into them a fourth time, rocking the truck with determined force.

"He's trying to run us off the road!" C.J. shouted.

The truck rammed them again. "He's doing a damn good job."

"Oh, no!" she cried.

"Just keep watching the road," he said. "You're doing great."

"It's not that. Sutter's Cliff is up ahead and it's a sharp drop to nowhere."

"We've got to do something before we get there."

"What?"

"Hit the brakes."

Her foot slammed on the brake. The tires squealed and her truck spun around, coming to rest in the ditch. The eighteen-wheeler zoomed by, unable to stop at such high speed.

The seat belts held them firmly in place, but they were stunned and shaken.

Still gripping the dash, Matthew gasped, "You okay?"

She let out a shuddering breath. "Yes."

Quickly assessing the situation, he said, "Try to turn it around. We've got to get moving."

She shifted into Reverse. The truck wouldn't budge. "There's something wrong." She shifted the lever on the floorboard into four-wheel drive. The truck moved awkwardly.

Matthew hurriedly undid his seat belt and jumped out. "Damn, we blew out a tire." In the distance he could hear the grinding of gears.

"He's turning around. Come on, we have to get out of here."

She killed the engine. "We'll have to go on foot."

He glanced at the barbed-wire fences and dense woods. "Anybody live around here?" he asked.

"Not for miles." C.J. yanked on her door. It wouldn't open, so she climbed out the passenger side. She stood beside the truck and surveyed the rugged land, then her gaze met Matthew's.

He lifted a dark eyebrow. "I guess it's over the fence and into the woods. I don't think he'll come after us on foot."

Matthew pressed down the bottom wire with his foot and raised the next one with his hand, making a hole for her. She gave him a sharp glance. She wanted to tell him she wasn't a helpless female, but decided this wasn't the time.

She crawled between the wires, then held the fence open for him. Their eyes met a second before he scrambled through. The engine of the big truck roared closer.

"Hurry," Matthew urged. Grabbing her hand, he pulled her behind him. The woods were thick with undergrowth and bushes that tugged at their clothes, hair and skin, but they pushed on. He wanted to get them far out of sight.

Suddenly a gunshot broke the silence and a bullet whizzed close by, embedding itself in a tree. "My God, he's shooting at us!"

They heard someone crashing through the undergrowth. "He's following us!" she cried.

Matthew squeezed her hand and started off as fast as he could, almost dragging her. A bramble bush caught her hair and jerked her backward.

"Ouch!" Her hands clutched her head as she tried desperately to untangle her hair.

"Be still," Matthew said, and tried to help her.

"I can do it myself," she snapped.

"Dammit, for once in your life let someone help you."

The harshness in his voice stilled her efforts. With gentle fingers, he deftly freed her hair from the bush.

"Come on." Matthew grabbed her hand again and began to run. If their pursuer got close enough, they'd both be dead; Matthew was certain of it. A strong sense of protectiveness surged through him. He wasn't going to let anything happen to her.

They emerged onto a grassy knoll. Taking several deep breaths, they raced to the edge. About a hundred feet below ran the Colorado River.

They heard the whine of another gunshot.

"He's getting closer," C.J. said.

Matthew glanced at her anxious face and back at the woods, then down to the river. "The river or the gunman? What's your choice?"

She stared down at the murky depths and wondered what lay beneath the surface—hidden rocks, snakes, a bottomless pit?

As a bullet sped past her, she said, "I hope you're a good swimmer, city man," and quickly removed her shoes and vest. If she was going to die, it wasn't going to be at some stranger's hand.

Even in a crisis she had a sense of humor. Oh, he liked this country lady. "I'm a damn good swimmer," he replied, grinning as he took off his jacket and tie, then jerked off his boots.

Matthew clutched her hand and stared into her green eyes. All the sparring humor disappeared. Seriousness gripped them. By mutual consent they were taking their chances with the river.

"At the count of three we make a run for it and jump," he told her.

"Okay," she said. The fear inside her dissipated as she

gazed into his confident dark eyes. She couldn't think of anyone she'd rather be with at that moment.

"When you hit the water, try not to come up immediately and don't fight the current. Swim to the edge and crawl onto the bank and flatten yourself against the cliff. That way he won't be able to get a clear shot at us."

"Okay," she said again and took a steadying breath.

"One, two, three!" he shouted. They set off at a run and sailed over the cliff into the water below. The last thing Matthew remembered was the green of her eyes.

C.J. held on to his hand as long as she could, but the impact of their bodies hitting the water forced them apart. Down, down she went into the dark water. The current immediately lifted and moved her body like a piece of driftwood. She didn't fight it, remembering what Matthew had said. When the current released her, her lungs were tight, and she tried to swim toward the surface. She was starting to panic. Where was the water's edge? She didn't know; there was no way to tell beneath the surface. She let her instincts take over and swam with all her strength. Her lungs begged for oxygen, but she held her breath. *Not yet,* she kept thinking.

Suddenly her head broke the surface and precious air gushed into her chest. As she struggled to stay afloat, she saw she was about fifty feet from shore. Relief swept through her and she swam swiftly toward the edge. Her feet touched bottom and she dragged herself through the mud and weeds to the bank and collapsed in exhaustion.

She lay there, sucking air into her starved lungs. Slimy mud coated her face, and the water tugged at her weak legs, trying to pull her back in. She dug her elbows into the mud and pushed. Her body slid forward. She was safe. She was safe. She was safe. Matthew! She lifted her head. Matthew wasn't on the shore. She looked up and down the lonely water's edge, feeling a shiver of alarm. He'd said he was a good swimmer. He should have been here, somewhere. What if he'd gotten confused in the water like she had and swum toward the center of the river and the current had taken him under so deep he couldn't— *Oh, God, no!* her heart cried.

"Matthew," she whispered, and tried to get to her feet, determined to go back into the water and find him. She had to. She couldn't go on without him. The realization trembled through her with amazing clarity.

Then, like the answer to a prayer, his dark head shot through the surface about fifty feet downstream. "Matthew," she sighed. The pain in her chest eased and she sagged onto the bank.

C.J. watched as he swam vigorously for shore. Then he began to wave his arms frantically, motioning for her to get to the cliff. In her terror she had forgotten his instructions. She scrambled to her feet, but before she could take two steps she tumbled back into the mud. Damn, her foot was caught in the undergrowth of viney weeds that grew along the water. As she struggled to free her foot, Matthew reached her and grabbed her around the waist, dragging her to the cliff. He wrapped his arms around her and flattened them both against a wall of hard rock and dirt.

As their wet bodies molded together, gunfire sprayed the water. Over and over the bullets kept coming. The place where she'd lain was now pitted with bullet holes. The constant firing was like thunder in her head. She tried to cover her ears, but Matthew tightened his arms around her.

Abruptly the shooting stopped. They remained perfectly still, knowing that if the man suspected they were below him, they'd be dead in an instant.

The firing started again, all over the water, the edge, as if to ensure they wouldn't make it out alive. Then the gunfire stopped again, echoes receding into the swift flow of the river. A satisfied laugh resounded along the muddy embankment.

C.J.'s skin crawled at that horrible sound. As they waited, they heard the man thrashing back through the woods.

They remained against the base of the cliff. After a while C.J. raised her head from Matthew's chest and stared into his dark eyes. Without a word they sank to the ground, but they still didn't speak, afraid that any noise could alert the gunman.

Their wet tired bodies huddled together. Everything was silent now, except for the steady gurgling of the water. Cradled between steep banks, the river had an eerie calm. They were in the middle of nowhere, a part of the Colorado where no one ever ventured except by boat. C.J. shivered. They were lucky they'd made it out alive.

Unexpectedly a cow trudged down a narrow trail on the other side of the river. She picked her way to the water's edge and drank thirstily. Lifting her head, she stared at the strange sight of two people crouched on the other side. She shook her head as if to dispel the image, then drank more water and went slowly back up the trail.

Something beside them moved, and C.J. realized it was a large water moccasin sunning itself.

Don't scream. Don't scream, she kept repeating to herself.

Panic rushed through her and she had trouble breathing. Ever since she could remember she'd been afraid of snakes. Living on a ranch she should be used to them, but try as she might, she'd never conquered her fear or revulsion.

Don't scream.

She stifled a gasp deep in her throat as the snake slithered back into the water.

Matthew saw the snake, then glanced at C.J.'s face and saw the stark fear in her eyes. She was afraid of snakes!

Another crack in the wall she presented to the world. He hoped he was there when that wall came tumbling down. He hoped that— Matthew pulled himself up short. He was acting as if C.J. had a place in his life. After this case was over, he'd probably never see her again. That thought brought little comfort.

They heard the distant roar of an engine and both sat up straight, listening closely.

"Do you think he's gone?" she whispered.

The sound receded into the distance. "Yes."

"Thank God." She pulled out of his arms and tried to wipe some of the wet mud from her face and clothes. The fear was completely gone from her face.

He watched her useless efforts to remove the river's grime. "Do you always take someone trying to kill you so calmly?"

C.J. reached for his hand and placed it beneath her breast. He could feel her heart thumping rapidly. "I was scared to death," she admitted. "I didn't think he was ever going to stop shooting and I was terrified he'd spot us."

The warmth of her body and the softness of her breast infused a need in Matthew so strong that he got stiffly to his feet. He had to concentrate on getting them out of this watery grave, instead of how she felt in his arms.

"Why was he trying to kill us?" C.J. asked. Matthew's eyes were shrouded and he wouldn't look at her. Suddenly it dawned on her.

"He wasn't trying to kill us. He was trying to kill *me*." She said the words she knew he was thinking.

"C.J." He tried to stop her from saying more.

"No, it's true, isn't it?" She leaped to her feet. "He was trying to kill me. You just happened to be there." She paused. "Who would want to kill me?" Glancing at his face, she answered her own question. "The Townsends."

"We don't know that."

"Oh, I forgot, you're their lawyer, so naturally you're going to take up for them."

He ran a hand through his wet hair in frustration. "C.J., I don't know what's going on, but right now my primary concern is getting us out of here. Then I'm going to find some answers." He studied the steep cliff. "It's not going to be as easy going up as it was coming down, but let's go." He started down the narrow embankment. It was about four feet from the water to the base of the cliff. "Look for a cow trail."

She followed, noticing their feet making imprints in the mud. She also noticed something else. His slacks were clinging to him, boldly emphasizing his muscled legs—and well-defined rear. Shaking her head, she wondered why she was thinking such things. She should be concentrating on their predicament. If they didn't find a way up the cliff, they could be stranded on this lonely river for hours.

They'd walked for about five minutes when Matthew stopped and pointed to a cow path that curved to the top.

"You go first," he instructed.

Slowly she started up. Her wet feet slipped a couple of times, but Matthew was always there to catch her.

"Do you know your clothes are clinging in a most revealing way?" he asked.

She sent him a secretive smile. "Have you looked at yourself?"

"Good God," he exclaimed, and she looked back to see him staring down at himself. "You should have said something.'' He tried to adjust his wet slacks, but they remained firmly in place.

She laughed. ''And spoil the view? I don't think so.''

Matthew thought he could listen to the sound of her laughter for the rest of his life. He now knew what it took to make C.J. laugh—danger, excitement and a good view of his body. ''Is that a feminist remark?'' he wanted to know. ''Or the opposite?''

''Just the truth.'' She laughed again, and the strange bubbly feeling inside her gave C.J. the extra strength to reach the top. With a sigh she sank onto the knoll. Matthew dropped down beside her.

''We made it,'' she sighed, and stretched out full-length on the grass, her face to the sky, letting the April sun warm her wet and weary body.

Matthew watched her face, then with one finger touched the mud on her soft cheek. She shifted toward him, her green eyes dreamy.

''We look like two drowned rats,'' he said, his brown eyes gleaming. Then they darkened with a passion she couldn't miss. ''But you have to be the most beautiful drowned rat I've ever seen.''

She knew he was going to kiss her, and every fatigued aching cell in her wanted his kiss. That recognition jolted her to her senses. As he bent his head, she turned hers. His kiss landed on her cheek. Abruptly she got to her feet.

''We shouldn't get emotionally involved,'' she stated briskly, and nervously brushed dried mud from her clothes.

''I was only going to kiss you.''

''Kissing leads to other things.'' How she wished she'd had the chance to voice her questions about his father earlier. Now wasn't the time. Maybe later.

He sat up and frowned at the confusion on her face.

"Besides, you're the Townsends' lawyer and—" She stopped as something occurred to her.

"And?" he prompted.

"You're the only one I told about taking the shortcut."

His eyes narrowed. "What are you saying?" he asked in a cold careful voice.

C.J.'s mind raced dangerously. "I'm saying that guy knew exactly where to find me."

Swiftly Matthew got to his feet, his eyes black with anger. "You think I set this up? That I enjoy getting shot at and endangering my life by jumping off a cliff into a treacherous river? Well, let me tell you something, lady. I might be the Townsends' lawyer, but I'm not stupid, and you and I have nothing else to say to each other."

"Fine," she shouted as he marched off angrily. She should have stayed away from him, she told herself. What did she really know about him except that he was Matt's son and that she was curious about him? Curiosity was going to get her killed.

Even though the sun was warm, her body trembled with exhaustion and fear. She took a shaky breath and clenched her grubby hands into fists. *Wait a minute,* she cautioned herself. *Think about this rationally.* Old Matt had integrity ingrained in his bones. She suspected Matthew did, too. Was she willing to take a chance and find out?

His proud figure strode farther and farther away. Slowly she followed. He reached their strewn clothes and sat down, then briskly scraped mud from his feet.

Sinking down beside him, she said, "You have to admit it looks suspicious."

He didn't say anything, just roughly jammed his foot into a boot. She knew she'd hurt him, and a heaviness settled in her chest. She tried to think logically about the whole structure of events, weighing possibilities. All that registered was the pain in those dark eyes.

"No one's ever shot at me before and it has me rattled," she said. "I can't imagine why anyone would want me dead, except the Townsends. But deep down I don't believe you had anything to do with it."

Without saying a word, he jammed his other foot into a boot. She wanted to scream with frustration. This man was stubborn. What more did he expect from her?

Then his eyes caught hers. "Do you really?"

On a shaky sigh she breathed, "Yes." She touched his face; she trusted him. That trust was tempered with feelings she didn't want to think about.

When he felt her hand on his cheek, he knew he'd forgive her anything. She had too powerful a hold on him, and there was nothing he could do to change it. He didn't even know if he wanted to.

"Let's get one thing straight," he said. His eyes didn't leave hers. "I would never do anything to intentionally harm you. Yes, I'm the Townsends' attorney, but I have your best interests at heart. And that's the most unethical thing I've ever said in my life."

A smile lit up her face. "How can it be unethical when it makes me feel so good?"

He gave her a smile in return, but shook his head. He didn't have an answer for her. The feeling was contagious. "Put your shoes on. We have to find our way back to the truck."

She tried to remove some of the mud from her feet by rubbing them in the grass, then she hastily slid them into her sandals. Her face creased in obvious pain.

"What's wrong?"

"This braid is giving me a headache." Her hands tugged at the wet muddy plait. Her efforts were in vain.

"Here, let me help," he offered, and she didn't protest. He knelt behind her, his hands unfastening the stubborn braid. As he pulled the ruined green ribbon free, long black hair fell down her back to the grass. He ran his fingers through the muddy tresses. "You have the most gorgeous hair I've ever seen."

C.J. heard the husky undertone in his voice and knew they were heading for trouble once more. She scrambled to her feet, not wanting to hurt his feelings again. "We'd better get going."

A strange expression crossed his face before he got to his feet. Without a word they started back through the woods. This time it was easier. They weren't running, so the branches didn't scratch their skin or tear their already-tattered clothes. They'd left a trail through the tall grass and followed it easily until it led them to the edge of the woods.

Matthew stopped, listened and looked in every direction. An eerie feeling crept over her. "You don't think he's waiting for us, do you?"

He glanced at her wary eyes. "No, I believe he thinks he got us in the river, but I'm just making sure."

Everything was quiet, just a gentle breeze teasing the trees and an occasional bird whistle. The remote country road stretched on and on; their stalker was nowhere in sight. Satisfied, they climbed through the fence. It didn't even bother C.J. when he held the wires for her.

The truck was sideways in the ditch with a blown-out tire. "Well, city man, can you change a flat?" she asked.

He grinned. "I was a country boy before I was a city man."

"I'll take that as a yes."

CHAPTER EIGHT

THEY CHANGED THE FLAT, then drove toward Austin. Matthew called the police from a pay phone, and they agreed to meet at Ryder Laboratories. Deputy Moore from the sheriff's office and Detective Beal from the Austin police arrived minutes after C.J. and Matthew did. When it was established that they were uninjured, the police ushered them into a conference room.

C.J. couldn't help but think of the picture they made. Torn and dirty clothes, mud trailing from their skin, Matthew's dark hair clinging to his scalp, hers hanging in knotted rattails.

Dr. Ryder sent his secretary out to buy them clean clothes, and the interrogation started. Deputy Moore remained silent while Detective Beal grilled them. Of average height with dark hair and intense blue eyes, Beal kept asking the same questions over and over. Could they identify the truck? Did they see the man? Who would want to kill them?

C.J. stated her suspicions about the Townsends, but the detective's stony gaze gave her little satisfaction. Dr. Ryder's secretary returned then, and C.J. hurried into Dr. Ryder's private bathroom. She stripped off her dirty clothes and stepped into the shower, welcoming the spray of warm water against her skin. She'd thought she would never want to come near water again, but it was heavenly to feel clean. After drying herself, she did the best she could with her hair. Someday she was going to get it cut; it was just too much bother. She brushed the damp strands, then, using a rubber band the secretary had given her, secured it at the nape of her neck.

Picking up the new clothes, she stared at them for a moment. A dress, panty hose and underwear. A dress? She hardly ever wore a dress, but she didn't ponder the issue. She was grateful for what she had.

The panty hose and underwear fit perfectly and she quickly slipped on the dress. Made of some silky fabric in a green print, it was a body-skimming design with a rounded neck and cap sleeves. She looked in the mirror and hardly recognized herself. Was this the same woman who'd left home with so many hopes this morning? Now someone wanted her dead. Who? Who hated her that much? The Townsends. Matthew's clients. Was she right to put her trust in Matthew? She shook her head, knowing she was going to drive herself crazy if she didn't stop thinking about him.

WHEN SHE OPENED the bathroom door, she was startled to find Matthew standing there, holding his own fresh change of clothing. His gaze slid over her. "My, my," he drawled, "it was worth the wait."

Self-consciously she ran her hands down the front of the dress. "It's a little revealing, don't you think?"

He examined the low neckline and the way the material clung to every curve. "Never ask a man that question."

Before she could form a suitable response, Dr. Ryder came into the office. "Good, you're dressed," he said, nodding at C.J. "The lab's ready for you."

Matthew gave her a reassuring smile, then disappeared into the bathroom. She followed Dr. Ryder down the hall. "It's good to see you again," Dr. Ryder said. A short thin man with a balding head and thick glasses, he was a typical researcher, studious and factual. "I'm just sorry you had to go through so much to get here."

"Thank you," was all she could say. She had met the man at one of the rare parties she'd attended in college. After a few dances she would search for a dark corner and watch the party from a distance. That was where she'd met Cliff Ryder, who'd been hiding in a corner trying to escape the noise and jocularity while waiting for his girlfriend. He had talked about his research in DNA and she'd listened. When she'd thought of the paternity test, his name was the first that had come to her mind. C.J. felt he couldn't be tempted by bribery from the Townsends or anyone.

The lab procedure was quick and simple, and soon she was back in Dr. Ryder's office. Matthew came out of the bathroom in jeans and a knit shirt. She stopped short. He looked so different.

He glanced down at his clothes. "Something wrong?"

"I've never seen you in anything but suits."

"Ah, this is the country-boy look," he teased. "I told you he was still alive and well."

They smiled at each other. A smile filled with humor and desire. Warning bells went off in her head and she had to ask herself again—was she right to put her trust in this man?

The impact of her smile shot through him, but despite the pleasure, he saw the uncertainty in her eyes. She wasn't sure she could trust him. Under the circumstances, he supposed she had a right to be wary, but God, he didn't like the hollow feeling it gave him.

Dr. Ryder's secretary came into the office. "The Townsends are being shown into the conference room," she told them.

"Detective Beal and Deputy Moore are having a cup of

coffee,'' Matthew replied. ''Would you tell them the Townsends are here and ask them to give me about ten minutes?'' Matthew turned to C.J. ''Stay here. This won't take long.''

''No, I want to face them.''

''C.J.,'' he said, ''it won't do any good. Please let me handle this.''

She stared into his eyes. She wanted to understand, to trust him. But why had he asked her not to see them? She needed to know if they'd hired someone to kill her. But realistically she knew they weren't going to admit anything, so it was best to let Matthew and the police handle this. For now at least.

MATTHEW DID A DOUBLE TAKE when he entered the conference room. He'd expected Rob and John, but the room was full of Townsends. Even John's nurse, the resistible Stephanie Cox, was there.

Rob walked over to him, glancing at his apparel with a disagreeable eye, then shook his hand vigorously. ''Matthew, I think you know everyone. Dad, Aunt Martha, Stephanie, my twin sister, Joyce, and baby sister, Clare.''

''Yes, although it's been years since I've seen Joyce and Clare.'' He was struck by the difference in the Townsend sisters. Joyce took after her mother, blond and beautiful, while Clare was dark and plain.

''Yes, it has,'' Joyce said, and gestured at everyone in the room. ''You're probably wondering what we're all doing here. We wanted to give Rob and Dad our support. This is so ridiculous.''

They could stand here and exchange pleasantries all day, but he had more important things on his mind. ''Rob, could I have a word with you in private?''

"You can speak in front of my family. We have no secrets."

He doubted that, but decided not to insist. "Okay," he said. "Someone tried to kill C. J. Doe today." A moment of silence followed. Matthew watched all their expressions. No emotion, nothing, just poker faces on everyone, except Clare. She appeared genuinely distressed.

"What's that got to do with us?" Rob muttered.

"The police want to ask you some questions."

"Why?"

"Because when it comes right down to it, there are very few people who'd want to see her dead, while you—"

"We had nothing to do with whatever happened to her!" Rob thundered.

"As your attorney, I *should* be inclined to agree, but since I was with her and they tried to kill me, too, I'm even more inclined to want some answers."

John's eyes narrowed slightly. "You were with her?"

"My truck broke down and she offered me a lift," he explained, and went on to tell them the rest of the ordeal. "So," he finished, "if anyone had anything to do with hiring this guy, I want to know now. Attempted murder is a serious charge and things could get ugly."

"I assure you no one in this room is that stupid." Rob almost spat the words at him.

"I sincerely hope not, because I don't take kindly to someone trying to kill me."

"Then maybe you should stay away from people like C. J. Doe," John snapped.

"Now, don't upset yourself, John." Martha gently rubbed his shoulder.

Stephanie threw her a withering look. Matthew felt like telling them how badly he'd like to drop this case. But he had to stick it out. For his father's sake—and for C.J.'s.

He took a deep breath. "The police will be here in a few minutes. Just answer their questions honestly."

The questioning went smoothly. The Townsends answered everything to the detective's satisfaction. Beal told Matthew later that he believed they had nothing to do with the shooting, but he would continue to investigate, as would the sheriff's department.

MATTHEW KNEW C.J. was furious that the Townsends got off so easily. They spoke little on the ride home, consumed with their own thoughts.

He wanted to say something to reassure her, but he also knew she had to come to grips with her own feelings.

The light was fading as she drove up in front of the Sloan house. Matthew studied her bleak expression for an extra second. "Dr. Ryder's putting a rush on the tests. By next week you may know something."

"Yes," she answered quietly, too quietly.

"C.J., are you all right?"

She glanced at him. "Someone tried to kill me, and I guess that's starting to sink in. I'll feel better once I get home to Pete and Harry."

Somehow that didn't make *him* feel better. He wanted her to feel safe in his presence, but he understood she needed to get back to the environment that was secure for her.

"Would you like me to follow you home? I could get my mom's car."

She shook her head. "That won't be necessary, but would you mind calling Pete and telling him I'm on my way?"

"Sure."

"And please don't mention what happened today."

He saw the worried frown on her face. "You intend to tell them, don't you?"

She rubbed the steering wheel with one hand. "Yes, but I have to do it very carefully. They both have bad tempers, and I'm afraid they'll go after the Townsends...."

Turning in his seat, he rested his arm along the back. "The police are still investigating, but they need proof before they can proceed with anything."

"Proof?" she echoed hollowly. "How about this feeling in my gut?"

With one finger he gently touched her face, although he could immediately feel her pulling away from him. "I'm afraid that's not enough. We gave the police a good description of the truck, but since it didn't have a license plate, that makes it difficult to trace. They just need some time."

She didn't say anything. Maybe she needed time, too. But he didn't let her go.

"When this is over and I'm no longer the Townsends' attorney, I'd like to call you. You can reacquaint me with the good eating places in Coberville."

Her eyes pierced him with an expression he didn't understand. "Are you asking me out on a date?"

One eyebrow darted up in amusement. "Yeah, I believe that's what they call it—even around here."

"I don't think I can go," she answered in that quiet voice.

"Why not?"

She sighed. "Don't push it, Matthew. I'm tired and I might just tell you."

He reached out and caught her arm. "Tell me," he urged. "Because every time I'm near you or I touch you, like now, I can feel you pulling away from me. Why, C.J.?"

"Please, don't," she said, yanking back her arm.

"Tell me," he persisted.

"I'll make you a deal. Tell your mother you asked me for a date, and if she reacts in a positive manner, I'll go out with you."

"Wait a minute." He frowned. "What's my mother got to do with this?"

"Just tell her."

"Not until you give me a reason."

"Oh, Matthew." She sighed again. "Why are you doing this? Can't you see I don't want to tell you?" She paused. "Besides, it's just something I feel."

He eyed her for a moment. "Tell me," he said, knowing he couldn't get out of the truck until she did.

"Okay." She slapped the steering wheel with both hands. "But remember, you asked." She took a deep breath. "Your father was nicer to me than anyone in this town. And yet your mother, a good Christian lady, dislikes me intensely. There has to be a reason for it."

"And you think it's...?"

She looked directly at him. "Your dad might also be mine."

"What?" He drew back as if she'd hit him.

"You heard me."

He shook his head as if to rid himself of the ugly thought. But so many things suddenly became clear in his mind—their talk on the way to Austin, her pushing him away. "Let me assure you of something. My dad is not your father."

"How can you be sure of that?"

"I just am. I know my parents. They were devoted to each other. My dad would never have been unfaithful to my mom."

"But you can't be positive."

"I am, dammit," he said, not liking where this conversation was going. "Besides, I thought you believed one of the Townsends was your father. Isn't that why we went through all this today?"

"You don't understand, do you?" Her eyes held his. "I don't *know* who my parents are. Because of Victoria's will, I thought the rumors might be true, but I don't know. Just like I don't know why your dad was so nice to me." Both hands gripped her head. "Can't you see I *just don't know?*"

Her pain was almost a tangible thing. He tried to comfort her. "C.J...."

"It's awful not knowing."

All the fears and doubts she'd lived with every day of her life were in her voice, and it tore at his heart. He had to take some of the pain away. "My dad is not your father."

She stared at him. "But you're not sure. I can see it in your eyes."

"I am, C.J. I'm very sure."

From the look in her eyes, he knew there was only one way to settle this. "Okay, I'll ask my mother," he told her. "Will that satisfy you?"

"Yes," she said, the tension leaving her face.

"Good." He forced a smile and climbed out of the truck. "And you get ready for that date, because I'll be seeing you when this is over. You can count on it."

He stood on the curb and watched the taillights disappear from view. He felt as if he'd just been kicked in the stomach and was still trying to catch his breath. She thought they could be blood-related. The idea almost paralyzed him. They *couldn't* be. No way in hell.

As he hurried up the walk to the front door, he repeated that to himself. But a disturbing question kept intruding.

Why didn't his mother like C.J.? She didn't normally dislike someone without reason. He would find out, he vowed, and put an end to this bizarre turn of events.

When he opened the door, the aroma of food cooking greeted him. His mom appeared in the kitchen doorway with an apron around her waist, and for once there were no tears in her eyes. She still had bad days, but he knew that soon she'd be able to handle things on her own.

"Oh, you're home. We're having meat loaf and…" Her voice trailed off as she noticed his clothes. "You were wearing a suit when you left this morning. What happened?"

"Just a moment," he said. "I have to make a phone call and then I'll be right with you." He went into his dad's study and called Pete Watson. Pete didn't ask any questions and Matthew was grateful for that.

His mother was waiting anxiously in the living room. He put an arm around her shoulders and led her to the sofa, telling her about his day. When he finished, she hugged him tight. "Oh, Mattie, I don't know what I would've done if anything had happened to you." Her blue eyes grew stormy. "It's all that girl's fault. She causes nothing but trouble. I tried to tell your dad, but he wouldn't listen."

Matthew's eyes narrowed. "It wasn't C.J.'s fault. Someone tried to kill her, not the other way around."

"I don't care. That girl is nothing but trouble." She twisted her hands nervously.

"Mom—"

"Please." She stopped him and got to her feet. "I don't want to talk about her anymore. Supper will be ready in a minute."

He watched her go into the kitchen, food the last thing on his mind. This wasn't like his mother. She was a loving, caring person who always tried to see the best in people. Why did she have such hostile feelings toward C.J.?

All through supper he tried to turn the conversation to C.J., but his mom always changed the subject. He could have forced the issue, but somehow—and it made him feel like a coward—he didn't want to know. He didn't think he could handle the thought of C.J. being his half sister. God, what was he thinking? There was no way! But still he couldn't shake that sense of foreboding.

TELLING PETE AND HARRY what had happened didn't go well. They were angry, very angry, but C.J. managed to calm them, and they promised not to do anything rash.

She went to sleep worrying about Matthew. Had he asked his mother? What did she say? And the most burning worry of all—how would she feel if they *were* related? No. They couldn't be. After all the years of looking and waiting to find her family, she knew she didn't want Matthew to be part of that family. She was beginning to feel things for him, and none of those feelings had anything to do with brotherly love.

HER LUNGS WERE TIGHT. She had a burning sensation in her eyes and throat. She couldn't breathe and she was being pulled down, down, to a dark watery grave.

"No!" she screamed, and sat bolt upright in bed.

Pushing hair from her face, she sucked air into her lungs. It was only a dream, she assured herself. She was safe. She crawled out of bed and looked at the clock. Barely six. Pete and Harry should be up, but the house had an eerie stillness about it.

She pulled on her jeans and dashed down the hall to the kitchen. Two empty coffee cups sat on the table, but Pete and Harry were nowhere in sight. Where could they be?

They wouldn't do anything crazy, would they? They'd promised.

Running outside, she checked the garage. The trucks were still there. But her relief didn't last. Glancing toward the corral, she noticed their horses were gone. Damn, there was only one place they'd go on horseback.

Seven Trees. The Townsends' ranch.

GUNFIRE JOLTED Rob Townsend awake. He sat up in bed and listened. The sound seem to vibrate through the walls.

Francine stirred. "What's that?"

"I'll go see." He got out of bed and slipped a navy silk robe over matching pajamas. "Go back to sleep."

A tap on the door caught his attention. He opened it to his agitated butler, Henry. "Sir, the Watsons are out front demanding to see you."

"Damn, what the hell do they want?"

"I don't know, but they have guns and seem very upset."

"Don't worry, Henry, I'll get rid of them," Rob said, and took the stairs two at a time. Just as he opened the door, a blast of gunfire shook the windowpanes.

"What the hell's the matter with you?" he exploded. "You're on private property and I want you off now."

Pete Watson leveled a shotgun at him. "I'd be careful who I was giving orders to, son."

At the venom in his voice Rob took a step backward. The two men were astride horses, wore long dark coats and held shotguns.

"Now you listen and listen good," Pete shouted. "Stay away from C.J. And you'd better call off your hired killer because if anything happens to her, I'll make sure you never draw another breath."

"My family had nothing to do—"

"I'm not interested in your excuses," Pete cut in. "Just heed my warning or you'll regret it." With that he kneed the horse and quickly rode down the drive, the clip-clop of hooves making an ominous sound.

But Harry didn't ride away. He glared at Rob with dark forbidding eyes. Rob took another step backward. Slowly and deliberately Harry spat tobacco juice on the pavement. Then in a threatening voice he said, "'Violent endeavors have violent ends.'" His free hand went to the big knife in a holster around his waist, then he picked up the reins, nudged his horse and rode off.

Rob gulped in a deep breath and stormed back into the house.

"Should I call the sheriff?" Henry wanted to know.

"I'll handle this," Rob said. "The sheriff is just as afraid of Harry Watson as the rest of the people in this town. I'll make damn sure those two wild men don't get away with this. Who do they think they're dealing with?" He went directly to his study and slammed the door. Reaching for the receiver, he dialed Matthew Sloan.

Matthew was sound asleep, dreams of C.J. filtering through his mind. She was running away from him, her long black hair flying behind her. As she turned to glance back at him, he saw tears in her eyes. *No,* he tried to tell her, *It's not true.* But the words stuck in his throat.

"Matthew, wake up." His mother shook him.

Through the remnants of sleep, his eyes focused on her. He wondered why she seemed worried.

"You were having a bad dream or something. You were thrashing around and I couldn't wake you."

"Sorry, Mom." He yawned and pushed himself into a sitting position.

"There's a call for you. Didn't you hear the phone?"

"No. I'll take it in here." As his mother left the room, he picked up the receiver.

Before he could say a word, an angry voice came down the line. "Those crazy Watson men came over here with shotguns, threatening me and my family. I won't have it. Do you hear me? If I have to call the Texas Rangers, I'll get them locked up for the rest of their insane lives."

The voice was unmistakable. "I'm sorry, Rob. I'll look into it."

"You'd better do more than look into it." That warning note in his voice riled Matthew. "As our lawyer, it's your job to protect us and our interests, so you'd better make sure they stay away from here."

"I'll talk to them," he replied with deceptive calm.

"I thought you would, since you seem to be on such good terms with C. J. Doe." The accusing words had Matthew biting his tongue. Patience, he told himself.

He gripped the receiver. "As you know, someone tried to kill C.J. yesterday, and that's enough to upset anyone. I'm sure after they cool off the Watsons won't bother you again."

"They'd better not," Rob growled, and the phone went dead.

Matthew got out of bed and shrugged into a terry-cloth robe. Glancing at the phone, he hesitated. He had to call her, but he didn't want to. Hearing her voice was going to play havoc with his senses. But what he had the hardest time facing was his cowardice of last night. He should have forced his mom to discuss her attitude toward C.J., should have asked the questions he knew he had to ask. God, he'd never had such a vulnerable feeling before. Slowly he dialed the number.

C.J. picked up instantly. "Hello?"

He took a deep breath. "C.J., I got a call from Rob

Townsend. Seems Pete and Harry were over there with their shotguns, threatening them.''

''I knew it.'' She sighed irritably. ''They promised they wouldn't, and they broke their promise.''

''Just make sure it doesn't happen again.''

''I will.''

''Thanks, C.J. I'll talk to you later.''

He hung up the phone feeling like a bigger coward than ever, but he just couldn't tell her he hadn't even asked. He would do it, though, and soon. He couldn't go on like this.

C.J. HUNG UP, wondering why he hadn't mentioned his mother. Surely he'd asked her. Why hadn't he said something? The sound of horses trotting into the corral diverted her attention.

She charged outside, anger in every line of her body. ''You promised!'' she yelled as they dismounted. ''You promised you wouldn't do this and yet you ride over there like the James brothers. This isn't the Old West and you can't do things like that. Don't my wishes mean anything?'' They both just gazed at her with woeful expressions. ''I guess not. Maybe it's time I moved on.''

As she whirled around, Pete grabbed her arm. ''Girl, try to understand. This was something we had to do.''

Her eyes blazed. ''But I asked you not to.''

''Sometimes a man has to do what he feels is right.''

''Don't you care about the way I feel?''

''Of course we care, but if anything happened to you...'' He stopped and turned away, but not before she saw the glistening of tears in his eyes. Seconds later, his feelings under control, he looked back at her. ''We only wanted to scare them.''

''Well, you did that.''

"Good," Harry mumbled.

She couldn't stay mad at them. Inwardly she wanted to do the same thing, but knew she had to let the police handle it. Still, Pete and Harry had spent years protecting her, and that wasn't going to change. "Why do I put up with the two of you?" she asked half-humorously, hugging Pete, then Harry.

"No more talk about leaving," Pete said.

"No more talk about leaving," she answered with a smile and walked between them to the house. As Pete's spurs jingled and Harry's shotgun brushed her leg, she felt as though she did indeed live in the Old West, protected by two men who would die for her. At that thought, she shivered uneasily.

"SHE CAN'T BE." Dale Weeks couldn't believe his ears. "I fired enough bullets into that water to kill an elephant."

"I assure you she is still alive and so is Sloan."

"You didn't tell me a man was going to be with her."

"I didn't know, you damn fool."

"Next time get your facts straight. If I have to kill two people, the price goes up."

"You can't even kill one, you idiot."

"Don't worry. I never leave a job unfinished."

"She's back at the ranch now, and you won't get near her with those two old fools around."

"She can't stay there forever, and when she leaves, I'll be waiting."

"If you want the rest of your money, you'd better not botch it this time."

"She's as good as dead."

"Just be careful. The police are on the alert. They're looking for that truck."

"They'll never find it. I covered my tracks."

"No more mistakes, Weeks."

"You just have the money ready, because I'll be leaving the country when I finish this job."

"Call me when you do."

CHAPTER NINE

AFTER HIS CONVERSATION with C.J., Matthew hurried downstairs, eager to talk to his mother. She was dressed, getting ready to go out. A visiting preacher was at the church, and she had agreed to act as hostess for the reverend. Damn, he wanted to talk to her!

His chance didn't come until Sunday night. By then he felt ready to explode. His mother had her feet up, resting, and Matthew knew this was his opportunity.

He took a chair opposite the sofa. "Mom, I'd like to talk."

She glanced at him. "Sure, what about?"

"C. J. Doe."

She sat up, a distressed expression on her face. "What about C. J. Doe?"

"Why don't you like her?"

Her shoulders stiffened defensively. "I didn't say I didn't like her."

"You're very hostile whenever I mention her name."

She shrugged it off. "That's just your imagination."

"It's not my imagination, Mom. Be honest with me."

"It's nothing."

"Okay," he said. "Then you wouldn't mind if I took her out on a date."

"A date?" Her eyes opened wide and she got to her feet. "If you need female companionship, there are lots of young women who'd be eager to go out with you. There's Shelly—''

"I want to go out with C.J.," he interrupted, feeling as if he were fourteen again, needing his mother's permission.

"Why?" She threw up her hands. "What's so special about her?"

"I like her. I like her a lot."

Weakly she sank back against the sofa. "It's happening all over again. She's trying to take you away from me, just like she tried to take your father."

"What?" Had he heard her correctly?

She twisted her hands, her words coming fast, her breath jerky. "It all started when that money began coming to his office. At first she refused to take it, said she didn't want money from anyone who hadn't enough guts to give it to her in person. Your dad said he admired her character and strength, and eventually he talked her into accepting it. He starting advising her on college, then he was helping her with her courses. It was C.J. this and C.J. that. He started meeting her after work and on weekends. Time he used to spend with me he was spending with her."

Matthew had a bitter taste in his mouth. "Are you saying they were having an…" He couldn't say the word *affair*. The thought would have been laughable if not for the look on his mother's face. "A relationship?" he finished.

"Yes."

The bitter taste spread from his mouth throughout his body, but he knew something was wrong with this explanation. There had to be another one.

Seeing the look in his eyes, she quickly added, "Not *that* kind of relationship. You know your father—he wasn't the type. It was more of a father-daughter thing. He liked her and wanted to help her."

Relief spiraled through his system, but he knew he couldn't leave it at that. His dark eyes held hers. ''Then why don't you like her?''

She twisted her hands again in that nervous gesture. ''You're going to think I'm a silly old woman.''

''Tell me, anyway.''

She shrugged. ''I was jealous. Matt and I always wanted lots of children, but after four miscarriages we only had you. And that was when we were already in our thirties. Suddenly he seemed to have the daughter he'd always wanted, and I felt left out. Especially when he wouldn't discuss her with me.''

The bile rose up in his throat and he wanted to forget the whole thing. But he couldn't. He had to know. He got up, crossed to the sofa and sat by his mom. He took her hands in his. ''I don't want to ask this question, but I have to. Please try to understand.'' He paused, searching for the right words, then he squeezed her hands and asked, ''Could Dad be her father?''

She jerked her hands from his, anger burning in her eyes. ''How dare you ask me such a thing? Your dad loved me and was never unfaithful. How could you even *think* such an awful thing?''

He reached for her hands again and held them tight. ''Mom, the mere thought is like acid in my stomach, eating away at me, but so many things don't add up. His involvement with the Townsends and with C.J., the money and so many other things. There has to be a reason he was so concerned about her.''

''He is not her father, Matthew.''

He closed his eyes, then looked directly at her. ''Can you be sure of that?''

Without blinking, without hesitating, she said, ''Yes.''

''Mom, I loved him, too, but he wasn't perfect, and

please don't dismiss this because of the way we felt about him. I like C.J., and my feelings toward her are not brotherly. So please help me believe it, too."

"You want proof?" she asked pointedly.

He was taken aback for a moment. "You have proof?"

She got up and went into his father's study. He could hear her opening drawers and rustling paper. In a few minutes she was back and handed him a manila folder.

Matthew opened it up and started to read. His eyes grew wide and he could scarcely believe what he was seeing.

"It's true," his mother said softly. "When you were about a year old, you dad came down with a severe case of mumps. At his age it was catastrophic. Dr. Haslow gave him a strong medication to get him over it. In the end the medication and the mumps rendered him sterile." She gazed down at her hands, as if reliving that time. "We were devastated, so we went to Austin to get a second and then a third opinion." She waved her hand toward the folder. "The results are all there. He was sterile."

He shook his head. "Why didn't I know about this?"

"It wasn't something your father liked to talk about. At first he felt as if it diminished his manhood, and we had kind of a rough time, but our love got us through."

"Oh, Mom." He wrapped his arms around her. "I'm so sorry to bring it all up again."

She sniffed into his shoulder. "We were lucky. We had you."

Matthew drew back and looked into her eyes. "I really couldn't believe he was C.J.'s father, but I had to ask. I hope you understand."

Her hand touched his face. "This girl means a great deal to you, doesn't she?"

"Yes," he breathed, knowing his feelings for C.J. were growing with every day. A smile curved his lips. "I wish you'd get to know her. She's really a unique person, so full of life and hopes and dreams.''

At the affection in his voice, she said, ''Matt used to say similar things about her. I guess I've let jealousy cloud my judgment. Well, maybe I'm not too old to learn from my mistakes. I suppose it's time I found out what y'all are talking about.''

''That would make me very happy,'' he replied, feeling as if a gigantic weight had been lifted from his shoulders.

Belle smiled sheepishly at her son. ''I don't know if your father ever told you, but you're not supposed to fall for the opposition.''

''Oh, Mom.'' He sighed and leaned back against the sofa. He knew she was teasing, but there was truth in her words. ''Being a New York lawyer, I thought I could handle just about anything, but this case has thrown me for a loop. I can't seem to think straight when I'm around C.J. I knew it was a lapse in judgment to ride to Austin with her, but I couldn't help myself. Now I'm so glad I did. At least I was there to help her.''

''I can't believe the Townsends would hire someone to kill C.J. I've known them all my life, and despite their dislike of the Watsons, I don't believe any one of them would go to those lengths.''

''As their attorney, I have to believe that, too.'' He kissed her cheek, eager to call C.J. But this type of news he wanted to tell her in person, so he settled for a quick phone call, asking her to be at his office first thing in the morning.

WHEN MATTHEW GOT to the office Monday morning, Miss Emma was already there staring at him over her rhinestone glasses. One thing about Miss Emma, she could be punctual, efficient and annoying all in the same breath.

"Pretty boy. Pretty boy," Matthew heard over his shoulder.

He turned to see Herman in his cage, sitting on a table by the window.

"Now, don't go getting your dander up," Miss Emma warned. "I only brought him in because Doc Lowe said he was lonely. He'd gotten used to my being at home when your father fell ill. I'll put him in the conference room if he becomes a bother."

Matthew flashed her a big smile. "Miss Emma, nothing is going to bother me today, not even Herman."

"Oh boy. Oh boy," Herman piped up.

Miss Emma cast Matthew a strange look. "Have you had too much coffee this morning?"

"No, I'm just in a very good mood," he told her. He couldn't remember the last time he'd felt this good. The whole world seemed brighter and clearer, and he had the ridiculous urge to keep on smiling.

"If you say so," she replied, still eyeing him with that strange look. "The Bower case is at ten. The file's on your desk. If you have any questions, just ask."

He was getting used to her brisk manner. It didn't bother him at all. "Isn't that the chicken thief?" he asked, and took the mail she was handing him.

"Yes, he was caught red-handed, so the best you can hope for is a probated sentence. He has a family to take care of, and usually Judge Mason is very lenient in these cases."

Normally he would be annoyed with Miss Emma for telling him how to handle a case, but he must be mellowing. He realized she knew these people much better than he.

The rattle of a trailer caught his attention and he glanced

outside. C.J. pulled up and parked along the curb with the long trailer, taking up several parking spaces.

"She's doing it again," Miss Emma grumbled.

Herman gave a low wolf whistle.

Matthew glanced at the bird and laughed. "Well, Herman, you and I agree on something."

"Herman, how many times have I told you not to whistle at girls?" Miss Emma scolded.

"Bossy lady. Bossy lady," Herman responded.

Miss Emma ignored the remark as she noticed Pete and Harry getting out of the truck. "I hope she's not bringing those two old coots in here with her."

"You got something against Pete and Harry?"

"Pete thinks he's a ladies' man, and Harry…well, I'd just prefer if Harry stayed outside."

Matthew suspected there was a story behind her words, but he didn't have time to dwell on Miss Emma and her peculiarities. He had more important things to concern him.

"Send C.J. in," he said, entering his office.

C.J. came inside, looking radiant and beautiful in tight jeans and a pink shirt. As she quietly closed the door, he saw a momentary look of discomfort on her face.

"If this is about Pete and Harry, they won't cause any more trouble." The first thing C.J. noticed, besides Matthew's warm smile, was his change of clothes. He wore jeans, a short-sleeved white shirt and his usual boots. The city man was becoming countrified. She liked the look. Oh, she liked it a lot.

"This isn't about Pete and Harry." He broke through her thoughts.

She frowned. "It isn't?"

"No." He waved a hand toward the chair opposite his desk. "Have a seat. I want to talk to you."

"What about?" The frown deepened as she sat.

He leaned against the desk and folded his arms across his chest. "I just need to know where you want to go on this date. Somewhere here in town? Or would you like to go to Austin for—"

"Date?" she interrupted. Suddenly her face cleared. "You asked your mother?"

"Yep." He couldn't help smiling. "And you can rest assured that my dad is not your father."

The frown reappeared. "How can you be so sure? I mean, your mother wouldn't come out and admit it, would she?"

Matthew held up his hand. "I had the same doubts." He reached for his briefcase and took out the folder. "I think this will answer all your questions."

Leafing through the folder, she said, "These are medical reports."

"Yes. Read what they say."

He waited while she did so.

"Your dad was sterile." She sighed, shaking her head. "I can't believe it."

"Yes. It happened when I was a year old. So there's no way he could be your father."

She fingered the folder, her expression hidden from him. So many emotions coursed through her, but relief was paramount. She and Matthew weren't related. Ever since the first day she'd met him, she'd searched his features, looking fearfully for a clue that would tie them together. Every time she got near Matthew, though, so many other feelings surfaced. He stirred strong emotions in her, and the idea that they might have the same father had torn her apart. Now she knew they didn't—knew absolutely, positively. But there was something else that nagged at her.

Matthew watched her bowed head. "Aren't you happy about this?" he had to ask.

She lifted her head, her green eyes troubled. "Yes, of course, but why doesn't your mother like me?"

"A simple case of jealousy."

"Jealousy?"

"You have to understand that my parents were always close, more so since I went away to college. Suddenly he was spending time with you, helping you. Evidently he knew something about you, and he didn't share that knowledge with my mom. They'd always shared everything, and she resented him for keeping this from her. And she blamed you."

"I never meant to cause problems between them."

"I know, and I think Mom knows it, too."

There was silence for a moment, then she asked, "Do you think your dad knew one of my parents?"

"Yes, I think he did," he said honestly.

"I thought so, too, but he would never tell me. Then I thought that since he wouldn't, *he* must be my father. I've believed so many things and none of them were true. I feel like a fool. Your mother must really hate me now."

Matthew pulled her to her feet, gazing into her eyes. "No, she doesn't. She feels like a silly old woman, and it's all because neither one of you knew what was going on. Maybe when we get the results of the paternity tests, we'll have some answers."

"I hope so," she replied.

"In the meantime we have a date to plan."

"Yes." Her eyes glowed.

Matthew brought her closer, his hands resting lightly on her waist. "It's such a relief knowing we're not related, but I wouldn't mind being kissin' cousins."

"You wouldn't?" she whispered, acutely aware of her pounding heart and quickened breath.

Staring at her lips, he breathed, "No."

Almost in slow motion she took the step that brought her body against his. He drew a sharp breath, and she could feel his warmth and the rapid beat of his heart. He bent his head and softly touched her lips. His were warm and gentle, just as she'd known they would be, but there was passion and fire simmering beneath the tentative caress. She trembled with a shiver of expectation, and she reveled in the sensual pleasures his lips promised.

At the feel of her quivering body Matthew groaned and pulled her tightly against him, his lips taking hers in a fiery hunger. She met his hunger with equal fervor, her hands tangling in his dark hair, giving herself over to the desires his touch had unleashed. It seemed as if she'd waited all her life to feel his touch, his kiss, his possession.

Her kiss, her touch was everything Matthew had dreamed of. He felt himself going up in flames, losing control, losing himself totally and completely in her sweetness. The kiss deepened as his mouth opened over hers, his tongue exploring, tasting.

The taste and feel of him danced through her and she didn't want to think, just abandon herself to all these feelings her body craved. But despite the swirls of pleasure, a nagging warning intruded.

Ignore it. Ignore it.

But the warning persisted.

Slowly she pulled back, her hand against her bruised lips, her eyes darkened with the passion they'd just shared.

There was something else in her eyes, something Matthew didn't want to see. Could it be fear? Did he frighten her?

He quickly said, "I didn't mean to go that far."

"It's all right. I wanted it, too."

His alarm disappeared and he reached for her again, but she backed away. "No," she said, an ache in her voice. "As much as I want to, I can't." At his puzzled look she explained, "My whole life is consumed with finding out who I am, and until I know who my parents are, I won't allow my emotions to be swayed by something I can't handle."

He took a step toward her, trying to understand what those emotions were, but all he could feel was the heady sensation of her touch. "C.J.," he whispered.

That soft note in his voice almost destroyed her resolve. She wanted to give in, feel all the things she knew he could make her feel, but there was so much standing between them.

"I have to be honest," she said with more strength than she really felt.

"I wouldn't want you to be any other way."

"Aside from the mystery of my birth, there are other things that bother me."

"Such as?"

C.J. looked down at her hands. "I have a feeling you could hurt me badly."

"I would never hurt you," he stated emphatically.

Her eyes met his. "Not intentionally, no. But your life is in New York and you'll be going back there soon. My life is here in Coberville and..." Her voice faded, her meaning very clear, and what bothered him was that he couldn't deny her words.

He *would* be going back to New York, and he knew she wasn't the type of woman to want a brief affair. He wasn't even sure it was what *he* wanted. Thoughts of taking her to New York flitted through his mind, but he knew her spirit would suffocate in the crowded city with its skyscraper canyons and dirty skies. She needed sunshine, clear days and the quiet, familiar environment of Coberville, Texas.

They stared at each other for several seconds, and he wanted to take her in his arms and tell her he could alleviate all her fears, but he couldn't. He couldn't lie to her.

A tap on the door interrupted the silence, and Miss Emma poked her head around. "Dr. Ryder's on the phone. Said it was important."

Matthew reached for the receiver, and C.J. knew she should leave, but if the call had something to do with her, she wanted to know.

She listened carefully to what Matthew was saying, but his clipped responses gave her few clues.

"Yes. When? Okay. Let me know of any other developments."

As he hung up she asked, "What happened?"

He scowled at the phone for a second, then said, "Someone broke into Ryder Laboratories last night."

She was dumbfounded. "Is Cliff okay?"

"Yes, Cliff's fine, but the security guard didn't fare so well. Someone drugged his coffee and he had an allergic reaction. He's in the hospital, but Cliff says he'll be okay."

"What was the thief after?"

Matthew paused again, wondering how much he should tell her. "Nothing was missing or stolen, but one of their tests had been tampered with."

"Which test?" she asked quietly.

"Someone switched your vial of blood."

Her eyes narrowed. "What?"

"Cliff said not to worry. They took several vials of blood, so they're throwing out the first test and starting over."

"How'd they know the vial had been switched?"

"Seems the Ryder Lab has a very up-to-date security system. Something the thief didn't count on. Their tubes have numbers etched on them, and the numbers run in sequence when they do a test. Your tube didn't have a Ryder Lab number on it."

She shook her head. "The Townsends just don't give up, do they?"

"As their attorney, I can't answer that, but I did promise Cliff I'd keep this under my hat until the tests are completed. He doesn't want his lab broken into again, and he felt he should notify someone."

"I see," she said. "What is it they're so afraid of? I don't want anything from them. I only want some answers." Her troubled eyes met his. "Is that so much to ask?"

"No," he answered, wanting to ease her distress.

"I've got to go," she said hurriedly, and turned toward the door. "We've got to vaccinate Mr. Gibson's calves."

Unable to stop himself, he threw out his hands and caught her. He pulled her to him and brushed his mouth against hers. Her lips quivered and he knew he should have let her go, but he needed that kiss—because in some way it felt as if they were saying goodbye.

"Goodbye," she whispered, echoing his thoughts, and left the room.

On heavy feet he followed her into Miss Emma's office. Pete Watson slipped off the edge of Miss Emma's desk and headed for the door behind C.J. Suddenly he stopped. "You know, Emma, Harry's eyeing that bird of yours like it's his next meal."

Harry could be seen through the window giving Herman a hard stare.

"Oh boy. Oh boy. Big man. Big man. Oh boy. Oh

boy." Herman pranced around in his cage in an agitated manner.

Miss Emma jumped to her feet. "You tell Harry Watson to stay away from my bird."

"Now, Emma, why don't you come out here and tell Harry yourself?" Pete cajoled.

Miss Emma marched over to Pete and shoved him toward the door, saying, "Get out of my office, Pete Watson, and take that brother of yours with you." The door slammed shut with the sound of jingling spurs and Pete's laughter.

Miss Emma was flustered, her cheeks as red as her hair.

"Not one word, young Matthew, not one word," she warned, and stalked back to her chair.

"I wasn't going to say anything," Matthew told her, the circuslike atmosphere relieving some of the tension inside him. "Except I like that shade of red in your cheeks."

She glared at him.

He laughed with a merriment he was far from feeling, and closed the door.

MATTHEW DIDN'T SEE C.J. the rest of the week. He wanted to call her, talk to her, but he knew it was best if he didn't. She was right. He could hurt her, and that was the last thing he wanted to do.

But she was always there, in his thoughts and his dreams, and he was beginning to wonder if she always would be.

C.J. KEPT BUSY. She didn't want to think. She worked every day until she was exhausted and fell into a deep sleep at night. She realized Pete and Harry were worried about her, but so much was crowding in on her that she couldn't talk to them.

One afternoon she rode down to the creek, dismounted and sat on the grass, staring at the slow-running stream. The only sounds were the babbling water and Midnight munching on grass. The scene was quiet and peaceful, just her and her thoughts.

Cober property filled the landscape, and C.J. glanced toward the thousand acres Victoria Townsend had willed to her. The legacy of that land triggered so many questions. Why would someone want her dead? Why would someone switch the test tubes? What was the secret someone would go to such lengths to hide? Victoria Townsend had known. So had Matthew Sloan, Sr. But they hadn't told her. They'd just left her to flounder in a world where she felt out of place. "Why?" she asked the silence that surrounded her. The question was lost in the breeze, and as always, it wasn't answered.

She lay back on the grass, hands behind her head, gaze focused on the wide Texas sky. Matthew. She was so relieved they weren't related. She knew she was falling for him, and she hadn't known how hard until he'd kissed her. Her body grew warm from the memory. But she had to keep her emotions under control. Until she found out about her past, she had no future; that knowledge was soul-deep in her.

Besides, she told herself, in a few weeks he would be gone, back to his own world, and she'd be here in Coberville dealing with the turmoil of her life. By then she'd have the answer she'd been waiting for. Was she a Townsend?

She closed her eyes and wondered how she would feel if she was, especially after everything that had happened. Would it ease the emptiness inside her? Or lead to more unhappiness? Somehow she couldn't dredge up any real feelings for either of those men. Both were so cold and ruthless. But then, a person didn't get to choose his or her parents. She couldn't help wondering if the truth she'd been searching for all her life would turn out to be a truth she wanted to hear.

CHAPTER TEN

ROB STOPPED ABRUPTLY as he came through the bedroom door. Francine was throwing clothes into a suitcase. Her brown hair hung loosely around her shoulders, and her face was made up. A blue dress clung to her slim curves. She hadn't looked this good in weeks. She was obviously going somewhere, but this was the first he'd learned of it.

His perfect features creased into a frown. "What the hell are you doing?"

"What does it look like I'm doing?" she asked, and marched back into the closet for more clothes.

The thought that she might be leaving him crossed his mind, but he quickly dismissed it.

He grabbed her by the shoulder as she came out of the closet, arms full of dresses. "Francine, why the packing?"

Pulling away, she said, "I'm going home to Evergreen."

He didn't like that answer. "Don't you think we should discuss this?"

"Yes," she replied, stuffing the dresses into her suitcase with quick angry movements. "Like you discussed agreeing to take the paternity test." She whirled around. "You didn't even stop to think about me or how it would affect our children."

He moved closer to her, finally realizing what the anger was all about. "The Doe girl is not going to be a problem much longer. Trust me."

"But she's a problem now. For years I've put up with your lies and affairs, but coming face-to-face with one of your bastard children is a little more than even I can take."

It had been a long time since Rob had seen her in such a mood. He had to do something, and fast.

"Francine, baby, you're blowing this out of proportion," he said, and tried to take her in his arms, but she whirled back and started shoving clothes into the suitcase again.

"I'm going home to Evergreen. When you get your life straightened out, give me a call."

"For heaven's sake, Francine, what's so damn special about Evergreen?"

"It's my home!" she cried. "I was born there. Our children were born there. It's where I feel at peace. This—" she waved a hand around the room "—has never been my home. Your mother was always mistress here. Now it's Martha. And there's something really strange about your aunt Martha, in my opinion. She needs psychiatric help. It's not normal the way she fawns over your father. This whole family isn't normal, and I'm getting away while I still have a bit of self-respect left."

Her words shook him; she'd never gotten up this much courage before. But he knew how to handle his wife. He wrapped his arms around her waist. "I need you here with me," he whispered.

"Need me? You've never needed me." She laughed scornfully. "Your father needed my dad's political support, and you got me as a consolation prize. Then you proceeded to show me that you could have more beautiful and sexier women in your bed."

Rob pulled her close. "You're wrong. I need you now more than I ever have."

"No, you don't," she told him, but her voice was weak.

"You have all your other women to keep you occupied."
He could see tears gathering in her eyes. "Why couldn't
you be satisfied with me? Why do you need those other
women?" She sagged limply against him.

"There will be no other women. I promise."

"For how long? Until another sexy young thing comes
into your life?"

He sighed his frustration, getting tired of trying to ap-
pease her. "Don't you understand how important this election is to me? I need you here, as my wife, to win. And
we have to spend time with the people in the area. Help
me, Francine, and I'll bring the kids home when the semester is over. We'll spend the summer campaigning, and
if all goes well, we'll spend Christmas at Evergreen. We'll
be a real family, just like you want."

She leaned away from him, her eyes bright. "I want that
more than anything."

"Mr. Rob, Mr. Sloan is on line one." Henry's voice
came through on the intercom.

Rob went over to the intercom on the bedside table and
pressed a button. "Thanks, Henry." He picked up the receiver, listened to Matthew for a few moments, then hung
up.

With a somber expression he glanced at his wife. "The
test results are ready. Ryder wants to see us at ten in the
morning."

"Why couldn't he just give the results over the phone?"

"For some reason he wants to see everyone involved."

"A bit melodramatic, isn't it?"

"I suppose."

There was a brief tense pause, then Francine asked,
"Are you the father of that girl?"

"Of course not," he denied swiftly.

"You answered that just a little too fast."

He walked toward her and tried to take her in his arms again, but she pushed him away and asked, "How can you be so sure?"

He ran a tired hand through his blond hair. "Francine, I..." He paused, then said, "What the hell, you don't believe anything I say."

As he walked to the door, she warned, "You'd better not be the father of that girl, Rob. If you are, I'll leave you and I'll make sure the people of this district won't elect you dogcatcher, much less a U.S. senator."

He turned back, his blue eyes flashing. "Don't threaten me, Francine. It doesn't become you."

"It's not a threat, Rob. It's a promise. And you know I can make it happen. All I have to do is pick up the phone and call Dad." Her voice was cold and defiant.

He watched her for a moment and wondered what had happened to the warm, loving girl he'd married. The woman looking back at him was hard and embittered. Had he done this to her? The idea woke a conscience he'd thought long dead. Somehow he had to put his family back together again. He had to, or he was never going to win the election.

He walked back to her and looked deeply into her eyes. If there was anything he was good at, it was handling women. "You don't mean that." He smiled sweetly.

"No, I don't," she admitted, and took a deep breath. "But sometimes you make me say and do stupid things."

Rob relaxed, knowing he'd won this little skirmish.

He slid his arms around her and nibbled on her ear. "We're good together, Francine, and you know it," he whispered into her neck.

"Yes," she breathed.

"So." He kissed her lips. "Unpack and we'll give this campaign our best shot."

Her eyes narrowed. "Campaign? It's always the campaign with you and your father."

He kissed her again briefly. "I've got to tell Dad about Matthew's call. We'll finish this discussion later."

As he hurried to the door, she called, "Rob…"

He turned back, a pleased look on his face.

"You've sweet-talked me into staying only because I've let you. Loving you is a weakness I'm not proud of, but I've taken all I'm going to take. You screw up once more, and I'll keep my promise. Remember that."

The pleasure vanished from his face. He knew she meant every word. He had finally pushed her to the edge and he could either go down with her or try to make their marriage work. With the election looming closer and closer, he had only one choice.

In the garden surrounding the large indoor swimming pool, Stephanie Cox watched John Townsend take stiff steps with the aid of a walker. "Oh, Johnny, you're doing wonderful," she cooed.

John sank weakly into his wheelchair, breathing heavily. "Damn legs just won't move the way I want them to," he complained.

"It's going to take time." She smiled and eased onto his lap. "Don't be so impatient."

"Stephanie, get off. Someone might see," he snapped.

She wrapped her arms around his neck. "What difference does it make? You promised as soon as you were back on your feet, we'd get married."

"I can't think about marriage right now. I've got too much on my mind. That Doe girl has the whole family upset."

She drew back. "That Doe girl is all you ever think about. Why does she scare you so much?"

His blue eyes darkened. "She doesn't scare me. She makes me angry. Angry my wife would freely give away part of our children's heritage. And angry that little nobody considers herself a Townsend. Never in a million years would that be true."

She ran a finger down the angry lines of his face. "Even in your seventies you're a very virile man. I can just imagine what you must have been like in your younger days."

"That girl is no seed of mine," he refuted harshly.

"If you say so."

"I do, and she's going to be sadly disappointed at the test results."

She eased closer to him. "Let's forget about her and talk about us."

"Stephanie, I told you—"

"I'm tired of being your nurse, maid and therapist." Anger flashed in her eyes as she interrupted him. "I want to be your wife."

He put his arms around her, trying to soothe her. "First I have to get these other matters settled."

"The Doe girl again," she groaned. "How I wish she'd never come into our lives."

"Me, too, honey, but it'll all work out. I promise."

"Okay." She kissed his cheek. "But I want you to tell Martha we're getting married."

"Martha? Whatever for?"

"Because I don't like the way she fusses over you. She's your sister-in-law, not your wife."

"She's just a lonely old woman."

"I want you to tell her." Stephanie paused, then added, "if you don't, you can find someone else to warm your bed."

"Now, Stephanie." He ran a hand up her thigh.

Rob watched from the doorway, anger churning inside

him. He jerked open the door and stormed toward them. "Have the two of you no decency?"

"Now, son—"

"Leave us, Stephanie," Rob broke in. "I want to talk to my father."

Stephanie scrambled off John's lap and hurried away.

"You just never stop, do you?" Rob railed, running both hands through his hair. "I can only imagine the pain Mother suffered putting up with your infidelities all those years."

"The apple doesn't fall too far from the tree."

Blue eyes stared into blue eyes. "I know," Rob said with a regretful sigh. "But I'm going to make my marriage work."

"You'd better, or you can kiss this election goodbye."

Rob gritted his teeth.

John watched his son. "In a lot of ways you're like your mother. That woman had too much pride. When she first found out I was cheating on her, she kicked me out of her bed, and no matter how much I apologized and promised to be faithful, she never let me back in."

"So to get even, you had an affair with her sister."

John's eyes opened wide in disbelief. "How do you know about that?"

"I was old enough to be aware of what was going on."

"It was a stupid mistake, and you're right—I only did it to get back at your mother. It was just a brief thing that should never have happened."

"But Aunt Martha is still in love with you."

"Yeah." John looked down at his hands. "That's the sad irony of the whole thing. Martha loved me and I loved your mother, but I could never make Victoria believe that."

all the Townsends turned up—and he felt sure they would, in fact, be here in force today.

He hadn't seen or talked to C.J. in days, except to tell her the results were ready. He should have called her to make sure someone was coming with her. What was he worried about? he asked himself irritably. The ordeal was almost over. No one was going to hurt her now. But he couldn't get rid of the uneasy feeling in his gut.

A red Camaro drove into the parking lot and a slim, beautiful woman in a white suit got out. Matthew blinked. Was that C.J.? He watched in awe as she walked across the pavement with an elegance and grace it took some women years to cultivate. She had to be the most striking woman he'd ever seen. As that familiar warmth curled through his body, he realized his feelings for C. J. Doe went deeper than he'd even begun to imagine.

C.J. pushed open the glass door and came to a sudden halt when she saw Matthew standing in the foyer. He had on a navy blue suit and a blue pin-striped shirt; the city man was back. But just the sight of him made the churning in her stomach dissolve into a warm pleasurable feeling.

She hadn't seen him since that passionate kiss in his office, and now the sight of his handsome face weakened her resolve to keep some distance between them. It was for the best, she'd told herself a million times, but that had never eased the ache inside her.

"Morning." He smiled tentatively as he walked toward C.J. He glanced at her with open approval; then forcing his eyes away, he asked, "Where're Pete and Harry?"

"At home."

He frowned. "They let you drive here alone?"

Her green eyes darkened. "They don't *let* me do anything. I make my own decisions."

"Okay, maybe I phrased that wrong," he conceded, "but I thought they wouldn't want you to go through this alone."

"I've been alone all my life."

He studied the fixed expression on her face. "You haven't been alone, C.J.," he said softly. "You have two old men who love you more than life itself. And you had Maggie."

"Yes." She gripped the strap of her purse, knowing she was being testy for no reason, but her nerves were tied in knots. "I've been lucky," she added, feeling guilty because Matthew had to remind her. "Not everyone has such loving people to look out for them."

"I'm not sure I'd use the word *loving* in connection with Harry." Matthew's mouth curved into a teasing smile.

She smiled back, some of her tension easing.

As they gazed at each other, the silence stretched. "I guess you're waiting for the Townsends," she finally said. "I'll just go and see if Cliff is ready."

As she walked away, he said, "C.J."

She stopped and glanced back.

"I hope it turns out the way you want."

"Thank you," she replied, feeling an edge of uncertainty. How *did* she want the tests to turn out? All she knew—all she'd ever known—was that she wanted some answers to the mystery of her birth.

DR. RYDER'S OFFICE was packed. Matthew sat on his right, close to the desk. C.J. sat on the left, and the Townsends filled the chairs in between. As Matthew had expected, they were all here: Rob and Francine, Joyce and Thurman, Clare, Martha, John and the ever-present Stephanie.

"I wanted to see all of you today for a reason," Dr. Ryder began. Several test tubes lay on his desk and he picked up one of them, "Someone has an avid interest in Ryder test tubes. They didn't like the one we were using and decided to replace it with another."

"What are you saying?" Rob asked coolly.

"I'm saying, Mr. Townsend, that someone broke into my lab and switched C. J. Doe's vial of blood."

"That's ridiculous!" Rob said.

"On the contrary, Mr. Townsend. You see, I have a unique security system. The Ryder tubes all have numbers on them, and when we do a test, the tubes are done in numerical sequence. That's how we knew the Doe tube had been switched." He twirled the tube in his hand. "This is the tube and if you'll look closely, you can see there are no numbers on it."

"Are you implying the Townsends had something to do with this?" John's voice was harsh, challenging.

"I'm not implying anything. I just want everyone to know what happened."

"Have the tests been done?" Rob asked impatiently.

"Yes. We try to guard for every contingency. So we draw three vials of blood from each person involved."

"Then what are you going on about?" John grumbled. "Do you have the results or don't you?"

"What I'm going on about, Mr. Townsend, is that I don't like my lab being broken into and my employees endangered."

"What's that got to do with us?"

"Who else would be interested in the test results?"

"Before you accuse anyone you'd better have some proof," John hissed, clenching the arms of his wheelchair.

"I don't. We checked the tube for prints, but of course there were none."

"Then give us the results so we can get this thing over with," John ordered.

Dr. Ryder scanned the room. "In case anyone's interested, my security guard is doing fine." Everyone, except C.J. and Matthew, stared back at him with indifferent expressions. Slowly he turned to the files on his desk.

He leafed painstakingly through them. Matthew knew he was stalling, making the Townsends squirm. He might not be able to prove they'd broken into his lab, but he was going to make them sweat before he told them anything.

Finally Dr. Ryder looked up. "Before I tell you the results, I want to say that we gave special attention to these tests, and I consider the findings to be accurate and precise. I want you to understand that the findings have to be in the upper nineties—like ninety-nine point nine or ninety-nine point eight—for a man to be considered the biological father. When the finding is lower, it's less likely the man is the father."

"You going to tell us or are you going to ramble on all morning?" John was getting impatient.

Dr. Ryder looked directly at him. "Since you're so curious, Mr. Townsend, I'll take you first." He opened a file and paused, then said, "In your case, the percentage was very low. There is no way you could have fathered C. J. Doe."

An audible sigh of relief escaped John and a satisfied smile spread across his face. But there was one Townsend left, and no one made a move or uttered a sound.

Dr. Ryder opened another file. "Now John Robert William Townsend. The percentage wasn't as low as your father's and—"

"You lying bastard!" Francine jumped up and began to slap her husband, hitting his face, his shoulders, anywhere she could reach.

Rob managed to capture her hands, holding them tight. "Stop it!"

"Mrs. Townsend, there's no reason to get this upset," Dr. Ryder interjected. "Please let me finish."

Francine leaned weakly against her husband.

"As I was saying," Dr. Ryder continued, "even though your husband's percentage isn't as low as his father's, it's still too low for him to have fathered C. J. Doe."

The Townsends broke into smiles and their tension decreased noticeably.

But not C. J. Doe.

She sat as if turned to stone. The pain in her chest became a sick and fiery gnawing. She'd never thought the truth would hurt so much. Losing the land and the money didn't matter as much as the agony of not knowing. After all she'd been through and after all she'd given up, she still didn't know who she was.

Dr. Ryder looked at C.J. "I'm sorry. We did the test twice. If you have any doubts, there's some more extensive DNA testing that can be done."

"That won't be necessary," she said, wondering if it was her own voice she heard or some person outside her body. She knew the results but was having difficulty assimilating them. Everything seemed unreal, like a bad dream.

"You're damn right that won't be necessary," John said, his blue eyes piercing C.J. "We all knew you weren't a Townsend, girlie."

C.J. saw the hatred in the blue eyes and suddenly relief surged through her numb body. She was glad she wasn't this man's daughter.

"You get the papers out, Sloan," John directed Matthew. "I want her to sign that land back to the Townsends today."

"I'll leave you to your legal matters," Dr. Ryder said, and left the room.

Matthew opened his briefcase and took out the necessary papers. He laid them on Ryder's desk and handed C.J. a pen. "Sign where the *X*'s are," he instructed, wishing he was anywhere but here. The pain in her eyes tore him apart.

C.J. signed in the indicated places, surprised her hand wasn't shaking because inside she was trembling as if she had a fever.

"This is the waiver, which we won't need," Matthew said as he sorted through the legal documents.

"No, we won't need that, will we, girlie?" John snarled. "You're not a Townsend. You're just a little nobody who—"

"Dad." Rob stopped him. "It's over. Let it be."

"Not after the hell she's put this family through," John shot back, his hard eyes still on C.J. "You thought my wife's lapse in judgment somehow linked you to the Townsend family. She only felt sorry for you, like everyone else in Coberville did. I never thought you'd be stupid enough to hand the land back without a fight. Whoever your parents might be, they aren't very bright."

C.J. stiffened, anger blasting through the shattered fragments of her ego. "I may not know who my parents are," she told him, her voice strong and unwavering, "but I can honestly say with every breath in my body that I'm glad a cold cruel man like you is not my father."

"How dare you!" John tried to get to his feet. "You little nobody, how dare you talk to me like that!"

Rob put a hand on his father's shoulder and pushed him back into the wheelchair. "Calm down, Dad."

"Don't distress yourself." Martha gently rubbed his arm. "You'll have another stroke, and she's—" her glance swung to C.J. "—not worth it."

"The money," John breathed raggedly. "I want her to

release her claim on the hundred thousand dollars. That was the deal. She'd give everything back to the Townsend estate."

Matthew spoke up. "It's the Cober estate."

"Cober? Townsend? What's the difference?" John looked at him through narrowed eyes.

"The Cober estate belongs to your children, and the Townsend estate belongs to you and your children," Matthew told him without blinking.

"You're splitting hairs, Sloan, and I don't like it."

"The money being held at the bank is from the Cober estate, and I'm only trying to keep things legal. Besides, she's already released her claim on everything." He wasn't sure why he was making such a big deal of it, but he felt John Townsend needed to be brought down a peg.

C.J. glanced at Matthew and their eyes locked. He wanted to help her and couldn't. He wasn't her lawyer.

She saw a spark of sympathy in his eyes and quickly turned away. He didn't understand what she was going through. No one could.

"I'll get the papers filed at the courthouse and that settles everything," Matthew said, closing his briefcase.

"See that you do," John muttered as the Townsends started to leave the room.

"Just one more thing." Matthew stopped them. "As of this moment I am no longer the Townsend attorney, nor do I feel inclined to ever be so again."

"You'd do well to remember which side your bread is buttered on, boy." John sent him a chilling look. "I know some influential people who could make life real hard for you."

Matthew's eyes darkened with a warning. "I've been known to keep some influential people out of jail—and put them in—so before you start making threats, you'd better be clear about who you're dealing with. Because there's one thing I can guarantee you, Mr. Townsend—you don't want to have to meet me in a courtroom.''

There was a dramatic pause as the two men faced each other. Joyce's voice broke through the tension. ''Come on, let's go celebrate! We just had a great victory.''

John Townsend was the first to look away. ''Yeah, let's get out of here.''

Stephanie quickly pushed him from the room with Martha by his side whispering, ''It's all right, John. Don't worry about those people.''

The rest of the Townsends quietly followed. Clare hung back a moment, giving C.J. a sympathetic look.

Rob lingered in the doorway, saying to his wife, ''Go ahead, I'll be right there.'' He spoke to Matthew. ''I'm sorry things got out of hand today.''

''You don't owe me an apology,'' Matthew answered stiffly. ''You owe that to C.J. All she wanted was some answers to the rumors that have been circulating around Coberville for years, and what she got was a flogging by the Townsends.''

Rob stared at C.J., and for a moment he looked about to respond, but then he turned and followed his family.

CHAPTER ELEVEN

THE ROOM WAS QUIET. Matthew watched C.J. as she sat with her head bowed, her whole demeanor one of despair. He knew he should leave, but he couldn't.

"C.J."

"Go away, Matthew."

"C.J."

She stood and walked to the window. Folding her arms, she stared outside. "Like they said, it's a great victory," she murmured, her voice bitter. "So why don't you go join the Townsends and celebrate?"

He frowned, not liking the hardness in her voice. "Didn't I tell you this could backfire?" he asked shortly. "I crossed the bounds of ethical conduct for you more times than I care to think about. So why are you blaming me?"

He was right. She was lashing out at him unfairly. But she was feeling so many painful things, she was barely conscious of her actions.

"I'm sorry," she said. "I'm so confused and mixed up. I just keep feeling I let her down."

"Who?"

"Victoria Townsend." C.J. swung around to face him. "She left me that land for a reason, and I thought I knew what it was. I thought she wanted one of the Townsend men to face his responsibility." She sighed deeply. "But it wasn't true. None of the rumors were true. Nothing makes any sense, and I'm still back where I started—not knowing who I am.''

''But you know you're not a Townsend.''

''Yes.'' She gazed off into space.

Matthew couldn't stand it. Her obvious distress was tearing him apart. He had to do something to alleviate it. ''Let's go have lunch,'' he suggested. ''You owe me a date, remember?''

She shook her head. ''No, I can't. I have to call Pete and get home.''

''Talking might help.'' He didn't want to let her go.

''I don't think so,'' she said. ''I need some time alone to sort through my feelings.'' She glanced at the telephone. ''I wonder if Cliff would mind if I used his phone.''

''I'm sure he wouldn't,'' Matthew replied, and picked up his briefcase. ''I'll wait for you outside.''

When she came out of the office, Matthew could see she was feeling better. The dejected expression was gone and the fighting spirit was back in her eyes.

''How did Pete take the news?''

''With his usual coolness.'' She gave a hesitant smile. ''He said the Townsends aren't good enough to lick my feet.''

''He might be right,'' Matthew said as they started toward the foyer.

''And he might be biased, too.''

''Sure you don't want to go have lunch somewhere?'' Matthew tried again, hoping she'd change her mind.

''I told Pete I was on my way home, and he and Harry will be clocking every mile.''

''I think the danger is over,'' Matthew replied as they walked through the front doors. ''Someone just got a little nervous about the test results.''

''But we'll never know, will we?''

"Probably not." They stood on the curb. "You got a good loaner," he said.

She frowned, not following his words, then realization dawned. "Oh, the Camaro. That's mine. I don't drive it much. I prefer my truck." Her eyes found his. "Thanks for helping me, Matthew, and I'm really sorry for snapping at you."

He smiled and watched her walk away with her usual grace. Suddenly his attention was diverted by the screeching of tires. A tan pickup slid into the parking lot and was headed straight for C.J.

"C.J.!" he shouted, and she glanced back, a look of terror on her face as she saw the truck. She tried desperately to get out of the way, but the truck was upon her too fast. It zoomed by, knocking her to the ground. Tires still screeching, the truck disappeared into traffic.

Matthew was already running toward C.J.'s still body. He knelt beside her, his heart beating so fast he could hardly breathe.

She lay on her stomach, her black hair all around her. As he moved his hand to push back her hair, she stirred, half sitting up.

"What happened?" she asked with a dazed look, holding a hand to her head.

Relief swept through him. She was okay. A little shaken, but okay. His trembling hand smoothed hair away from her face. "Someone tried to run you over."

"You shouted and I saw the truck," she choked out. "I barely had time to get out of the way. If you hadn't…"

Matthew saw the tears swimming in her eyes. He scooped her up in his arms, and hurried back into the clinic.

Several people ran to see what was happening. "Call the police," he yelled. "Ask for Detective Beal."

He carried her inside and carefully sat her in a chair. As Dr. Ryder examined her, Matthew paced the room, waiting. He removed his jacket and loosened his tie, pacing again.

Finally Dr. Ryder said, "She seems fine, but it might be best to get her over to the hospital."

C.J. heard him. "I just need a few minutes to recover and then—" She stopped speaking as Detective Beal came through the double glass doors and Matthew quickly went over to him.

"What happened?" Beal pulled out a notebook.

Matthew ran his hands through his hair. "God, I wish I knew. This tan late-model Ford pickup came out of nowhere and tried to hit her. It made straight for her. It wasn't an accident."

"Someone's still trying to kill her?"

"Evidently," Matthew answered.

Beal studied Matthew's haggard expression and said, "Let me call this in so we can start searching for the truck."

In a minute he was back. "Could we sit down? I'd like to ask you both a few more questions."

Matthew sat by C.J., taking her cold hand in his. They answered questions for the next thirty minutes. At the end C.J. asked, "Who would do this?"

"I don't know, ma'am, but we're going to find out," Beal vowed. "I'll check and see if they've found anything."

When Beal left again, Matthew placed his arm carefully around C.J. She rested her head on his shoulder. "Why, Matthew, why?"

Beal came back into the room and interrupted. "The truck was found about a mile away. It was stolen. We're running it for prints. Keep your fingers crossed."

"There won't be any," Matthew said. "This was a professional. I feel it in my gut."

"Could I speak with you a moment?" Beal asked Matthew.

Matthew got up and followed Beal some distance away. "If the person who tried to kill her finds out she's still alive, he could try to finish the job."

"Oh, God, I hadn't thought of that."

"I want a doctor to check her over, and then I need you both at the station to sign some reports. A policeman will escort you to the hospital and back to the station."

"Thanks, Beal. I won't let her out of my sight."

"I'm sure you won't," Beal said.

BY THE TIME THEY FINISHED at the police station, it was late. Beal strongly advised against traveling back to Coberville in the dark. It was too risky. He persuaded them to check into a hotel with police protection.

The policeman who escorted them to the hotel was Officer Carter, a man in his early thirties with a ready smile. He was all business, accompanying them to the restaurant for a quick meal, then making sure the rooms were safe and secure. Afterward, he stationed himself outside their doors, reassuring them that no one would get past him.

C.J. looked like a shadow of the young woman who had stepped out of the Camaro this morning. Matthew was worried, although the Emergency Room doctor said she was fine. She had bruises on her head and arm that would heal in a few days, but she was clearly still shaken up.

They had rooms with an adjoining door. At first C.J. had asked to go home, but Matthew knew what she needed now was rest. She didn't protest when he explained things to her, and that bothered him, too. It wasn't like her to be so meek.

Matthew waited while she undressed and crawled into bed. All he could see was black hair framing a white face against equally white sheets. He picked up her limp hand.

"Are you sure you're okay?" he asked.

"Yes," she whispered.

He held her hand, going over and over the events of the morning. Who would do this to her? Who wanted her dead?

As if reading his thoughts, she said quietly, "None of this makes any sense. The Townsends have their land and their money back. Why would they want to hurt me now?"

"Maybe it's not the Townsends."

Her eyes grew wide with disbelief.

"It could be anyone," he told her. "That's why we have to be careful until we find out who hired this guy."

"Pete was right. I should have listened. Oh, no! Pete!" she wailed. "I have to call him. He and Harry are probably worried sick."

"Don't get upset," he said in a soothing tone. "I called while you were in the ER. But you might want to call him yourself now—to reassure them."

She did and felt much better after she'd talked to Pete. He'd wanted to come to Austin to get her immediately, but she'd calmed him down and promised she'd be home the next morning.

She was so tired she couldn't think. Matthew would take care of everything, she told herself, feeling safe. The thought shocked her. She'd never depended on anyone, and yet, putting herself in his care was the easiest thing she'd ever done. She looked at his haggard disheveled appearance and raised her hand to lovingly touch his face. "You need to get some rest, too."

"I will," he murmured, and watched her drift off to sleep.

C.J. SLEPT FOR A WHILE, then woke to the sound of voices. Matthew was talking to someone in his room. A warm feeling came over her and she listened closely to the other voice. Detective Beal.

"My men are talking to people in the neighborhood where the truck was left. Someone must have seen something. I'm also going to have a talk with the Townsends, to see if anyone acts suspicious."

"I don't think the Townsends are involved."

"Why?"

"They got everything they wanted. They have no reason to want her dead."

"Maybe someone didn't count on the way the tests came out. Maybe someone wanted all the bases covered."

"Could be." Matthew sounded hesitant. "But it doesn't ring true. No matter how the tests came out, the Townsends had nothing to lose. I just have a feeling that one of C.J.'s real parents has something to do with this."

"But no one knows who her parents are."

"Yes, and that's the way someone wants it to stay. But I believe once we find out who hired that man, we'll have some answers to the mystery of C.J.'s birth."

Matthew's words rattled around in her aching head. It couldn't be true. Her real parents wouldn't want her dead, would they?

Dear God, she didn't want to know.

MATTHEW SHOWERED and put on a bathrobe furnished by the hotel, then checked on C.J. The lights were out and she was fast asleep. Good, he thought; it was what she needed. He tried the door, making sure it was locked, then went back into his own room. He lay down and stared at the ceiling. Sleep would not come easily tonight.

But he must have dozed off because he was awakened

by a sound from C.J.'s room. He jumped instantly out of bed and ran in. She was thrashing her head from side to side, moaning, "No, no."

He sat on the bed and tried to wake her gently. "C.J., it's Matthew. Wake up. You're having a bad dream."

Her eyes popped open and she had a glazed puzzled look, as if she didn't know where she was. Her face cleared as events came rushing back and her trembling arms reached for him. "Matthew, please hold me," she cried.

His arms went quickly around her waist, drawing her close. "It's okay," he murmured against her hair.

He didn't know how long he sat there holding her trembling body, but he soon became aware that she was wearing only her bra and panties. He could feel the softness of her skin against his fingers as he breathed in the fragrant scent of her hair, her body. He was in trouble and he knew it. He should be concentrating on protecting her, not allowing his mind to fill with such delicious thoughts.

He leaned back slightly. "Can you sleep now?"

In answer she wrapped her arms tightly around his neck. "Thank you, Matthew. Thank you for being here."

"You're welcome." He kissed the side of her face.

They held on to each other, but Matthew knew he had to leave her and fast. She felt too good in his arms.

When he went back to his room, he heard something—a pop followed by a thud. He walked to the door, listening. There was a faint rattle, as if someone was trying C.J.'s door.

"Carter!" he called out. He wanted to open the door, but he had strict orders not to, under any circumstances. When he got no answer, he called again. Still no response, but the rattling stopped. "Carter, answer me or I'm calling Beal!"

Silence. He went to the phone and dialed Beal.

"Don't open the door," the detective ordered. "I'm coming over."

Pacing the room, Matthew couldn't take it any longer. He had to know what was going on outside in the hall. Finally he snatched up the phone and called security. He waited five minutes, then opened the door.

Carter was sitting in a chair with his head propped against the wall. He was asleep. "Damn," Matthew cursed, and walked over to him, intending to give him an earful.

When he reached him, Matthew stepped back in horror. There was a single bullet hole in Carter's head. Blood streamed down the side of his face. Matthew knew without touching him that he was dead.

"Oh, God, no!" he cried.

The elevator doors opened, and Beal and the security guard rushed out. Noticing Matthew's pallor, Beal asked, "What's wrong?"

"Carter. He's…he's dead."

Beal went over to the policeman. "Damn, damn." He drove one fist into the other. His eyes swung to Matthew. "I thought I told you not to open the door!"

Matthew didn't answer. He was too shaken by the sight of Carter.

"Are you listening to me?" Beal asked.

Matthew blinked. "Sure."

"The man who's been trying to kill C.J. has obviously been following her since the accident. He knows she's here. You probably scared him off. We have to move her *now*."

Matthew collected himself. The man—the intruder—had been trying to get into her room. If he hadn't been awake, C.J. would also be dead. His whole body felt cold.

"Get her up," Beal said. "I'll make arrangements."

Matthew ran into her room, turning on the light. "C.J."
She sat up, bleary-eyed.

"Get dressed," he said. "We have to get out of here."

"What?"

"That man has found us. He shot Carter. Beal's moving us."

"Oh, no!" she cried, thinking of the young policeman.

"Hurry," he called, and ran back to his room.

He dressed quickly and Beal appeared in the doorway.
"Let's go."

Matthew darted into C.J.'s room just as she finished
dressing. He grabbed her hand, and they headed for the
door.

In the hall were ambulance personnel and two police-
men with guns drawn. There'd been no sirens. Matthew
blocked the scene with his body, trying to prevent C.J.
from looking at Carter, but as he moved to let her on the
elevator, she saw the body.

"Oh, no," she moaned again, her hands against her
trembling lips. "Why?" She buried her head in Matthew's
shoulder.

The same question was running through Matthew's
mind as they were rushed from the elevator through the
lobby and into a waiting car. The car sped off into the
night with Beal driving and another policeman in the passenger seat.

They drove around and around, in and out of traffic,
onto the freeway, then onto a series of backstreets.

"No one's following us," the policeman informed Beal.

"Good," Beal answered, and picked up a cell phone.

"Who are you calling?" Matthew asked.

"Just making sure a secure room is ready."

Beal drove into the parking lot of a small hotel. He

turned to Matthew. "We're going through a side entrance to an elevator and up to the room. One of my men will be there with the key. Don't talk to anyone and don't stop for anything. Let's go."

They got out of the car. Holding hands, Matthew and C.J. followed Beal through the door and into an elevator. Beal had his gun drawn, watching, listening, making sure they were safe. Within minutes they were in a room.

Beal shoved his gun back in his shoulder holster. "Two of my men are in the room across the hall. They'll be guarding this room the rest of the night."

"Excuse me," C.J. said, and ran into the bathroom. Her nausea was mounting and she thought she was going to be sick.

Matthew swung back to face Beal. "Why can't you catch this guy?" he asked urgently.

"Sometimes it just takes time. But we'll get him."

Matthew ran a hand through his tousled hair. "We don't *have* time. He's already made three attempts, and the next one…"

C.J. came out of the bathroom and he stopped. Her hair hung in disarray around her, her white suit was streaked with dirt from the parking lot, and a tear on her left sleeve showed evidence of blood. Yet to him she still looked enchanting.

"Try and get some rest," Beal said. "For now, you're safe. I'll see you in the morning."

Matthew closed the door and made sure it was bolted tight. For a moment he got a glimpse of the men across the hall with their automatic weapons, and his blood ran cold. In a split second C.J. could be dead, just like poor Carter. He had to keep her safe, and he hoped those men were more attuned to danger than Carter. It was obvious the gunman was a professional with all the tricks of his trade.

He turned and surveyed the room. Small, with twin beds, the room lacked the ambience of their other accommodations. On either side of the only window were two chairs separated by a small coffee table. C.J. was curled up in one of the chairs. She didn't say anything, just stared at him with a lost-little-girl look that twisted his insides.

He knelt in front of her and caught her icy hand. She blinked, as if disoriented. This wasn't the C.J. he knew. Her stubborn fighting spirit was gone, and she seemed defeated, afraid. He wanted to take her in his arms and ease her pain, but he knew the worst wasn't over.

"It's going to be okay," he said. The reassurance sounded hollow to his own ears.

"Okay," she echoed doubtfully. "How can it be okay when one of my parents is trying to kill me?"

His eyes narrowed. "Where did you hear that?"

"I heard you talking to Beal earlier."

"Damn," he muttered. "I'm sorry you heard that."

"Why? If it's true, I should know."

"It's just a theory, C.J., nothing more."

"Why would they want me dead?"

"I don't know, but don't get upset about something that might not be true."

"The truth is *someone* wants me dead."

He saw the terror in her eyes. "Don't do this, C.J."

"Running from that man a couple of weeks ago was like an adventure. The danger didn't seem real, and even today, when that truck almost ran over me, I told myself it was probably an accident. A drunk driver or something. But tonight, when I saw that nice young cop with a bullet hole in his head, it was real, too real. Every time I close my eyes, I see his face. He's dead because of me."

Matthew gripped her hands. "Stop torturing yourself," he said roughly. "He died because some crazy bastard shot him. You couldn't help what happened."

She gazed into his eyes. "I'm scared, Matthew. I've never been this scared in my life."

Swallowing hard, he admitted, "I'm scared, too. I've been responsible for people's lives before, but that was in a courtroom where I had a fighting chance. This is like fighting a ghost because we don't know who we're fighting, and your life hangs in the balance. That's what frightens me. When you were lying in that parking lot, I didn't know if you were dead or alive."

She heard the pain in his voice and turned to him, her hand lightly stroking his cheek. At her touch his eyes darkened and a spark of desire flared between them, as it always did.

"I don't want to be alone tonight," she whispered.

"I'll be right here," he assured her.

"No, that's not what I mean." She shook her head. "I want to sleep in your arms."

He stood up. He had to. He couldn't be that close to her and be rational.

Matthew looked at the naked longing in her eyes—and the trust that was there, too. She trusted him, needed him. Her defenses were down and her emotions were free and unfettered by pride or disillusionment. The wall had completely crumbled. The effect was everything he had imagined it would be. Powerful, spellbinding and yet oddly disconcerting. She was opening her heart to him, and suddenly he felt unworthy of such a gift.

"C.J.…"

Getting to her feet, she glided into his arms, stilling his protest. Unable to stop himself, he welcomed her body against his, just holding her, but he knew that wasn't enough. There was something between them, a feeling they couldn't deny.

She heard his sharp intake of breath as she kissed his neck. She ventured farther, teasing his cheek and jaw with featherlike kisses.

His body trembled with a need only she could create, but he had to be strong for both of them. "C.J.," he whispered into her hair, "this has been a horrendous day. You don't know what you're asking."

"Yes, it's been horrible," she agreed, resting her head against his chest and listening to the beat of his heart. "But I know what I'm asking. I want you to love me until the nightmare goes away." As she finished speaking, her hand gently stroked his chest through his shirt.

He drew back and looked into her eyes. "This isn't right. It's for all the wrong reasons."

She stared back at him, her eyes misty. "I want you. Isn't that enough?"

At the honesty and yearning in her eyes, he sucked air into his lungs, feeling his resistance ebbing. "Everything we talked about in my office is still true," he reminded her. *You're still searching for your parents. I'm still returning to New York.* "Nothing's changed."

"Things *have* changed since then. I don't know if I'll have a tomorrow, so please let me have tonight."

"C.J.," he groaned, and closed his eyes. A feeling of utter despair washed over him.

"You can't deny we're attracted to each other," she said, reaching up and gently pressing her lips to his.

Her soft kiss ignited the flame he was trying to keep under control. His hands tightened around her waist. He was tired of resisting an emotion that was more real than anything he'd ever felt. "You have to be my wildest fantasy come true."

She laughed and started to unfasten the buttons on his shirt, her lips caressing his naked chest.

Desire darted through him, intense and unabated. "Are you sure?"

"Yes," she whispered, her hands and lips still working their magic.

"I don't want to take advantage of you and this situation," he breathed with a catch in his voice. "In the morning you might feel differently."

"I won't, but…" Her hands stopped and she rested her forehead against his chest. One finger played nervously with a button. She had to tell him. They couldn't go any further until she did.

"But?" he prompted.

"I, ah…I'm not very experienced."

"Oh," he said into her hair, knowing exactly what she was trying to tell him.

"I did the usual things in college, but I couldn't bring myself to take that final step. I never felt the passion and fire that sweeps a girl away and makes her forget everything." She paused, then added deliberately, "Until now."

Matthew's first instinct was to run, to get far away from her and the power she had over his emotions. Then he realized he'd been doing that all his life—running from women when they wanted something from him he wasn't willing to give. Commitment. Permanence. But C.J.—he was willing to give her anything she asked. The thought scared him to death, but he couldn't turn away from her.

"An unwanted pregnancy was always on my mind," she said.

Her voice wavered as she spoke, and Matthew knew she was thinking about her mother.

He sifted his hands through her hair and turned her face

toward him. At her heartbreaking expression he couldn't speak.

"I'm not on any…you know…" Her voice faltered, but she told him everything.

Her admission sent a warming shiver through him. "It's all right, I'll take care of it. Trust me," he said, knowing that what they did tonight, here in this room, would change them both forever. He felt it in his soul. But he didn't have the strength to deny her anything.

C.J. knew he was experienced, and she didn't want to think about the women before her or those who would come after. She wanted to think only about now, this moment.

She slid her arms around his neck, softly kissing his lips again. "All I'm asking for is tonight. No commitments, nothing, just tonight."

All her life she'd lived with one desire—to find her parents. Now that desire was matched by something equally strong—Matthew. Loving him. She couldn't face the uncertainty of tomorrow without knowing that special intimacy her body craved and her heart needed above all else.

She whimpered as his mouth moved over hers, and her pulse pounded in her ears from the delicious assault on her senses. Their lips took and gave until it was no longer enough. His hands stroked her body through her clothes. She shuddered, feeling a need so great that the nightmare began to drift away. This was what she wanted—Matthew, only Matthew.

Clothes became a hindrance and quickly their hands pulled at the restricting barriers. Her white outfit mingled with his dark suit on the floor. He released a ragged breath as he paused and gazed at her smooth golden body silhouetted by the single lamp burning in the room.

"God, you're beautiful," he murmured, staring at her long black hair cascading over her breasts.

He swung her up in his arms and carried her to the narrow bed. As he gently laid her down, she felt the rough spread underneath her and heard the squeak of the bed-springs, but her emotions were absorbed by the power and magnificence of his naked body.

With one knee on the bed Matthew looked down at her loveliness, almost afraid to touch her. She seemed so fragile, so feminine, and his every instinct cried out to possess her. His hand trembling, he lightly brushed the bruise on her forehead and gazed deeply into her eyes.

C.J. saw that beneath the passion in his eyes was a question. *Are you sure?* She reached up and pulled him down to her, knowing only one way to reassure him. Her lips met his, driving away all his doubts until the passion took over completely. All her inhibitions and fears floated free, and she ached for him, ached for that intimate closeness of lovers. The world started to spin away, leaving just the two of them in this room, alone, together....

Afterward they lay without moving or speaking, her black hair all around them. Matthew drank in the sweet scent of her, knowing he'd never experienced this wild abandonment with any other woman. Was it the danger, the mystery—or the woman? He had a feeling it was the woman. There was something magical about her. She drew him, captivated him until all he could think about was her.

He wanted to look into her eyes, but he couldn't. If he saw regrets, he wouldn't be able to stand it. But...he knew he had to face her. Slowly he raised his head.

She smiled, a gorgeous smile that lit up his soul. *No regrets.* He buried his face in the warmth of her neck.

She held him tightly, three little words hovering on her

lips. She had never said them to anyone, not even Pete or Maggie, but she wanted to say them to him. She loved him, but she wouldn't tell him. Couldn't tell him. She had only asked for tonight.

CHAPTER TWELVE

AS DAWN CREPT SILENTLY through the window, Matthew lay watching C.J. sleep. She lay nestled against him with her head on his chest, her hair covering them like a black sheet. His arm rested on her waist, and his hand fingered the silken tresses as he savored these last moments with her.

They were still naked, lying on top of the bedspread; sated and relaxed, they hadn't even bothered with the covers. They felt completely at ease with each other, as if they'd been lovers forever.

Forever. He wondered how long that was. What dangers waited outside the door? As he stared at the ceiling fan turning, slowly and methodically, he wanted to stop time, to keep her here with him.

She stirred, then raised her head. For a moment fear clouded her eyes, then it quickly vanished. "Morning." Her smile was radiant. "How early is it?"

He glanced at the gold watch on his wrist. "Almost six."

"How long can we stay here?" she asked, her eyes taking in his growth of beard and the dark hair falling over his forehead.

At her wandering gaze every muscle in his body came alive, and a lazy grin spread across his face. He wouldn't mind waking up like this for the rest of his life. He cupped her face in his hands and pulled her down to kiss her.

"C.J.," he breathed against her lips.

"Don't say anything that will let the outside in," she warned him. "This is our time, and let's not waste a second of it. Love me as if there were no tomorrow."

He was eager to do her bidding. Their hands and lips became frantic, searching, tasting, finding all those intimate places they had discovered the night before. Wrapped in a cocoon of neverending pleasure, the only sounds they made were sighs of fulfillment.

Matthew lay beside her, exhausted, yet replete in a way he had never felt before. They had made love as if it *was* their last time, and the thought broke his heart.

C.J. lazily traced the contours of his back, knowing he had chased away the nightmare for a while and given her a night she'd never forget. She was safe while she lay in the haven of Matthew's arms.

REALITY INTERVENED QUICKLY and the pleasures of the night faded into the dangers of morning. They barely had time to dress before Beal was banging on the door.

The detective believed the safest place for C.J. was back in Coberville on the ranch. He'd had C.J.'s Camaro driven back to Coberville during the night, to see if anyone would follow it. No one had.

Matthew's truck was waiting outside, and they had a police escort to the city limits, then the highway patrol took over. When they reached Coberville, Sheriff Watts was waiting. Beal was thorough; he'd taken care of everything.

Matthew stopped at the Watson ranch entrance and talked to the sheriff, a short stocky man Matthew remembered from his schooldays. He assured them everything was under control and the sheriff's department would keep a close eye on C.J.

Halfway to the house, Matthew stopped again. He turned in his seat. "You're far away."

C.J. forced a smile. "I was just thinking how good it feels to be home."

Matthew knew he had briefly eased her fears, but now they were back, and she was trying very hard to be brave. He patted the seat between them. "I meant the distance between us."

The smile this time was real as she undid her safety belt and scooted along the seat until she was next to him.

He slid one arm around her, holding her, and all he could think about was making love to her. But morning had brought reality and once again he had to curb his feelings.

"You'll be safe here," he whispered against her hair. "No one's crazy enough to come in here after you."

"I know." She sighed and ran a hand through his hair, needing to feel him. She wanted to cling and beg for…what? All she knew was that he'd come to mean so much to her, and letting him go wouldn't be easy.

They kissed tenderly, then kissed again. Matthew rested his forehead against hers. They sat in silence for a few seconds, and then he drove them to the house.

Pete and Harry were at the passenger door before the truck even came to a halt. Pete jerked open the door. He paused for a moment and stared at the bruise on C.J.'s forehead, taking in her pallor and disheveled appearance.

"My sweet girl, what have they done to you?" he cried, his voice shaky.

"I'm fine," C.J. assured him, and got out.

Matthew followed.

C.J. threw her arms around Pete's waist and leaned her head on his chest. Harry moved closer, stroking her dark hair, and she turned, hugging him, too.

Matthew watched this scene with a lump in his throat. These menacing giants had tears in their eyes, and suddenly they didn't seem so menacing, just two old men who loved C.J. more than anything on this earth.

The trio walked around the truck. At the sight of Matthew, Harry's shaggy brows knotted together in a sinister look. "You should have taken care of her," he thundered at Matthew, his hand going to the knife around his waist. "Maybe I'll take this knife and teach you a lesson."

"Harry, stop it!" C.J. shouted, and wedged herself between Matthew and Harry. "You should be ashamed of yourself! If it wasn't for Matthew, I'd be dead. He called a warning to me, and I was able to get out of the way before the truck could hit me full force. Then he kept me safe during the night. Now apologize."

Harry glanced off into space, his bearded jaw tight.

"It's okay," Matthew said.

"No, it isn't." C.J. turned to Harry. "If you don't apologize, I'll never forgive you."

There was a tense silence, then Harry muttered, "Sorry," and stomped off to the house.

Pete stepped in front of C.J., and Matthew's tired muscles tightened. "Harry's just upset," he said. "We both are, but C.J. says you helped her." There was a long pause. "Thank you." He shook Matthew's hand before following Harry to the porch.

Matthew let out a deep breath.

"They don't mean anything. They're just worried about me," C.J. told him.

"I wish they'd try to understand I'm not the enemy."

Her eyes held his. "Oh, I think they do, but they see you as another danger."

Matthew knew exactly what she meant, and after last night he knew they weren't wrong.

Her hand touched his face, lightly stroking his stiff growth of beard. Her fingers ignited so many delightful sensations, but he knew he had to control them, to walk away.

"I guess I'll be going," he said awkwardly.

At the hesitant look in his eyes she replied, "Don't worry, I'll be fine here."

He knew she would be, yet it wasn't easy to take that step away from her, to leave her behind.

"But I'm not so sure about you," she added, pointing at his wrinkled shirt and rumpled suit. "You're a mess. The starched city man is looking a little wilted."

He grinned, and unable to resist, gave her a quick kiss, then forced himself to get into the truck.

"WHO WOULD WANT to kill that lovely child?" Belle asked as Matthew explained what had happened yesterday.

"Well, you've changed your attitude."

"Don't remind me," she sighed. "She's quite lovely, as I'm sure you've noticed." She darted him a knowing look.

His mouth twisted into a tender smile. "I've noticed, Mom."

"I think I'll go see her tomorrow, take a pie or something. Would that be okay?"

"Sure," he said, trying not to let his surprise show. This was what she'd wanted, he realized—to be a part of the relationship his father had had with C.J., which for some reason his father hadn't allowed. Another missing piece in the puzzle.

"You know, I had a terrible crush on Pete Watson once."

"You had a crush on Pete?" Matthew echoed in disbelief. Then vague stories started to filter through his mind. "That's right, you all grew up together."

"Yes. Pete, Harry, your dad, Emma, Victoria, Martha and me. Pete was a ladies' man back then. A handsome cowboy and rodeo rider, but as soon as your dad looked my way, that all ended."

Matthew was reminded of the scene in his office a few days ago. "Did Miss Emma have a crush on Pete, too?"

"Emma and Pete?" Belle looked shocked. "Heavens, no. It was always Harry for Emma."

"Harry?"

"My, yes, they were a couple back in high school. They used to fog up the windows on Harry's old pickup many a night."

"What happened?"

"Emma's mother found out and put a stop to it. She made Emma choose between her and Harry. Emma chose her mother. That decision changed their lives forever. Emma became an old maid and Harry was never the same."

Matthew sat lost in thought, hardly able to believe his ears. Miss Emma and Harry. No wonder she hadn't wanted him in the office. They probably hadn't spoken to each other in fifty years. He remembered her words about not letting life pass him by. Evidently Miss Emma regretted her decision. And Harry? Well, Harry had gone off the deep end a long time ago.

"Harry withdrew from the world." His mother's words cut through his thoughts. "He became a strange man who frightened everyone." Belle paused for a moment, then added, "No one will get near C.J. with him around."

"That's why I left her there. It's the safest place for her."

After a short silence his mother said, "It was hard for you to leave her, wasn't it?"

"Yeah," he murmured, amazed at her insight. But then, she was his mother and probably knew him better than anyone else.

"YOU IDIOT, WEEKS."

"It wasn't my fault. That Sloan guy helped her, and the detective lost me on the backstreets of Austin."

"I want her dead."

"It's not gonna be so easy now. They'll be guarding her. I'm gonna need more money."

"You're not getting another dime until the job is finished."

There was a pause. "I think you'll change your mind. I still have the will."

"You bastard! I knew I couldn't trust you."

"Hey, I have to look out for myself."

"What do you want?"

"An extra twenty-five grand for the will."

A long pause. "Fine. Come to Coberville, but I want that will and I want C. J. Doe dead."

"Sure thing."

BEAL CALLED the next day. They'd turned up nothing on the truck. Every lead was a dead end. With Beal's caseload Matthew knew this one would probably be put on a back burner, and he hated that. Someone stalking C.J. was a danger he couldn't ignore.

Matthew picked up the phone and called his office in New York. He informed them he wouldn't be back as soon as he'd expected. His urgency to return to New York was superseded by his concern for C.J. Gail wanted to ask questions, he could tell, but his private life was his own, and he didn't have to answer to anyone. He told her what he wanted done on the Peterman case and requested daily updates.

THE NEXT FEW DAYS weren't easy for C.J. Sleep was filled with nightmarish dreams. But she was starting to feel better, and she clung to that.

Everyone was treating her so kindly, especially Matthew and his mother. Belle Sloan's manner was so different from before, warm and friendly, and C.J. found they had a lot in common. They both loved flowers, old movies and Matthew. C.J. enjoyed talking to her, and especially enjoyed hearing stories about Matthew when he was a boy. Mrs. Sloan helped pass the days.

The nights were awful. She couldn't stop thinking that one of her parents might want her dead. The thought was too depressing and she didn't want to face it. Coward, she told herself, wondering where her strong fighting spirit had gone. She felt as though everything had crashed down around her feet, and she didn't have the strength to pick up the pieces of her life.

She hated herself for that weakness.

"WHAT ARE YOU DOING?" Belle asked. It was one o'clock in the morning and Matthew was in his dad's study, pulling out boxes, going through his papers.

"There has to be a clue here somewhere," he mumbled.

"What are you talking about?"

"Dad knew something about C.J. and it has to be in his private files. I've got to find it."

"It's after one, Matthew. Go to bed and tomorrow I'll help you."

"Tomorrow may be too late." He pulled another box out of the closet. "There were no prints on the truck and the police haven't turned up anything. I have to find out what Dad knew. It's my only hope.''

She quietly closed the door.

At three o'clock Matthew trudged upstairs, falling fully clothed onto the bed. *There has to be something,* he kept saying to himself as he drifted off to sleep.

HE WAS UP AT SEVEN, showered and had breakfast with his mother, then headed for the sheriff's office. He needed some clues and the best place to find those would be at the beginning, when C.J. was abandoned.

''Good morning,'' Watts said as Matthew walked into his office. The sheriff's bald head glistened and his smile was friendly. He got to his feet and shook Matthew's hand. ''Hope this early visit doesn't mean anything's wrong.''

''No, I'm just looking for some answers.''

''Answers to what?''

''C.J.'s birth,'' Matthew told him. ''I'd like to see the file on her—on when she was abandoned.''

A look of discomfort appeared on the sheriff's face.

''What is it?'' Matthew asked.

Watts rubbed his bald head. ''What the hell,'' he finally said. ''Things have gotten out of control and I think it's time it all came out in the open.''

''What are you talking about?''

''I was a deputy when C.J. was left on the Watsons' doorstep. Sheriff Miller was determined to find the parents. Then, all of a sudden, he told me to get rid of the file, the basket and the baby clothes.''

''He had orders from someone?''

''Yeah, someone with a lot of power, because Miller told me if I knew what was good for me, I'd keep my mouth shut.''

''Do you know who it was?''

"No, but I always thought it was John Townsend. He was the only one with that much power. But since I heard he's not her father, I'm in the dark."

Matthew took a moment to digest this information. Somehow he knew this wasn't everything. There had to be more. "What happened to the file and baby clothes?"

That look of discomfort appeared again.

"I can get a court order," Matthew told him.

The sheriff glanced up sharply. "You don't have to do that. I hid them in the storeroom. I'm only thinking about C.J."

"You'll have to explain that one to me."

"Ever since Maggie died, C.J.'s been on this quest to find her parents. I can't tell you the number of times she's been in here asking for the file and those baby things."

"And what was she told?"

"Miller lied to her. Told her the file had been misplaced and that Maggie had kept the baby clothes. She knew he was lying about that, because Maggie had told her the sheriff took the items for evidence." He paused, shaking his head. "When she was eighteen, she saved enough money to hire a private investigator. After talking to the sheriff, the man took her money, told her the same lies and left town."

"What was the sheriff afraid of?" Matthew asked.

"I don't know. He never told me, but after his death, I'm ashamed to say, I kept up the lies. C.J. never gave up, though. She used to drive me crazy. When the money started coming for her education, she staked out your father's office. I'd go over there and try to make her go home. Then she started leaving the truck on the outskirts of town and walking to the courthouse. She'd sit there and watch Matt's office. I don't know when she slept. Finally Matt made other arrangements with the money. I'm sure the only reason she took the job at the bank was to go through the records, trying to find the name of her benefactor.''

Matthew's heart ached for the girl so desperately searching for answers and being lied to at every turn. He got to his feet and looked directly at the sheriff. ''I'll be back after lunch. Have the file and baby things ready.''

''I'm not even sure I can find them. It's been so long.''

''You'd better, and that's all I have to say.'' Matthew flashed him a dark look as he headed for the door.

He checked on C.J., then spent the rest of the morning clearing up some minor cases. After lunch he returned to the sheriff's office.

As Matthew sat down, the sheriff placed an old file in front of him, saying, ''Not much there. Never understood why it was so important to get rid of it.''

He quickly opened the file and scanned its contents. After a moment he said, ''You're right, there's not much here. It says the baby was left in a basket, wearing a dress, booties and bonnet.''

''Yeah, it was the strangest thing. The basket and outfit were traced back to Neiman-Marcus in Dallas. The sheriff hit a brick wall after that. Whoever purchased the items paid cash and there was no record.''

''But they were expensive,'' Matthew guessed.

''Sure were. The basket alone cost over five hundred dollars.''

Matthew rubbed his temple with a forefinger. ''Did the sheriff question the Townsends?''

''The Townsends?'' Watts snorted and leaned back in his chair. ''You know as well as I do that they control this town and the sheriff wasn't about to jeopardize his career.''

''Only a few people in Coberville would have the kind

of money to buy those expensive items, the Townsends being at the top of the list.''

''I told you what I thought about John Townsend, but that wasn't true.'' The sheriff's eyes narrowed. ''I hope you're not expecting me to question them now.''

Matthew glanced at Sheriff Watts, knowing he wasn't willing to put his job on the line any more than Sheriff Miller had. The Townsends wielded immense power.

''No,'' Matthew sighed. ''But I'd like to see the baby things.''

The sheriff called a deputy, who brought in a big dusty plastic bag. He took off the tag and pulled down the plastic. Matthew's breath caught in his throat. The basket was beautiful—white and delicately woven. White satin lined the inside and fine lace decorated the edges of the soft material. A small dress, booties and bonnet, also white with ruffles and lace, lay inside.

As he stared at the lovely things, it crossed his mind that these items were bought by a woman with money. Suddenly something C.J. had said popped into his head. *I thought Victoria Townsend wanted one of the Townsend men to face his responsibility.* That was it, he told himself. Why hadn't it occurred to him before?

MATTHEW HEADED for the Watson place. He had to see C.J. Driving up to the ranch gate, he honked the horn. Within minutes Harry rode up and unlocked it. Matthew waved as he drove through, but Harry didn't respond.

He saw her immediately. She was sitting in the swing, drinking a glass of iced tea. He noticed that the bruise was gone from her forehead. Her skin had a vibrant glow and her black hair was glossy, hanging over her shoulder into her lap. All he could think about was a hotel room in

Austin, and the two of them lying in bed with those masses of dark hair falling about their naked skin.

C.J. watched him as he came up the steps. Tall and handsome in jeans and a blue plaid shirt, he looked very different from the man she'd encountered a couple of months back, but he was still just as devastating to her senses. Her heart beat a little faster, and she couldn't hold back the eagerness she felt at seeing him. As her heartbeat slowed, she noticed he was carrying a plastic bag.

"Hi," he said, placing the bag between them and sitting in the chair opposite her. How he wished they were alone and he could touch her and hold her the way he wanted to. Since that night in Austin they hadn't had any time together. There was always someone around.

His gaze traveled every inch of her creamy skin. "You look wonderful."

"I feel wonderful," she said, and set her glass on the porch railing.

Still, there was something in her eyes that bothered him. The old C.J. had retreated into herself, blocking out the pain, along with her hopes and dreams. The fighting spirit that was such a part of her nature had taken a severe blow, and he wanted to see that light in her eyes again.

He moved from the chair to sit on the swing beside her. "Hire me as your lawyer," he said in an urgent tone.

She drew back. "What?"

"I'm going to find your parents, and to do that I need you to be my client."

She looked at him for a long moment. "The police haven't found anything, have they?"

"No," he replied. "I'm starting my own search."

She shook her head. "Why? This isn't your specialty. And no one's been able to find my parents. What makes you think you can?"

"Because my dad knew something about you, and he was the type to write everything down and never throw anything away. I'm going to keep looking until I find out what he knew. I've also checked with the sheriff."

"Oh."

That one word said a lot and he didn't know how she was going to react to the baby things, so he plunged right in. "He had something that belongs to you." He pulled the bag toward her.

The name on the tag leaped out at her. *Baby Girl Doe.* Underneath was the date she'd been found on the Watsons' doorstep. Christmas Day. Her hands started to tremble.

"How did you get this?" she asked in a barely controlled voice.

"It's been in the storeroom at the sheriff's office all this time."

"No." She frowned at him. "That's not possible. I've asked and asked and I even hired someone to find it."

He took a deep breath. "They all lied to you."

She jumped up, eyes blazing. "Those bastards! How could they? How could they do this to me?" The fight was back in her, and he could see she wanted to scream and rant, maybe hurt someone.

He caught her hands. "It's here now, C.J. That's all that matters."

She jerked her hands away. "No, it isn't," she snapped, then her voice changed. "I'm so tired of the lies. Why doesn't anyone want me to know the truth?"

"I do," he said, and their eyes met. He grabbed her hand, urged her back into the swing and kissed her softly. "Look inside the bag, all right?"

She didn't speak, so he unfastened the tag and removed the plastic.

She gasped when she saw the white basket. She reached

out and lovingly touched it, then saw the dress and picked it up. "Oh, God, it's so beautiful." Her eyes filled with tears.

Matthew caressed her cheek with the back of his hand.

"Thank you," she whispered, feeling her anger ebbing away as she held the small dress.

Matthew sensed her relaxing and tried to make her smile. "Now are you ready to hire me?"

"I can't afford you," she said, wiping the tears from her face.

"In your case I'll make an easy-payment plan."

"Like what?"

"A kiss a day."

She laughed, and the sound was music to his ears. "Matthew, have you been drinking?"

"No, I'm just high on excitement."

She watched the light dance in his brown eyes. "A kiss a day, you said?"

"Yes, we can start with those sweet chaste kisses on the cheek and forehead, then move on to the lips, then deep passionate kisses, then—"

"Okay." She held up her hand, smiling. "I get the picture, but when we reach that last part, I expect to receive exactly what you've promised."

"Oh, you will," he said with a playful grin.

She shook her head comically. "Matthew Sloan, I do believe you *have* been drinking."

"I haven't," he said, fingering the dress in her hands. His voice sobered. "Remember when you said you thought Victoria Townsend had given you the land and money because of one of the Townsend men?"

"Yes, but we found out that wasn't true."

"Look at these things. Seems obvious they were purchased by someone with money."

"Yes, probably," C.J. mused. "Maggie said the things were beautiful. That's why I tried so hard to find them." Frowning, she added, "They were bought by someone who had money but that doesn't put us any further ahead." She held the dress to her chest, wishing she could see the person's face.

He leaned forward, gazing at her intently. "What if it wasn't a Townsend man, but a Townsend woman?"

C.J. shrugged loosely. "If you're talking about Joyce and Clare, I already checked them out. Clare was a shy teenager who didn't date, and Joyce was in Europe at the time." She paused for a second. "But since everyone's so good at lying to me, I'm not sure of anything anymore."

"I'll check them out once more, just to make sure."

Her eyes flew to his. "I'll help you."

"No, no," he stated emphatically. "Our number-one priority is keeping you safe. That means you have to stay here. It's too dangerous in town."

From the look in his eyes and the tone in his voice she knew not to pressure him. But that didn't mean she had to do what he said, either.

Getting to his feet, he murmured, "I've got to get going. I have a court hearing." Moving closer, he asked, "You think I could get a small down payment?"

"I think that can be arranged." She smiled mischievously and reached up with one hand, pulling his head down to hers. Their lips met in an eager kiss.

"Did I say *one* kiss a day?" he whispered against her lips. "I think we need to renegotiate." Out of the corner of his eye he saw Pete and Harry approaching the house. "Or maybe not," he said, straightening with a grin on his face.

"Thank you," she called as he went down the steps. Glancing back, he saw she was still clutching the dress.

CHAPTER THIRTEEN

THE NEXT MORNING Matthew went right to work. After calling his office in New York, he spoke with Miss Emma. "Pull all the files Dad had on the Townsends and anything he might have had on C. J. Doe. Even if it's just a note, I want to see it."

"Whatever for?" She glared at him over the rim of her glasses. "I thought that was all settled."

"It isn't. Someone's still trying to kill C.J."

"You think the Townsends are involved?" she asked in a secretive whisper.

"Just pull the files," he said curtly, then something occurred to him. Why hadn't he questioned her before? If anyone around here was likely to have any information, it was Miss Emma Stevens. He stopped her as she made to leave. "I'm sorry, I didn't mean to snap at you." A little groveling never hurt as a means to an end.

A shadow of annoyance crossed her face, but she didn't say anything, which was a first.

He leaned back in his chair, twirling a pencil thoughtfully. "What did Dad know about C.J.'s parents?"

Her eyes grew enormous. "Why would I have any idea?"

Leaning forward, he rested his elbows on the desk. "You were Dad's right hand."

"Yes, but that was one thing he kept very confidential.

He wouldn't even tell your mother, and believe me, she didn't like that one little bit.''

"Surely you overheard a phone call, saw a letter, *something*," he persisted.

"The only thing I saw was the money that came here once a month for her education. It was always put through the mail slot sometime during the night." She adjusted her glasses pensively. "I remember the envelopes were always the same—cream-colored, expensive and scented. You can't buy that kind at the local convenience store."

"Do you have any of those envelopes?"

"No, your dad took them. I guess he threw them away, because I never saw them again after they were delivered."

"Thanks," he said, knowing that was all he was going to get out of her.

Reaching for the phone, Matthew heard the front door open, but he figured Miss Emma could handle whoever it was. He glanced up and his body vibrated with new energy. C.J. stood in the doorway, looking like her old self in jeans and boots. Her eyes were bright and her hair was pulled back and held in place with a blue ribbon.

She smiled, and he felt an ache in the pit of his stomach. She stirred his senses like no woman he'd ever known. She was fresh, exciting—and here, the practical part of his brain finally kicked in.

He came quickly around the desk. "What are you doing here? Where's Pete and Harry?"

"It's nice to see you, too, and Pete and Harry are right outside," she answered sassily, and he knew for sure the old C.J. was back.

He ran a hand through his hair. "I'm sorry, but you surprised me. You shouldn't be out. It's too risky."

"Please don't start." She rolled her eyes. "I'm about to go stir-crazy at the ranch."

"It's only until the police catch this man."

"*If* they catch him," she corrected. "Sheriff Watts has his men patrolling our road half a dozen times a day, and they haven't seen anyone suspicious. After three failed attempts he probably got scared and left the county."

"But we don't know that."

"I don't want to argue. I came to help you search for my parents."

He sighed in exasperation. "C.J.—"

"I can help, Matthew. I *can*."

"C.J.—"

Miss Emma strolled in with an armload of files and dumped them on his desk. "Have fun," she said—a little impudently—and left the room.

Matthew glanced at the files, then at C.J.

Her chin jutted at a stubborn angle. "I'm staying, Matthew."

"Fine," he said, knowing it was pointless to argue. Besides, he could use her help. "Start looking for anything that has to do with you or the Townsends. In particular, look for notes Dad scribbled in the margins."

For two days they went through file after file, starting with the year she was born and the year after that. They found nothing. His dad had done a lot of work for Victoria Townsend, but none of it pertained to C.J.

Even his office in New York hadn't been able to turn up anything on Joyce or Clare.

C.J. sat in middle of the floor, files all around her. Matthew sat at his desk, files stacked high on either side. Both were tired and frustrated.

Matthew rubbed his aching neck and looked at C.J. She

sat cross-legged, a file in her lap, avidly reading its contents.

"Listen to this!" she said eagerly, scrambling to her feet and pushing a file in front of Matthew. "There's some scribbling to the side about Joyce Townsend and a flight to Florida. The date is November of the year I was born. Surprise, surprise," she muttered. "Joyce wasn't in Europe, after all."

Matthew studied the scribbling and couldn't make much sense of it, but he knew someone who could.

"Miss Emma," he called.

"What?" she answered impatiently, coming through the door. "It's getting late. I'm ready to go home."

"In a minute," Matthew said. "I'd like you to look at something." He gestured at the file on his desk. "Can you tell us what this means?"

She peered at the writing. "Good God, you're not asking much. That was so long ago."

Matthew thought talking about the Townsends might help jog her memory. "What were Joyce and Clare like when they were growing up?" he asked.

She blinked at the quick change of subject, then shrugged. "I don't know. Joyce was the beautiful one with her blond hair and blue eyes. The boys were all crazy about her, but she wouldn't give them the time of day. She considered herself too good for the local boys. Victoria sent her away to school when she was about thirteen. I didn't see much of her after that, except on holidays."

"And Clare?"

"She was the sweet one, not stuck up like her sister. Of course she wasn't as attractive as her sister, either, and people were constantly reminding her of that. So I guess it's understandable she preferred books to people."

He pointed to the margin. "What does that mean?"

She studied it for a moment. "Flight 202. Joyce Town-send. Miami, Florida," she read, wrinkling her brow in thought. "Oh, I remember now. Victoria always had your dad handle her problems. Even when he was busy with his judge duties, she'd call him. That year Joyce was studying art in Europe. She must have been in her early twenties. She came home for Thanksgiving and stayed hidden at the ranch, didn't want anyone to see her. Victoria was worried about her. So your father arranged for her to go to a resort in Florida to get some rest and pampering. Joyce came here in sunglasses and a big floppy coat to get the details from your father. At first I didn't even recognize her. She'd put on a lot of weight and looked pretty bad. Only time I ever remember seeing her look that way."

A spark of excitement ran through Matthew and he could see the same spark on C.J.'s face.

"Did she come home for Christmas?" he asked.

"No, I don't think so. Next I heard, Victoria had sent her back to Europe."

"Think, Miss Emma. Are you *sure* she didn't come home for Christmas?" C.J. asked, unable to stay silent any longer.

"I can't be sure. It's been so long," Miss Emma shook her head. "Now, I need to get home to Herman."

"Wait a minute." Matthew grabbed a folder he'd put aside. "There was something here about Clare. Dad arranged for her to go to the Golden Light in Dallas the February after C.J. was born. What kind of place is that?"

"Lordy, Lordy, why do y'all have to dig this up?"

"Please, Miss Emma, help us," C.J. begged.

Miss Emma leaned in close and whispered, "I don't want this to get out, but Clare's had all kinds of problems. Poor thing, the only time I remember seeing her with a boy was Benny Joe Johnson, the blacksmith's son and—"

"No," C.J. broke in, "she didn't date anyone. I went to the high school and got her year book. I talked to some of her classmates and teachers. They all said the same thing. She was shy, introverted, and like you said, she only had an interest in books. No one even remembered her having a date."

"Well, they didn't see what I saw."

"We need facts, not gossip," Matthew said.

"Gossip? I don't gossip," Miss Emma returned indignantly.

"Okay." Matthew sat back. "Tell us what you saw."

"Well, I had Ben—Benny's father—build a big birdcage for the parrot I had then, but one of the rods came loose and I took it back for him to weld. There was no one in the shop, so I went to the little room Ben uses as an office and kitchen. I thought he was eating his lunch. The door was ajar and I peeked in. Lordy, did I get an eyeful. Clare and Benny were on the sofa doing some heavy necking. I immediately went back to the shop."

Matthew straightened. "Are you sure it was Clare?" he asked slowly.

"Yes!" Miss Emma snapped. "I'm not blind. Besides, when I left I drove around back, and there was the white Porsche Victoria had bought her for her birthday, hidden behind some bushes. I saw it parked there a lot of times after that."

C.J. threw up her hands. "I don't believe this. No one remembers her even looking at a boy."

Miss Emma shrugged. "I guess they wanted to keep it a secret, but Victoria must have found out, because she sent her off to school in Switzerland a month before school was out. That would've been some time the previous April. Martha went with her because Victoria wasn't well." She stopped, then added, "When Clare came home, she was a mess. Tried to kill herself that February. Sure did.'' Miss Emma nodded. ''Took a bottle of Victoria's sleeping pills. As always, Victoria called your father and he arranged for Clare to get some help at the Golden Light. It's a private clinic for people with problems. Of course your dad always registered the girls under assumed names, because of John's political career and all.''

That was it, Matthew thought. That's why his firm couldn't find anything on them. But something wasn't right.

''Dad wrote their real names in the margin,'' he reminded her.

''That's a note to himself, so he could remember who was going where. All the flights and homes were in another name.''

''Do you know the names Dad used?''

''Lordy, no. He kept that to himself.''

Damn. Matthew brought his attention back to the matter at hand. ''Clare tried to kill herself the February after C.J. was born?'' Matthew repeated, scribbling bits of information on a pad.

Miss Emma's eyes narrowed. ''I think it was. The date should be in the file.''

C.J. ran around the desk to look.

Matthew's finger pointed to the date.

''It is!'' C.J. clapped her hands together, almost afraid to think what that meant.

''I'm going home—you two can sort this out,'' Miss Emma said, heading for the door. ''You know, that pair of old fools have been out there every day, sitting over at the courthouse, talking to people, drinking coffee. They're starting to get on my nerves. So please take them home. And, young Matthew, remember you have an early call at the courthouse. Joey Barnes, fourth speeding ticket.''

He frowned. "Is that in the morning?"

"Yes, but it shouldn't take long. Joey's sixteen, and he has six brothers and sisters. His dad passed away about a year ago and he's having a hard time adjusting."

"I'll remember that."

As the door closed on Miss Emma, Matthew turned to C.J. "Pete and Harry don't have to stay here all day."

"I've told them that, but they're getting up two hours earlier to do the chores. Harry goes home during the day to check on things. They're stubborn. They won't listen to me."

He raised an eyebrow. "Must be contagious."

"I'm not stubborn," she denied.

"Yeah, right." He grinned and leaned back and stretched his arms. "Time to quit for the day."

"No!" C.J. cried. "We're just getting started. We have to find out more about Clare and Joyce."

"C.J." He pulled her onto his lap. "Everything's closed for the day and we need to get some rest. We'll start again tomorrow."

"Oh, Matthew, tomorrow's so far away," she complained. "Just think about it. Joyce mysteriously comes home at Thanksgiving and Clare has a secret boyfriend. There has to be something in all of that. It's just too many secrets."

His hand smoothed her hair. "We'll find out, I promise."

"I thought I could find out, too, but everyone lied to me."

He lifted her hair away from her neck. "I know, and I'm sorry about that, but now things are starting to happen. We're going to find your birth mother." As he finished speaking, he kissed the hollow of her neck.

She moved against him, unable to think when he

touched her like that. "Matthew," she breathed. Her lips grazed his jaw, then his chin and lingered on his mouth.

His arms encircled her waist and brought her closer, and he kissed her long and hard. So long and so hard she had trouble catching her breath.

"We haven't been together since…" he whispered into her neck.

"I know," she answered on a ragged breath.

"Let's lock the door and—"

"Okay," she agreed.

Before either could move, they heard the front door open.

"Damn," Matthew cursed.

"It's Pete," she moaned. "I'd better go."

She gave him a brief kiss and slid off his lap. At the door she blew him another kiss.

He caught it in his hand, thinking that wasn't exactly what he had in mind.

"HAVE YOU TOLD HER?" Stephanie asked John as she massaged his legs. After a vigorous swim in the pool he sat in his wheelchair, relaxing.

"Now, Steph, don't start," he said.

"You promised to tell Martha we're getting married. You said you'd do it as soon as the Doe thing was over with."

"That was a big day." His lips twisted into a cynical sneer. "Victory was so sweet, and that little nobody got exactly what she deserved."

Stephanie eyed him closely. "Yes, she did." She put an arm around his neck. "Now let's talk about us. I'm tired of being treated like dirt around here. I want to be your wife."

"Rob's election is coming up and I have to concentrate

on that," he said, running a hand up her arm. "Why don't we buy you that sports car you've been wanting? I believe red is your favorite color."

"I don't—"

"John." The sound of Martha's voice stopped her, and she quickly removed her arm a moment before Martha Cober came through the door.

"There you are." Martha smiled at John. She was dressed for horseback riding, in jeans and boots. Even in her seventies she was still an ardent horsewoman. "How are the exercises coming?"

"Fine, just fine," John answered.

"You're getting so much stronger."

"John has something he'd like to tell you," Stephanie said, breaking into the conversation.

"Oh?" Martha glanced at her disdainfully.

"Now, Stephanie," John intervened.

"John and I are getting married and we wanted you to be the first to know," Stephanie blurted.

Martha's blue eyes narrowed on John. "Is this true?"

John scowled at Stephanie before looking back to Martha. "Nothing is settled. My first priority is getting Rob into the senate, but yes, Stephanie and I have talked about marriage."

"I see." Martha suddenly looked feverish. "Well, I only want your happiness."

"I can make him happy," Stephanie said.

Without another word Martha turned and stormed back into the house.

Stephanie smiled with satisfaction and tried to climb onto John's lap, but he pushed her away, saying, "I don't like being manipulated, especially by a woman. Since you're always talking about leaving, maybe it's time you should."

Stephanie paled considerably. "Johnny," she cooed, "I only did it because I love you."

"You love my money, Stephanie, and we both know it."

"Johnny." She slid onto his lap without any problem. "I can make you happy and you know it." She wound both arms around his neck and kissed him deeply.

"Steph…"

WHEN MATTHEW GOT BACK from the courthouse the next morning, C.J. was sitting on the curb outside the office. Pete and Harry were sitting in the truck with the doors open. He greeted them, and C.J. followed him inside.

"Now what?" she asked, her eyes bright with anticipation.

Looking at her, his mind veered in a completely different direction, but he quickly masked his feelings, knowing there was little chance of their being alone.

He made a sweeping gesture at the files. "We start putting all these away. I'm sure that would make Miss Emma happy."

"Shouldn't we check out Clare first? There has to be a reason she tried to kill herself."

"All in good time, C.J. Be patient."

"I can't," she told him. "We're too close to finding something."

He saw the eagerness on her face and hoped, for her sake, they were. "I have to call New York to ask about a few things."

"I'll start with these."

"Good," he said, as she carried a box into the storeroom.

After his phone call, he helped her with the files. They

worked side by side in silence, and Matthew was amazed at the peace he felt just being with her.

As he gathered files from his desk, Miss Emma bustled through the door. She was late, she explained, because she was having problems with Herman. "How'd it go at the courthouse this morning?" she asked.

"Got him a year's probation with a restricted license. He can drive to school and with his mother in the car."

"I'm sure his mother was pleased."

"Yes," he answered absently, his mind on other things.

"Are you still interested in Joyce?"

He glanced up. "Yes, why?"

"I saw her big Cadillac at the Cober mansion in town, and the maid was getting suitcases out of the trunk."

"Does she always stay at the place in town, instead of the ranch?"

"Usually, especially if her husband's with her. He and Martha don't get along."

"Thanks," he said thoughtfully, picking up a pencil and doodling. He didn't have a lot to go on, just a gut feeling.

"Joyce," he wrote. "Gained weight. Thanksgiving. Clare. From spring to Christmas, nine months."

Could both Joyce and Clare have been pregnant that same year? What were the odds?

Hearing the conversation, C.J. came out of the storeroom. "So Joyce is in town," she breathed. "What a break."

"Yes," he said. "I think I'll pay her a visit."

"I'm coming with you."

He grabbed her before she could reach the door. "C.J., I have to do this alone."

"Why?"

"Because she's not going to say anything with you there."

"Why not?"

He sighed heavily.

"If you think you're going without me, you're sadly mistaken," she told him.

"C.J.—"

"Don't you understand? I *have* to confront her."

"With what?" he asked patiently.

"I don't know, but I want to look her in the face and ask her if she's my mother."

"And you expect her to tell you—" he snapped his fingers "—just like that?"

"Maybe," she answered, angry pride filling her voice.

The pain in her eyes twisted around his heart. But he had to convince her that confronting Joyce couldn't possibly lead to the completion of the quest.

"C.J., I know how important this is to you, but we have to be careful. We have no facts, just some scribblings and Miss Emma's memory about what happened all those years ago. If Joyce knows anything, it's going to take some finesse and tact to get her to admit it. Let me do this. One on one. Joyce and me. It's what I do for a living. I'm good at questioning people."

C.J. bit her lip, hearing his words but not wanting to accept them. "Matthew," she said intensely, "I have to know. She—"

"Yes, I hear you, but Joyce isn't going to tell you anything."

"It's all so frustrating," she murmured in a small voice.

He cupped her face with his hands. "I know," he whispered, his thumbs caressing her cheeks. "But think about this. If Joyce *is* your birth mother, she's not going to admit it without some pressure."

"I suppose," C.J. mumbled, knowing he was right, but hating to give in.

"Will you let me do this?"

She swallowed her pride. "All right," she murmured without enthusiasm.

He kissed her softly. "It shouldn't take long."

C.J. nodded, then watched him leave with a frown on her face. Would she ever know? She was beginning to think the secret was buried so deep they'd never be able to unearth it.

THE COBER HOUSE was the biggest house in town, covering most of a block. An impressive three-story building of white limestone, it was fronted by large Ionic columns. The fence around it was white wrought iron with stone corners.

Matthew pushed open the gate and walked up the stone path to the front doors. A maid in a starched black uniform answered the door.

"Mrs. Joyce Brown, please," he said politely.

"Do you have an appointment?" she countered stiffly.

"No, but I'm Matthew Sloan, an attorney. I recently handled a case for the Townsend family."

"Come this way." She escorted him to a large marble-floored foyer. A huge crystal chandelier hung from the ceiling. To the right was a grand living room with an identical chandelier, and he could see a staircase winding to the top floors.

She showed him into a small sitting room with antique chairs, sofas and a stone fireplace. "I'll tell Mrs. Brown you're here."

"Thanks," he replied, glancing around the austere room. Everything in it must have dated back to Jeremiah Cober and his mistress, Nora Babbish. The old story was that after the deaths of their two daughters from cholera, Jeremiah's wife lost her mind. He found solace with an actress from Boston; he moved her to Texas and built this house for her. Various Cobers had occupied it over the years. He remembered his mom saying Clare used it as a residence when she was in town.

A painting caught his attention. William Cober. Jeremiah's grandson. He was unmistakable with his blond good looks.

"Rob resembles him, don't you think?" Joyce asked from the doorway. She was dressed in an elegant outfit of beige loose-fitting slacks and blouse that had Paris written all over it.

"Yes, he does," Matthew replied. "And so do you." Since they were twins, Joyce and Rob had similar features.

Joyce ignored the compliment. "But I'm sure you didn't come here to discuss family portraits," she said.

Right to the point, with a chilling tone to boot. Clearly he wasn't welcome here.

Matthew also got right to the point. "I'd like to talk with you about C. J. Doe."

A look of impatience flashed across her face. "I thought that was settled."

"Not quite. Someone's still trying to kill her."

"That doesn't have anything to do with us." She waved a hand angrily. "Why can't you people believe us? That detective's been hounding us day in and day out. We left the city to get some peace. Now *you* show up."

"C.J.'s life is at stake. Doesn't that mean anything to you?"

"After what she did to this family?" Her blue eyes flared. "I have very little sympathy for her."

"What did she do?" he asked, his expression one of pained tolerance. "She gave back the land and money in exchange for one small favor, which turned out to the

Townsends' advantage. I fail to see any hardships she's caused.''

''You don't understand,'' Joyce said quietly.

''All I understand is that you seem to hate a woman you hardly know.''

''What do you want from me?'' she exclaimed.

''Some answers.''

''I can't help you.'' She turned abruptly and headed for the door.

He had to call her bluff on a hunch; it was all he had. But he'd learned a long time ago that when you threw something unexpected at people, they reacted instinctively. He was hoping Joyce would do the same.

''What happened to the baby you had at twenty-three?''

''What?'' She whirled to face him.

''You heard me.''

She glanced nervously around, then quickly closed the door. ''How did you find out about that?'' she asked in a vicious tone.

Inside he felt a moment of victory, but he didn't let it show on his face. ''I have my sources,'' he said.

Walking to the window, she twisted her hands together. ''Nobody knew but my mother and me. How could you have found out?'' she asked, almost to herself.

''What happened to the baby?'' he probed, feeling as if his very life hung in the balance.

''What?'' She looked distractedly at him.

''The baby, Joyce. Where is the baby?''

Her eyes darkened. ''None of your damn business.''

''I'm going to find out, so you might as well save yourself and your family a lot of pain by telling me.''

''My family,'' she echoed in distress. ''They don't know! You can't say anything to them.''

''Tell me about the baby, Joyce.''

She turned back to the window. "I was studying art in Paris and met this Italian count. I fell head over heels in love, but he forgot to tell me one small detail. He was married and already had a family. I got pregnant and I didn't know what to do. At my age I should have known better."

"And?" he prompted.

"I was almost seven months pregnant before I came home. Everyone thought I'd just put on a lot of weight, eating all those French pastries, but Mother figured it out. After Thanksgiving she made arrangements for me to go to an exclusive home for unwed mothers."

She paused and he waited, almost afraid to ask, but he had to. "Is C.J. your daughter?"

She swung around, her eyes enormous. "My God, is that what you think? That I'd abandon my own child?"

"Is she?"

"No! How dare you even suggest it!"

"What happened to the baby?" he tried again.

"My baby died," she said quietly. "And it wasn't a girl. It was a boy with dark hair and eyes. He came early and had a congenital heart problem and..." Her voice broke and she started to cry.

"What was the name of the home? And what name did you use?"

Angry tearful blue eyes flashed, "You don't believe me?"

"The name."

She hurried over to a small desk in the corner and scribbled something on a piece of paper. Shoving it into his hand, she said, "Go ahead and inquire for yourself, because I can assure you I am not C. J. Doe's mother." She glanced down at her hands, then back at him. "Please, don't tell my husband," she begged. "He doesn't know anything about it, and if it got into the papers it could ruin his political career.''

''If this checks out, no one will hear it from me.''

''Thank you,'' she said, then quickly left the room.

Dammit. He'd felt sure she was C.J.'s mother. How could his instincts be so wrong? For a brief moment he'd tasted victory, felt rejuvenated. Now he was back to square one.

He stared at the paper in his hand. He was positive she wouldn't lie about something like this. But he'd check it out all the same.

As the maid showed him to the door, it opened and Clare Townsend came in carrying a stack of books. She was in town, too. He hadn't expected this, it would save him a trip to Austin.

He hurried to help her, taking the books from her and setting them on the entry table.

''Do you need any assistance, ma'am?'' the maid asked Clare.

''No, thank you, Della,'' she answered. ''I can manage now.''

When the maid left, Clare smiled tentatively at Matthew. ''Thank you, I didn't realize they were going to be so heavy.''

She wore a simple long brown dress with a high neck. Her hair was in its usual cropped-off style, close to her head. She didn't take much time with her appearance, and he wondered why. He had a feeling her plainness was deliberate.

''No problem,'' he said.

She lovingly touched the books, which were more than a little ragged. ''I've been to the library and I promised Mrs. Tate, the librarian, that I'd take these to Austin and get them repaired. It's a shame what some people do to books.''

"Yes," he answered, knowing this was his chance to ask her about the past. The task didn't hold much appeal. She wasn't strong like her sister and might crumble right before his eyes, but he had to keep probing.

"Could I speak with you for a minute?"

Her blue eyes widened. "What do you want to talk to me about?" she asked as she walked into the sitting room.

"C. J. Doe," he replied, following her.

She sat in a chair, her back straight, hands folded in her lap. "Have they found out who's trying to kill her?"

"No, not yet."

"That poor girl. It must be awful for her."

Matthew was taken aback at her response. Sympathy from a Townsend. That was unusual. Although he recalled a glimmer of compassion on Clare's face that day of the revelations in Dr. Ryder's office.

"Yes, it is awful, and I'm trying to help her."

"How?"

"By finding her parents."

"Really?" She looked surprised.

"Help me," he implored.

"How can *I* help you?" she asked in disbelief.

"I was hoping you'd fill in some blanks."

"About what?"

He chose his words carefully. "That spring before C.J. was born. You were sixteen and seeing Benny Johnson."

Her eyes narrowed, but that was her only reaction.

He waited.

"So what?" she finally said.

"Why did your mother send you away a month before school was out?"

"She wanted to break us up," she answered immediately. "He was a working man's son and not good enough for a Townsend."

She squeezed the arms of the chair so hard her knuckles were white. She was lying. He knew it, and he realized she wasn't going to be as easy as Joyce. He'd been wrong; Clare wasn't weak at all. There was a lot more to her than met the eye. He had broken tough witnesses before, but he hated pressuring her like this. For C.J. he had to.

"Wasn't there another reason?" he dropped into the silence.

"Like what?" she countered, not giving an inch.

"Like an unwanted pregnancy."

Her eyes defiantly met his. "You're reaching, Mr. Sloan."

"Am I? I don't think so," he said, holding her gaze. He knew he had to pull out all the stops. "I'm sure Benny wouldn't think so, either."

She lowered her eyes and folded her hands in her lap again. "Have you talked to him?"

He hesitated, wondering how to answer that question. Obviously it was important to her. "Not yet."

"Please don't," she entreated.

"Give me a reason, Clare."

There was complete silence as she resumed studying her hands. He knew he was close to getting her to admit the truth. He had to keep up the pressure.

He put his hands on the arms of her chair and leaned toward her. "Tell me what happened to that unwanted child."

"I wanted—" She stopped, obviously realizing what she'd said. Not raising her eyes, she said, "I can't. I promised, and you don't know anything."

"But I can find out. I'm a good lawyer and I can find out all the sordid little details."

"Please leave me alone," she whispered.

With one hand he lifted her chin and stared into her stubborn blue eyes. "Help me, Clare. Tell me what happened to your baby."

"I can't." Her bottom lip trembled and she quickly caught it between her teeth. "She'll be so angry with me."

"Who?" he asked, straightening a fraction.

"Aunt Martha," she replied angrily. "Oh, I just don't care anymore! It happened so long ago."

He wasn't quite following her, but he knew she was ready to talk. "Why would Martha be angry with you?"

"Because I promised never to talk about it again."

"Tell me," he urged.

She linked her fingers together, watching their movement as if mesmerized. "You're right, I was pregnant. I was so in love it didn't seem to matter. Then I found out Benny wasn't in love with me but with my money. I was devastated and wanted to confide in my mother. But somehow Aunt Martha found out and she said I couldn't tell Mother. You see, Mother was sick a lot and Aunt Martha said she couldn't take the news. It would make her worse."

When she stopped talking, he asked, "What happened next?" He could hardly wait for the words to come out of her mouth. Would they be the words he wanted to hear?

"Aunt Martha handled everything. I was so scared, but Aunt Martha said no one would ever find out, not even the family. We flew to Houston and—" she paused for a second "—she made me have an abortion."

Matthew drew in a sharp breath. This wasn't at all what he'd expected. "Who was the doctor?"

"Dr. Giles. Then we flew to Switzerland and I spent the summer recovering. Aunt Martha said I'd forget about it, but I couldn't. I even tried to kill myself to stop the guilt.

The nightmares. But nothing stops them. A day doesn't go by that I don't think about my baby.''

He dragged a hand through his hair, feeling the pain of defeat surge through him. She wasn't lying. Clare Townsend was not C.J.'s mother.

As if reading his mind, she said, "You thought I was the mother of C. J. Doe, didn't you?"

"Yes," he admitted frankly.

"I wish I were," she shocked him by saying. "Then my child would be alive and I wouldn't have this empty feeling inside.''

Her sincerity was unmistakable, and he didn't know what to say. "I'm sorry if I've upset you," he finally murmured.

A fleeting smile brushed her lips. "I hope you find her parents. It has to be terrible not knowing who you are and feeling like you don't belong. I sympathize with her. I know who my parents are, but I still feel like I don't belong. Everyone in my family is so beautiful and I'm so…different.''

"Hey, beauty's only skin-deep.''

She laughed, and it made him feel better. "I haven't heard that line in years.''

He smiled. "Benny Johnson was a fool.''

"And you're a charmer, Matthew Sloan.''

His smile broadened. He liked this woman. Life hadn't been kind to her, and he now understood her a little better. She'd been suffering from guilt for years, punishing herself for a teenage mistake. He wished only the best for her and told her so before he left.

WHEN HE GOT BACK to the office, he expected C.J. to meet him at the door, but she wasn't anywhere around; neither were Pete and Harry. He felt a moment of apprehension.

"Miss Emma, where's C.J.?"

Miss Emma looked up from the letters she was proof-reading. "That girl was about to drive me crazy. Back and forth to the window, waiting for you. Finally I told her to take those bothersome men to the diner for something to eat. She said she'd be right back and, believe me, she'll be right back."

He went into his office, glad for a few minutes to sort out his thoughts. What was he going to tell her? He'd gotten her hopes up for nothing and now he'd have to disappoint her. Again. Damn. Damn. Damn. How could everything go so wrong? He swung his hand, knocking folders to the floor.

Miss Emma eyed the mess from the doorway. "I take it things didn't go well with Joyce."

"No, they didn't," he snapped, glaring at her. For the first time he noticed the color of her eyes. Green. *She had green eyes.* The realization struck him like a bolt of electricity.

"You have green eyes." He didn't realize he'd spoken the thought aloud until he saw the expression on Miss Emma's face.

"So? A lot of people have green eyes," she said, then caught the question lurking behind his remark. "Don't even go there, young Matthew," she warned. At his silence, Miss Emma added, "If she was my daughter, do you think I'd be a lonely old woman with only a parrot for company?" She stepped closer, her eyes holding his. "If you get any more absurd ideas like that in your head, I'm gonna put you over my knee and spank you like I should've done when you put that frog in my purse years ago."

A grin spread across Matthew's face. What was wrong with him? He'd known her all his life, and she had to have been in her late forties when C.J. was born. Anyway, she certainly couldn't have hidden a pregnancy from his father or mother. God, he must be losing his mind!

"I'm sorry," he apologized. "I'm just a little crazy right now."

Miss Emma studied him for a moment. A small smile curved her lips. Then, as quickly as the insanity had started, it ended.

She bent to pick up the scattered papers.

"Leave them," he said. "I'll take care of it."

Straightening, she said, "Suit yourself. If that's all, I'll be heading home. It's suppertime for Herman."

"Fine," he said absently. He scooped up the papers on the floor and slapped them on top of the filing cabinet. Where were the answers? he kept asking himself. Both girls pregnant and yet neither of them C.J.'s mother. How could that be? He'd had it right in the palm of his hand and now he had nothing.

Picking up the phone, he called his office in New York. He gave his legal assistant, Tom, the added information about Joyce and Clare Townsend, but he already knew what he was going to find. Still, he couldn't just take their word for any of this.

He had to have proof.

CHAPTER FOURTEEN

C.J. RUSHED THROUGH THE DOOR. "What did she say?" she asked, her voice filled with excitement.

This was the hard part, telling her. He got to his feet and described his visit with Joyce and Clare.

She backed away. "No, no!" she cried. "That can't be! Both pregnant that same year and neither turns out to be my mother? One of them's lying."

"They're not," he said.

A defeated look glazed her eyes. "But how is that *possible,* Matthew? That leaves us with nothing."

"I know, but I'm not giving up. Dad knew something about you and I'm going to continue searching until I find it."

Her eyes cleared. "Yes, he did." She glanced around the room. "Where do we start? The files again?"

"No, not tonight. I need to think a few things through. Get Pete to take you home and—"

She clapped a hand to her face. "Oh, no! Pete—I forgot. I only came in here for a second to see you. I've got to go. Pete and I have to bail Harry out of jail."

"*What?* What's Harry doing in jail?"

"He carried his gun into the diner and someone called the sheriff."

"Why did he carry a gun into the diner?"

"He wanted to be ready in case anything happened."

"Didn't the sheriff realize he was only protecting you?"

"Yeah, and the sheriff was real nice at first. He said if Harry put his gun in the truck, he'd forget all about it."

"And Harry didn't?"

"No," she answered with a grim look. "He said he'd put a bullet in the sheriff's brain before he'd give up his gun."

"Oh, God."

"It took the sheriff and three deputies to put handcuffs on him, and Harry's probably madder than mad by now. I'd better go."

"I'll come with you. He's going to need a lawyer."

She turned, a gleam in her eyes. "I can handle this on my own. The sheriff and I will be having a long talk."

He knew what she meant. It was payback time for all the lies. He didn't envy the sheriff; when she got through with him, he'd probably be apologizing to Harry.

She planted a brief hard kiss on his lips. "See you tomorrow."

"C.J."

"Yes?" She glanced back.

"We'll find something."

"Yeah," she answered, hope gone from her eyes and voice.

GOD, HOW HE HATED that defeated look. He'd felt so sure that either Joyce or Clare had given birth to C.J.; now they had nothing. He sighed and flexed his shoulders. He'd talked to the sheriff, eliminated all the Townsends. Who was left? He snapped his fingers. Doc Haslow. That was it. He delivered every baby in this town.

Matthew drove quickly to the Cober Clinic, where Doc worked, while C.J. was busy elsewhere. It was late, but Doc Haslow's car was still there. After parking his truck,

Matthew hurried through the front doors and to the offices in back.

Tapping on Doc's door, he felt a moment of relief as he heard his customary "Come in, come in."

Tall and thin, Dr. Edward Haslow was in his early seventies. Even though his son, Edward, Jr., had taken over the clinic, Doc still helped out part-time. He was a man of boundless energy, and he'd probably work until the day he died.

"Matthew, my boy." Doc smiled as he stepped into the room. "Good to see you. How's your mother?"

"She's getting better every day."

"Good. I told her it would take time."

"Yes," Matthew murmured.

"Have a seat. How can I help you?"

Matthew sank into the chair in front of Doc's desk. "I'd like to talk to you about C. J. Doe."

Doc leaned back in his chair. "What about her?"

"I've taken C.J. on as a client. I'm trying to find her parents, and I desperately need some help. Do you remember any girls who could've been pregnant that year?"

"Not any who delivered at Christmas. I've already told C.J. that."

Matthew nodded. "Still, it's strange that in a town of less than five thousand people no one knows anything about an abandoned baby," he mused. "The mother couldn't have given birth all by herself and then put the newborn on someone's doorstep in freezing weather. She had help."

"The sheriff thought so, too," Doc said, "but no one was talking. It was the biggest scandal that ever hit this town, and all the people here wanted to distance themselves from the baby."

Matthew shook his head. "There has to be *something*. That baby didn't just appear out of thin air."

"I always thought it strange the baby was left on the Watsons' doorstep, instead of the Townsends'."

"Why?"

"The houses aren't that far apart, and if I was going to give my baby to someone, I'd give it to the richest people in the area. Everyone knew Victoria loved children, but sadly she wasn't able to have any more after the twins."

Matthew frowned. "Victoria Townsend couldn't have any more children after the twins? What about Clare?"

Doc shifted uncomfortably. "I meant after Clare."

"You're not a very good liar, Doc."

"And you're a very sharp lawyer."

"So what gives?"

With a wave of his hand Doc shrugged it off. "Nothing. Just an old man's suspicions that I should keep to myself."

"I'm up against a brick wall here, Doc, and C.J.'s life is at stake. If you can help me, I wish you would."

"This has nothing to do with C.J."

"But it's about the Townsends, and I think C.J. and the Townsends are connected somehow."

"Don't know, but I shouldn't have made that slip. My mind must be going."

"Your mind is like a razor," Matthew said. "So tell me what you suspect."

"I shouldn't." He hesitated, then said, "I guess it doesn't matter. Victoria's dead, but I don't want Clare to get hurt. She's a sweet lady and does a lot for this town."

"I'll keep everything confidential, unless it somehow pertains to C.J.'s parents."

"It doesn't." There was silence for a moment, and Matthew could see the doctor was wrestling with his conscience. Finally he started to speak. "Victoria had a hard time conceiving. She had some female problems and went to see a specialist in Austin. Finally she got pregnant. It was a hard pregnancy, though, and the babies came six weeks early. I had to deliver them. For a while, I thought I was going to lose her *and* the babies, even after I did an emergency C-section to deliver John Robert and Joyce. But Victoria wasn't so lucky. She started hemorrhaging and I had all kinds of complications. It was a long night, but she pulled through. I told her she was lucky she had a girl and a boy because she wouldn't be able to have any more children. The doctor in Austin told her the same thing.''

He paused, thinking back. ''The twins were about seven when I met her on the street one day. She said she was pregnant. I was shocked and told her to come to the office. I wanted to examine her. She said the doctor in Austin was handling everything. I was taken aback because she'd had problems before and I thought she'd want me to be in on what was happening, but I could see she didn't want me involved in the pregnancy.''

Doc drew a deep breath. ''About three months before the baby was due, she and Martha flew to a special clinic in California so Victoria could be monitored on a daily basis in case of problems. Then one day I saw Victoria in town with the new baby and I started to believe in miracles.''

''But something changed your mind,'' Matthew said.

''Yeah.'' Doc sighed. ''About two weeks later Victoria's maid called me. She said Victoria was real sick. I went out there. She was so pale and weak I thought she might he hemorrhaging like the last time, so I examined her. She wasn't, but I could tell she hadn't just given birth. I told her as much. She laughed it off, saying I'd made a mistake because she had a baby to prove it. I let it go, because it really wasn't any of my business. If Victoria had a secret, then it was hers to keep.''

"What's your feeling? That she adopted Clare?"

"Yeah." He scratched his head. "Why would the doctor in Austin send her to California? He was a specialist. Seems to me he'd want her in Austin to keep an eye on her."

"Makes sense to me."

"I figure the clinic in California was a place for unwed mothers, and Victoria went there to wait for a baby."

"Why would she go to such lengths to keep an adoption a secret?"

"Probably wanted Clare to feel part of the Townsend family. Some people are funny about things like that. Cobers and Townsends—family name and family heritage is more important to them than anything else on earth."

Matthew thought of Clare and what she'd said about not belonging. She knew. Subconsciously she knew.

"Do you remember the clinic or the doctor's name?"

"Not sure of the clinic, but it was in Santa Monica, I believe—and the doctor had a common name. Frank Jones."

Matthew got to his feet, as did Doc. "Thanks, Doc. This might help."

"It's all just doubts in an old man's head."

"I think you're right on target."

"Sad." Doc shook his head. "Victoria went through so much to get Clare, but then she became so ill she couldn't care for her. Martha was the one who raised her."

He shook his head again, as if to free it of the past. "I hope you find C.J.'s parents, son, I really do."

"Thanks," Matthew said, clasping Doc's hand.

"Again, this is all confidential," Doc murmured.

He nodded. Then he headed for the door, his mind reeling. Was Clare adopted? But what difference did it make? The answer wouldn't help him find C.J.'s parents.

But he couldn't shake the ambiguous feeling. It gnawed at him all night. He was missing something; he knew it. He went over and over Doc's story and could find nothing, no fact or clue. What wasn't he seeing?

BY MORNING Matthew had devised a plan of action. Or at least a place to begin. With Dr. Frank Jones. Although whether that would lead to any productive information…well, he just didn't know.

C.J. called and said she was going to be late. A buyer was coming to look at some horses and she had to show them for Pete. It gave him time to clear the doubts in his head; he didn't want to get her hopes up again.

He called his office in New York. Tom was a computer whiz, and if the answer was in a computer somewhere, Tom would find it. He told him what he wanted, then he waited.

Walking to the window, he gazed out into the alley. There was nothing to look at, only trash cans and a wooden fence. But over the fence he could see the chimney tops of the Cober mansion. What secrets did those walls hold? Was he insane for digging into something that had no obvious connection to C. J. Doe? He had to go with what he had—and he had to go with his gut feelings, hoping for the one piece that would make the whole puzzle fall into place.

The phone rang and he turned to answer it.

"I've got it," he shouted to Miss Emma.

"Yes?" he said into the receiver.

"Hey, boss, you answering the phone now?" Tom's jovial voice came down the line. "I guess that's what they mean by a one-man practice."

"What have you got?" Matthew asked, not in the mood for humor.

"Dr. Frank Jones had a clinic in Santa Monica, all right."

"Had?"

"The clinic's still there, but he retired about ten years ago. I'll fax his mailing address and phone number."

"Thanks. Did you find out what type of clinic it was?"

"It's for women with problem pregnancies. Dr. Jones is apparently well-known for his work in helping women who wouldn't otherwise be able to have children. The clinic catered to wealthy ladies back then—and still does."

Matthew was dumbfounded. It was just as Victoria Townsend had said. Could Doc be wrong?

"Boss, are you there?"

"Yes, I'm surprised, that's all. I thought this was a clinic for unwed mothers."

"No way. It's very exclusive."

"Thanks, Tom, I appreciate your help."

"No problem. Gail said to remind you that jury selection for the Peterman case starts in a few days."

"Tell her to try and get another postponement."

"Will do, and hurry home. The place isn't the same without you."

Matthew hung up the phone. Home? New York was his home, had been for a long time, but it didn't feel like home anymore. Coberville was getting into his blood. No, he corrected himself. It was C.J. He'd dated a lot of beautiful women who'd attracted him, mentally as well as physically, but with C.J. it went beyond that. She touched a part of him no woman had ever been able to reach—his heart. Over the years he had guarded it well, not wanting to end up in divorce court like so many of his friends. But with her sweet smile and stubborn pride C.J. had managed to slip through his defenses, and he couldn't help thinking that he wanted to keep her smiling for the rest of her life.

He heard the fax machine and hurried over to get the information on Dr. Jones. He stared at it. Was it possible that Victoria Townsend had given birth? Could Dr. Haslow be mistaken about something like that?

There was only one way to find out. He went back to his desk and dialed the phone number. This had happened more than forty years ago, but he was hoping Dr. Jones would remember a woman from Texas.

"Hello," a woman answered.

"Could I speak with Dr. Jones, please?"

There was a moment's silence, then the woman said, "Dr. Jones passed away two years ago."

He should have expected this. "I'm sorry. I wasn't aware of that."

"Obviously you didn't know Frank very well."

"No—I didn't know him at all. My name is Matthew Sloan and I'm an attorney from Texas."

"Texas? What's this about?"

"I'd hoped Dr. Jones could tell me something about one of his patients."

"He would never divulge confidential information."

"I wouldn't expect him to," Matthew assured her. "I just wanted to know if this woman actually *was* a patient of his. It's very important."

"I guess there's no harm in that," she said. "Maybe I can help you. I was his nurse, not to mention his wife, for more than fifty years."

Finally a little luck. "I'd appreciate it."

"What's the woman's name?"

"Victoria Townsend from Coberville, Texas. It was in the late 1950s."

"Oh, I don't believe my memory's that good. What did she look like?"

"She was petite and beautiful with white-blond hair and blue eyes."

"Doesn't ring a bell, but Frank and I were working on a book about his most difficult cases before he passed away. Recently I decided to finish it, and I have all his files in the study. If you could hold for a few minutes, I'll check for that name."

"Thank you," he said. "I'll hold."

He tapped his fingers on the desk, waiting, hoping for an answer that would make some sense of this strange situation. If Victoria Townsend had been a patient and given birth to Clare, then Doc had made a big mistake. But Matthew felt sure he hadn't....

"Mr. Sloan." Mrs. Jones was back on the line.

"Yes." He sat up straight.

"I found it. Victoria Cober Townsend."

Matthew frowned. "She *was* a patient, then."

"Yes, and I always made notes on each one. I vaguely remember the case. Her sister came with her, and they were completely different."

"Yes, that's it."

"Something's not right."

"What do you mean?"

"You said Victoria was beautiful with blond hair."

"Yes."

"We keep a photo of each patient and her baby, that's not the woman I'm looking at."

Matthew gripped the receiver. "It isn't?"

"No, this woman has brown hair and is rather plain. My

notes say she was obnoxious and mean, especially to her sister. Yes, I remember now. Her sister was the beautiful one.''

''Wait a minute,'' Matthew said. ''Let me get this straight. The plain one gave birth to a baby girl.''

''Yes, and had a relatively easy pregnancy.''

''Why was she there?''

''Back then, to keep the clinic open, we also catered to wealthy women who liked being pampered in the last stages of pregnancy. She was one of them. Oh, dear, I've probably said more than I should.''

''No, you haven't. I appreciate your help. You've solved an old mystery. Thanks, Mrs. Jones.''

As he hung up, the truth stood out clearly in his stunned mind. Martha Cober was Clare's mother. Doc was right, but no one had ever guessed, and the Townsends had gone to great pains to keep it a secret. Why? Because Martha was unmarried? Maybe she couldn't face the scandal; at that time it wasn't as accepted for unwed women to have babies.

Fast on the heels of that thought came another. Who was the father? Even as he asked himself the question, he knew the answer. John Townsend. He'd bet money on it. But why would Victoria agree to raise the child resulting from an adulterous affair between her husband and her sister? Did she want another child that badly?

He rammed frustrated hands through his hair. God, what did all this have to do with C.J.? Suddenly he sat bolt upright. How old was Martha when C.J. was born? Fifty? Could she still have children? It happened occasionally, didn't it? Could she have gotten pregnant again, and this time Victoria refused to bail her out? Could Martha Cober be C.J.'s mother? Was it possible?

Was this the piece of the puzzle he'd been looking for?

NOW WHAT? HE ASKED himself. He needed time to decide what to do next.

Miss Emma knocked on the door.

"Not now, Miss Emma, I'm busy," he said irritably.

"Well, pardon me." She poked her head into the office and set a plastic bag on the floor. "This came from the hospital. Do you want it or not?"

"What is it?"

"Your dad's briefcase. Belle picked up everything else, but she forgot the case."

He got to his feet. "Thanks, Miss Emma."

Lifting the bag, he pulled out the briefcase and set it on the desk. He ran his hand lazily over the fine leather. On the front were his dad's initials. He tried the latch, but it was locked. He went to the filing cabinet and slid his hand along the bottom and found the spare key. In a second he had it open. The scent of cigars filled his nostrils; an open pack lay on top of some court papers. In a side pocket were pictures of his mom and him. In another were clippings of all his legal victories in New York. Suddenly tears stung Matthew's eyes and he sank into his chair. Until that moment he'd never realized how much he missed his dad. He could always depend on him for solid advice and, God, did he need it now.

He cleared his throat and started to close the case when something caught his eye. A small book, a journal of some sort.

Opening it, he recognized his father's handwriting. Excitement raced through him. This was what he'd been looking for; he felt sure of it. Quickly he scanned the first few pages—notes and more notes about old cases. Toward the middle of the book, he noticed a scribbled notation:

"Victoria adamant about money. Wants C.J. to have an education she says—doesn't matter who her parents were. Wish V. could trust someone besides me. Problem too big for her to handle. Should let it be.

"Agreed Victoria will bring money to office. Leave so Emma can find."

That's where the money came from, he told himself, then read on. There were several more entries about Victoria, followed by: "C.J. graduated with honors. Took her out to lunch. Should have asked Belle. Too risky. Can't get her involved. She's too perceptive. Would guess truth."

That was it. His dad didn't want his mom too close to C.J. in case she recognized some familiar traits. Whose?

"Saw Victoria today. Upset. Wants new will. Advised her to see Reed in Austin. Disinterested party. Less chance of breaking it."

Another will? Where was it? What was in it? Questions zipped through Matthew's mind and he swiftly turned the page.

"C.J. stopped by today. Breaks my heart every time I see her. Wish I could tell her, but I'm honor bound."

Tell her what, Dad? Matthew's eye found another note:

"Belle's upset about C.J. again. Light of my life, try to understand. Can't share things that are not mine to share. Maybe Matthew will call. Always perks her up."

He stared at his father's writing, feeling the love his parents had shared. A love like that was so rare. Slowly he turned the page.

"Victoria looks bad. Worried. Something wrong. Wish she'd talk to Martha and resolve things. So much anger between them. V. can't go on like this."

Matthew kept reading. "Saw Victoria. Weak. Troubled."

Then: "Coberville lost its finest citizen. Sad day. Why did it have to end this way?

"Victoria's old will the only one at bank. Shocked. Where's new will? Need to do some checking."

A later entry: "Townsends furious. Want will broken. Have to stall for time. Reed out of country."

So his father *had* been stalling for time. That was the reason he hadn't mentioned the date on the old will, the reason he'd been dragging his heels. He knew there was another will.

"Feel tired. Weak. Have to get will settled. Promised Victoria. Maybe I should call Matthew."

Another page: "So tired. Can't breathe. Reed will be back soon."

Then: "Should call Matthew. He's so busy. Maybe tomorrow."

Two weeks after the last entry his father died. Closing the book, Matthew sat gazing off into space, feeling a mountain of guilt. Why hadn't his father called him? Was his life so busy that he didn't have time for his parents? God, he should have been here. His father had needed him. Matthew sighed deeply. Guilt wasn't going to help the situation. Anyway, he was here now—that was what mattered.

Matthew fingered the pages of the book. What exactly was the secret his father and Victoria Townsend had shared? Was it about Martha Cober? Was Victoria trying to force her hand, make her take responsibility for her actions? Could that be the answer to the mystery that hung over this town?

He read through the scribblings again, making sure he

hadn't missed anything. There was nothing here that could really help him, except the mention of a new will. That was crucial.

Reed? A first or last name? He had to find out. He had to find the will. Maybe the reason someone was trying to kill C.J. had something to do with Victoria's secret will.

HE HAD JUST put the briefcase away when C.J. came in. As always she looked great in a green T-shirt and jeans. Her long hair was braided and hung down her back.

"Hi." She smiled and kissed him slowly.

His body tightened with desire and he wondered if it was always going to be this way.

"Hi," he said, short of breath. "How'd it go with the sheriff?"

"Got Harry out without paying a dime."

"How'd you manage that?"

"Cashed in on some old lies."

"Somehow I knew you would," he murmured, and bent his head for another kiss. But she noticed something on the desk and pulled away. She picked up the pad he'd been scribbling on while talking to Mrs. Jones.

He tried to take it from her, but she jerked away, reading. God, why hadn't he torn it up? He didn't want her to read it until he had more facts. She'd been upset enough about the dead end with Joyce and Clare. He didn't want to disillusion her again.

Staring at him with huge eyes, she asked, "What does this mean, Matthew? 'Martha Cober. Clare's mother.'"

He couldn't lie to her. "Sit down and I'll explain."

When she handed him the pad, he tore the sheet off, crumpled it into a ball and threw it in the trash. She took a chair and watched him with a perplexed expression on her face.

He told her about Martha and Clare. "It's critical to keep this information confidential. If it got back to Clare, it could hurt her deeply."

"I would never tell anyone," C.J. said quietly. "But—" she frowned, her gaze holding his "—you wrote something else. 'Fifty years old. Menopause. C.J.' What does that mean?"

"Nothing," he said immediately. "Just rambling. Doesn't mean a thing."

"I think it does."

"Just leave it, C.J."

"No." She stood up, her eyes narrowed. "You think Martha Cober could be *my* mother, too. Don't you?"

He didn't answer. He couldn't.

"You think she got pregnant during menopause, and this time her sister wouldn't help her out, so she left the baby on Pete and Maggie's doorstep."

"C.J., stop this! I was doodling my thoughts and you should never have seen that."

"But it makes sense." Her eyes grew troubled. "That's why Mrs. Townsend left me the land and the money. Because she knew her sister would never acknowledge me, and as a Cober I had a right to at least something. I let her down." Her voice deepened with anguish. "I gave it all back. Dear God, how could I have been so foolish? I wasn't a Townsend, but a Cober."

He caught her by the forearms. "C.J., listen to me. I want you to put this out of your head. We have no proof— it's all just guesses. The woman was in her fifties, for God's sake, remember that."

"I hope she's not my mother," C.J. said weakly. "I

know it's terrible to say that, but Martha Cober makes me uneasy. She looks at me with such cold eyes and she never seems to see me. She looks right through me. It's eerie."

"Try not to think about her." Matthew softened his tone. "It's very unlikely she's your mother."

"Maybe," she mumbled, then asked, "What do we do now?"

"Gather more information. Get some facts, then—"

"You and your facts." She rolled her eyes. "I want to do something. I want to—"

His lips curved into a smile.

"Why are you smiling?"

"Because you're the most hardheaded impulsive wonderful woman."

"I'm not sure that's a compliment."

His gaze was warm. "It is."

When he looked at her like that, she couldn't think. She could only feel—delicious sensual feelings.

She swallowed and asked, "So how do we get those facts?"

"I've got to think about our next move."

"Fine. I'll be back later." She turned toward the door.

"Where are you going?"

"My Camaro's still at the sheriff's office where Beal left it. Since I got my truck back, I haven't needed it. I told the sheriff I'd drive it home, then we promised Mr. McIntosh we'd haul his calves to the auction."

"I don't think it's wise to be out so much."

"Pete and Harry are always with me. So stop worrying." She blew him a kiss and headed for the door.

"C.J."

"Yes?" She looked back.

"Try not to think about Martha Cober."

"I'll try, but it won't be easy."

Matthew went back to his desk and sat down, cursing himself. How could he have been so careless? He tended to scribble notes, just like his father, but he always tore them up or put them away. He didn't like C.J. being upset, and he knew his feelings for her went deep—very deep. She consumed his heart, his body, his soul, and New York seemed a lifetime away.

CHAPTER FIFTEEN

THE ODDS OF MARTHA COBER being C.J.'s mother were very slim, he knew. But he had to get to work finding proof if he wanted to relieve C.J. of her fears. Martha's medical history was the place to start, and Dr. Haslow could help him with that. He reached for the phone, only to discover that Doc was on a house call. Damn.

To allay his frustration he tried to remember all he knew about Martha Cober. There wasn't much. She was Victoria Townsend's sister and she stayed pretty much in the background.

Where could he learn more? Just as the question crossed his mind, his mother walked into the office. He grinned. He had the best source right here, right now. His mother had grown up with the Cober sisters.

He got up and walked around the desk to kiss her cheek. "Just the person I want to see. You can help me with something."

"Really?" Her eyes were suspicious. "I came over to see if I could get you to have lunch with me."

Giving her another kiss, he went back to his desk. "Not today, Mom. I'm too busy."

She sat down, smoothing her dress over her knees. Her salt-and-pepper hair was naturally curly and she wore it in a short neat style. Matthew thought how young she looked. In her seventies, she looked much the same as she had when he was a boy.

"You're working very hard to find C.J.'s parents," she commented.

"It's the only way I can think of to free her from this nightmare."

"I get the feeling it's more than that...." The words hung between them and he knew she was asking him a question, but it was a question he wasn't ready to answer. He couldn't help contrasting the difference in her attitude toward C.J. now with that earlier reaction. He thought of showing her the book, but felt it wasn't the right time.

"Don't play matchmaker, Mom," was all he said.

"I don't think I have to," she answered smugly.

Matthew didn't want to discuss this right now. "I need your help," he said urgently.

"So you mentioned." Her eyes narrowed. "With what?"

"Martha Cober. Tell me everything you know about her."

"Martha Cober?" She frowned. "Why in the world would you want to know about Martha?"

"In the search for C.J.'s parents, everything leads back to the Townsends. I'm checking out every one of them, but I know very little about Martha. Since you went to school with her, I'm sure you know something about her personality, her childhood, her life."

A puzzled expression settled on her face. "I'll tell you all I know, but for the life of me I can't imagine what Martha has to do with C.J.'s parents."

"I'm just looking for clues," he told her.

"Well, let's see," she started thoughtfully. "Martha is the oldest of William Cober's three children. Martha and Will, Jr., were from his first marriage."

"William Cober was married twice?" he asked, sur-

prised. When he'd been at the ranch, he had seen a painting of only one wife. "I've never heard that before."

"It was a short marriage. His first wife died when Will,
Jr., was about a month old. Within six months William
Cober had remarried, and Victoria was born nine months
later."

"What happened to his second wife?"

"She died giving birth to their next child. A little boy.
He died, too."

"Really," Matthew murmured. "I don't believe there's
a painting of her at the ranch."

"I've never seen a picture of her. But they say when
his first wife died, he didn't shed a tear, but when his
second wife died, he cried like a baby."

Matthew realized they were getting offtrack and started
to veer the conversation back to Martha, but his mother
began speaking again. "When Will, Jr., was killed at
twenty-one in a riding accident, old Will took to his bed.
No one could comfort him, not even Victoria, the child he
worshiped. Martha took over the running of the estate. She
made a lot of bad business decisions with the Cober newspapers and banks. The Cober empire was crumbling fast.
The impending demise of the Cober estate brought old
Will out of his bed. He took over the reins again, and with
Victoria's help he made the Cober empire what it is today."

"I don't remember much about this."

"It's not common knowledge, but Matt and I were close
to Victoria and she shared a lot of her problems."

"What happened next?"

She paused a moment, then continued, "Martha hated
the thought of her younger sister succeeding where she'd
failed. She took to drinking and gambling. She spent a lot
of time in Vegas and Atlantic City. She'd stay away for

months at a time, and when she came home, she'd always have some man in tow, trying to impress her father. That's how John Townsend came to be part of the Cober family. Martha brought him home one weekend, but the moment he set eyes on Victoria, he never looked at Martha again.''

"John Townsend was Martha's boyfriend?"

"Yes, and Martha never forgave Victoria for taking him from her. After Victoria and John were married, Martha left home and didn't come back until old Will died, but she got a big shock at the reading of the will. Victoria was named executor and had control over everything. Even Will, Jr.'s share was left to Victoria. Martha was so furious she vowed never to come back to Coberville."

"But she did come back."

"With her tail tucked between her legs, begging for Victoria's help. They say her gambling debts were in the millions and she was in a lot of trouble. Victoria agreed to pay off her debts if Martha signed over her interest in the Cober estate. Martha did, and Victoria let her live at Seven Trees. Ever since, Martha's been very docile, puttering in her flower garden and taking care of her horses."

"She never married or had children?"

"No, John Townsend was the love of her life. She's happy now that she can take care of him in his old age."

"Did she ever date anyone from Coberville?"

"No, the men in Coberville were never good enough for Martha."

"Think, Mom. Even in her fifties, did you ever see her with anyone?"

Belle shook her head. "No. After Clare was born, Martha's life centered on her. Since Victoria was sick so much, Martha practically raised her. She worships that girl, though she smothers and dominates her at times."

Matthew had heard the story about Victoria being ill

before, but no one had ever said from what. "What was wrong with Victoria Townsend?"

Belle shrugged. "Don't really know. I guess having Clare drained her of all her strength. I went to see her one time, and she was so weak she couldn't get out of bed. She had bouts of severe stomach pains and numbness in her hands and feet. The doctors never could figure it out. She'd be real sick for a while, then suddenly she'd get better. The last bout finally killed her. I shouldn't say that," Belle corrected herself. "She was ill, but she managed to get out of bed during the night and fall down the stairs."

"Victoria Townsend died from falling down the stairs?"

"Yes. No one ever knew what she was doing out of bed at that hour."

"Was there an autopsy?"

She frowned. "An autopsy? Whatever for?"

"To find out why she died!"

She glanced sharply at him. "You don't have to shout, Matthew."

"Sorry, Mom," he said immediately. "This is all so frustrating. Why wouldn't the Townsends want to know what was wrong with their mother?"

"After her death I suppose they just wanted to let her rest in peace. After all, the doctors were never able to diagnose her problem."

"Maybe," he murmured, his head filled with questions. "How did Victoria and Martha get along?"

"Like cats and dogs. They argued all the time. Martha was always jealous of Victoria. That's why I've never been able to figure out why Martha loves Clare so much. But human nature is a funny thing."

"It sure is," he mused, knowing exactly why Martha

loved Clare. He wondered if he'd ever manage to untangle the Townsends' lies and deceptions.

SHERIFF WATTS PULLED UP behind the red sports car that had been driven into the ditch. He got out, drew his gun from the holster and motioned his deputy to go around to the other side. Slowly he walked to the driver's door and peered through the shattered window. He quickly jerked back, taking several gulps of air.

"What is it, Sheriff?" the deputy called.

He took another deep breath and shoved his gun back in the holster. "She's dead. Half her face is blown off. Call an ambulance and get a crew out here to check for evidence. This is clearly a homicide."

"A homicide," the deputy echoed in dismay. "We haven't had a homicide in Coberville for ages."

"I know," Watts replied, walking back to his car. "What the hell is happening here? Who would want to kill that beautiful young woman? Such a waste. Now I have to notify the next of kin. I don't even know who that is. And I have to call Matthew Sloan. He's not going to like this one little bit."

"SHERIFF WATTS IS on the phone. Says it's important," reported Miss Emma through the intercom.

Matthew grabbed the receiver. "Yes, Sheriff? Is something wrong?"

"You could say that," the sheriff answered. "I got a call a little while ago about a dead woman in a red sports car on Fulton Road."

Matthew stopped breathing and pain ripped through his chest. Oh, God, C.J.! She was driving her sports car home.

"Matthew, are you there?"

He swallowed the constriction in his throat, realizing the sheriff was still talking. "Yes, I'm here."

"I naturally thought of C.J. She left my office in her red sports car, but when I got to the scene, I found the woman was Stephanie Cox."

Matthew took a couple of deep breaths. "Stephanie Cox? The woman was Stephanie Cox?"

"Yeah. Seems Mr. Townsend just bought her a new Corvette and she was trying it out. Someone pulled alongside her and shot her through the window. The windows are tinted, so the shooter couldn't see his victim too well. I figure he got the wrong woman."

"What are you saying?" Fear slammed into his stomach.

"The shooter was after C.J. is my guess. Probably thought he had her alone, away from Pete and Harry, and he seized his chance."

"What makes you so sure?"

"It all fits. Who'd want Stephanie Cox dead? C.J.'s the one whose life has been threatened. Our shooter's in Coberville and he's not leaving until the job's done. I went by the Watson place to warn them, but wasn't a soul around."

"They're hauling Mr. McIntosh's calves to the auction."

"That's in the middle of nowhere. I guess she's safe enough."

"Or it might be the perfect place to finish a job. By now the shooter probably knows he's made a mistake."

"You could be right, but I can't get loose just yet. I've got my hands full with this Cox murder and the Townsends, but I'll have a deputy free as soon as C.J. gets back into town."

"That may be too late, Sheriff. I'm going out there to make sure she's okay."

"Fine. That'll put my mind at ease."

Matthew hung up and headed for the door. He had to find C.J., and fast.

He climbed into his truck and drove toward the outskirts of town. Raised in Coberville, he knew all the back roads. He turned onto Boggs and drove for what seemed like hours as the old road twisted between one thicket and the next. Nothing much lived out here except wildlife.

Behind him dust swirled like dark clouds, and the truck bounced on the uneven dirt road. Hell on the suspension, but he didn't care. He had to get to C.J.

As he drove, he thought of Stephanie and her desire to be different, to be something more than she was. Such a loss. He and C.J. had to solve the mystery of her birth before someone else got hurt.

His nerves were taut by the time he saw a small white house—the McIntosh place. An old man in overalls and a straw hat walked toward him with the aid of a cane.

Matthew parked the truck and hurried over to him. "I'm looking for C. J. Doe," he said.

Mr. McIntosh eyed him from behind thick wire-rimmed glasses. "She's in the bottom, loading my calves."

"Thanks," Matthew said, and turned back to his truck.

"You'll never make it in that," the old man told him.

Matthew stopped. "Why not?"

"Need a four-wheel drive to cross Boggs Creek. It's up after the rain we had last week."

Matthew smacked the side of the truck. "Damn!"

The old man watched him for a moment, then said, "Come on, I'll take you in my Jeep."

"Thanks, I'd appreciate it," Matthew said, walking to the dilapidated vehicle. The frame was so rusted that when he climbed in the passenger side, he could actually see the ground through the floorboards.

It took the old man a while to get in behind the wheel, but soon the engine sputtered to life and they were off.

They charged around the barn and then through a corn-field and finally hit a road, all without slowing down. Mr. McIntosh squinted to see through a windshield splattered with mud.

"You're Judge Sloan's boy, aren't you?" Mr. McIntosh shouted above the roar of the engine.

"Yes," Matthew answered with a smile. Judge Sloan's boy. Growing up, he'd hated people calling him that; he realized now that he'd been running away from it all these years, trying to make his own identity. But he didn't need another identity; he already had one. He was Judge Sloan's boy from Coberville, Texas, and nothing was ever going to change that. Hell, he didn't *want* to change it. He was proud to be Matt Sloan's boy.

In searching for her identity C.J. had helped him realize how important his own was. For the past few years he'd felt a restlessness, and he finally knew why. All his life he'd been trying to prove something—but he understood now that he didn't have to prove anything to himself and certainly not to his parents. They loved him unconditionally.

"Good man," Mr. McIntosh muttered.

"The best." Matthew's smile deepened. The very best, he said to himself.

As they came to Boggs Creek, Mr. McIntosh shouted, "Hold on," and the Jeep plunged in.

They hit the water with a splash and Matthew gripped the sideboard. The creek rose midway up the wheels, but that didn't faze the old man as he whizzed through the water and mud, which splashed onto the windshield and all over the Jeep.

As they climbed the opposite bank, the old man still

didn't stop, just pointed to a rag on the floorboard. "Better wipe the windshield, boy. I can't see diddly squat."

Matthew grabbed the rag and holding the windshield with one hand, he wiped with the other. The wind whipped through his hair and the rough ride jostled his body, but he managed to get the job done.

Sinking back in his seat, he gave the man a dark look, but Mr. McIntosh was busy contemplating the road. Through twists and turns, they finally roared into a clearing and there was C.J., along with Pete and Harry. She was safe; that was all he cared about.

Pete already had his trailer loaded with calves bawling for their mothers. C.J. was leading her horse into the back of her trailer with more calves. She slammed the gate shut and locked it, then caught sight of the Jeep.

Thunder suddenly rumbled in the distance, making the calves jumpy. "Tell them they'd better get out of here before the rain starts," Mr. McIntosh instructed, shifting gears as Matthew climbed out. In a roar he was gone.

C.J. watched Matthew as he walked closer, wondering what he was doing out here in this weather. As he reached her, lightning streaked the sky, followed by a clap of thunder.

"Load up, girl, we're outa here," Pete called, climbing into Harry's truck.

"Come on, city man." C.J. smiled, noting his disheveled appearance. "I'll give you the ride of your life."

Settling into the passenger side, he said, "Old man McIntosh beat you to it." He brushed mud from his shirt, glad he'd changed into casual clothes. "The guy uses that Jeep as a weapon."

"You'll live." Her smile broadened as she started the truck. Pete and Harry pulled away and she shifted into gear, slowly following them across the field.

Matthew glanced back at the trailer-load of calves and marveled at her competence. She was so slim, so feminine, yet she handled the truck with the ease of any man.

"Are you going to tell me what you're doing out here in the middle of your workday?" she asked. "Did you find out something about Martha?"

He took a deep breath, combed his hands through his hair and told her the events of the morning.

"Stephanie Cox is dead?" she asked in a faint voice, negotiating her truck and trailer onto the road.

"Yes."

"Someone else dead because of me," she murmured sadly. "The nightmare's starting all over again."

"That's why I came. I had to make sure you were safe."

"My knight in shining armor," she said. "Thank you." But he knew she was upset from the way she white-knuckled the steering wheel.

They turned a corner and saw a man standing by a brown pickup, waving his arms.

"What the hell?" Matthew exclaimed.

"He must need help," she said, slowing.

"Don't stop," he ordered.

"Why not?"

"Do you know him?"

C.J. peered through the windshield. "No."

"Evidently he wasn't here when Pete and Harry went by. So where did he come from that quick? Just keep going. If he's in trouble, we'll send someone back to help him. It's just too dangerous to stop."

"Yes, sir," she said, picking up speed. As they reached the man, they both watched in horror as he pulled out a gun and started shooting. The bullets hit the side of the truck with a sound that equaled the thunder.

"My God, it's him," Matthew yelled. "Can you speed up?"

Through the side mirrors they could see the man climbing into his truck. "He's coming. God, not again." Matthew groaned, feeling they'd been through this already and wondering if, this time they'd make it out alive.

C.J. concentrated on keeping the truck and trailer going as fast as was safely possible. The truck hit a hole and bounced sideways, but she managed to control it, bringing it back onto the road.

Suddenly raindrops spattered against the windshield. Lightning ripped across the sky, and the floodgates opened.

"Oh, no!" she cried, turning on the windshield wipers. "If this keeps up, we won't be able to make it across Boggs Creek."

"Maybe Pete and Harry will be waiting for us."

"I don't think so. They're going to get those calves out as fast as they can. They know I can manage on my own."

Matthew saw the brown truck gaining on them. "Do you have a rifle in here?"

"No. The guns are in Harry's truck."

He leaned forward. "Can you see through this downpour?" he asked as rain blanketed the windshield. The frantic to and fro of the wipers was futile now.

"Barely," she answered, bringing the truck and trailer to a stop on the bank of the creek.

"Damn!" he breathed in disbelief. The rain had let up enough in the past minute so he could actually see the creek. "It looks like it's risen a foot since I crossed it with McIntosh. Can we make it?"

She shifted into first gear, her eyes on the brown truck behind them. "We don't have a choice," she said. "If you believe in God, this might be a good time to pray."

"C.J.—"

"We're going across," she said with determination. "I'm *not* making this easy for him."

"Okay, I'm with you," he told her.

Luckily the rain had diminished to a drizzle and visibility was better. The truck inched into the creek and Matthew held his breath. Water was coming in through the bottom of the door. As it reached the calves, they bellowed and moved around in fear. The trailer started to sway.

"C.J.!" he shouted.

She shifted into second gear. "We're not done yet." Her foot hit the gas pedal and the engine sputtered in protest, but miraculously kept going, pulling them and the trailer onto the bank in an explosion of water and sound the like of which he'd never heard before. Without a pause, C.J. hit third gear and the truck responded, taking them farther and farther—to safety.

"He's not coming across," Matthew said, as the brown truck stopped on the other side of the creek.

"Thank God," she replied. She kept the truck moving at a steady speed.

"You were wonderful." He touched her cheek.

"Don't compliment me now. We have to get off this dirt road before it becomes impassable."

"Whatever you say." He laughed, releasing the pent-up tension. He didn't even protest when they left his truck behind in the farmyard.

As C.J. negotiated the muddy road, the weather cleared and made driving easier. When they got to the highway, Pete and Harry were waiting.

"*Now* they stop," Matthew said furiously, jumping out when the truck came to a halt.

"Matthew!" she called, but to no avail. He was already confronting Pete and Harry, who were standing at the back of the trailer.

"What the hell is the matter with you two?" Matthew yelled. "Ever since I've met you, you've been down my throat about protecting C.J.—and then you drive off and leave her to fend for herself. My God, the shooter was lying in wait for her!"

"Calm down." C.J. touched his arm, but he twisted away in an angry gesture.

"What happened?" Pete asked quietly.

"At the second bend a man hailed me to stop, and when I wouldn't, he started shooting," C.J. explained. "He followed us until we crossed the creek. He decided not to chance the rising water."

"He wasn't there when we came through," Pete said. "Where'd he come from? There's only one other way into that bottom, and you have to be from Coberville to know about it. I never dreamed you'd be in any danger."

"She was, dammit," Matthew shouted, pointing a finger at Pete, "and you're supposed to be protecting her!"

"Are you all right?" Pete moved close to C.J, his skin visibly pale.

"Sure." She tried to smile.

"No thanks to the two of you," Matthew snarled.

"Better calm down, boy," Harry said in a threatening tone.

"Or what, Harry?" Matthew challenged him, close to his face. "You going to pull a gun on me again, or slit my throat? Well, come on, I'm in a mood to take you on."

As the two men confronted each other, C.J. stepped between them. "Stop it, do you hear me?"

When neither man acknowledged her plea, C.J. sighed, throwing her hands in the air. "Fine, go ahead and kill each other. I'm taking these calves to the auction."

As C.J. headed for her truck, Pete said, "We all want the same thing—to keep C.J. safe. So let's stop fighting."

Cars zoomed by. Calves bellowed and shifted in the trailers, but Matthew's dark eyes never wavered from Harry's brooding ones.

"Brother," Pete coaxed, placing a hand on Harry's shoulder.

Something flickered deep in Harry's eyes, something Matthew thought he'd never see—a look of respect. In an abrupt movement Harry stuck out his callused hand.

That was it. All the anger in Matthew dissipated. He drew in a deep breath and shook Harry's hand.

It was about more than just anger, though. It was about acceptance. Pete and Harry had finally acknowledged Matthew as a part of C.J.'s life.

Matthew climbed into the truck with C.J., but she didn't say anything and he knew she was annoyed.

"I'm sorry. I couldn't help myself. I had to let off some steam," he apologized.

She turned to look at him. "Feeling better, are you?"

"I'd feel a lot better if you'd smile at me."

A smile broke out on her face. "Let's get these calves to the auction before you hurt yourself."

Soon they were at the auction barn. Matthew called the sheriff, and after that, things started to happen fast. The sheriff had a deputy ready to escort Pete, Harry and C.J. back to the ranch. As usual C.J. had a different point of view. She didn't want to go.

Matthew held both her hands. "Please don't fight me on this," he said, gazing into her stubborn eyes. "The sheriff says Detective Beal is at my office. He may have some information that'll help us find this man. I want you safe until we can put it all together."

"I want to hear what Beal has to say, too," she said with a touch of anger. "I should have some say in all of this. It's my life!"

"C.J.—"

"I'm really not safe anywhere," she told him.

"But you're safer at the ranch with someone guarding you."

"He's right, girl," Pete said, and Matthew sighed gratefully.

C.J. looked at Pete. In all the years he'd raised her, he'd never told her what to do. He'd always let her make her own decisions.

"Let's go, girl, so these men can do their job," Pete added at her startled look.

"Okay," she finally agreed, knowing it wasn't the time to make a scene. Everyone was worried about her. She turned back to Matthew. "You'll call me as soon as you find out anything?"

"You'll be the first to know," he promised, cupping her face and kissing her right there in front of everyone. He didn't care who saw.

She walked to her truck and he watched as she pulled away, the deputy following. That sad look in her eyes tore at his heart, but at least she'd be safe this way.

She had to be.

CHAPTER SIXTEEN

THE SHERIFF GAVE Matthew a ride back to the law office and went inside with him. Beal was pacing the outer office, looking impatient.

They shook hands, and Beal, obviously noting Matthew's disheveled muddy appearance, asked, "Something wrong?"

"Yes." Matthew opened the door to the inner office, and the three of them entered. Matthew moved to his chair and sat. "That man tried to kill C.J. again."

Beal opened his briefcase and pulled out a manila envelope. From it he extracted a photograph and laid it in front of Matthew. "Is that the guy?"

Matthew studied the mug shot. The man had a hawk-nose, round face and narrow eyes. He was partially bald. "That's him," he said. "How did you identify him?"

"An old lady saw him get out of the truck that hit C.J. in Austin," Beal answered. "She was waiting for her daughter to pick her up, so she was watching the street. It took so long to locate her because she stayed with her daughter for a while and didn't come back until this week. We left messages at all the houses where we couldn't reach anyone. When she got home, she called us. She remembered the man well and picked him out of some mug shots."

"You haven't found him, have you?"

"No, but his trail leads to Coberville."

"I know that much," Matthew said angrily.

"Calm down, Matthew. I'm only trying to help."

"I know." Matthew shook his head. "It's just so frustrating."

"I've got more information. Just bear with me."

"What have you got?"

"His name is Dale Weeks. An ex-con. A security guard identified Weeks as the man who shot him. The guard works for a big law firm in Austin—Dylan, Kent and Reed. Stephen Reed was killed several weeks ago and the guard was critically wounded. It was touch-and-go for a while, but he finally pulled through and was able to look at some mug shots. We haven't yet figured out a motive for the shootings. The firm didn't keep large sums of money. It's still a puzzle, but Weeks is wanted for that murder."

Reed? That was it. *The will.* The pieces were beginning to fall into place. Matthew immediately told Beal about his father's notes.

"You believe Reed was killed for Victoria Townsend's will?" Beal asked, disbelief tingeing his voice.

"Yes—a new will never showed up."

Beal nodded slowly. "It all fits, doesn't it. What was in that will that would make someone go to such measures? And who are we talking about, anyway?"

"I don't know, but I'm going to find out," Matthew said.

"One more thing." Beal frowned. "A fact I haven't mentioned yet. Weeks worked at the Townsend ranch several years ago."

"The Townsend ranch," Matthew echoed, not really surprised at all. "It's time to have another talk with the Townsends," he said, getting to his feet. "They probably all know Dale Weeks. We just have to find out which one hired him."

"They're pretty upset about Stephanie Cox's murder."
The sheriff spoke for the first time. "I don't think you're
going to get anything out of them today."

"There's been a murder in Coberville?" Beal asked.

As the sheriff told him about the shooting on Fulton
Road, the phone rang. Matthew ignored it, knowing Miss
Emma would get it.

Miss Emma knocked at the door and came in, looking
nervous. "There's a man on the phone. He says if you
want to keep C. J. Doe alive, you'd better talk to him."

Matthew yanked up the receiver. "This is Matthew
Sloan."

"You think you're pretty smart, don't you, Sloan?
You're always around when that pretty thing needs help.
Like this afternoon…"

"Who is this?"

"Come on, Mr. Hot Shot lawyer, you're not that
dumb."

"What do you want?"

"I've got something *you* want."

Matthew's hand gripped the receiver. "What?"

"A will. Victoria Cober Townsend's last will and tes-
tament. It makes for very good reading."

"You have the will?"

"Yes, I have the will. How many times do I need to
say it?"

Matthew took a deep breath. "Why are you calling
me?"

"Money, Sloan. I want money and I want it fast. Thanks
to you, the cops are hot on my trail and I have to get out
of the country."

"How much?"

"Fifty thousand. In one hour."

"I can't get that kind of money that fast."

"You don't think I'm stupid, do you, Sloan? The bank is right across the street and your father was loaded, not to mention you've got money of your own. So don't give me that crap."

"Okay, but I need more time."

"One hour, or I'll change my mind and finish the job I was paid to do. Be a shame to kill that pretty young thing, wouldn't it?"

"Who hired you?"

"I'll call in one hour with instructions." The phone went dead in Matthew's hand.

Matthew turned to the sheriff and Beal and related the conversation.

"You're not seriously thinking about doing it, are you?" the sheriff asked.

"I have no choice. If I want to keep C.J. alive and get my hands on that will, I have to go along with him."

"It's suicide," Beal stated flatly. "He'll kill you. Think this through."

Matthew was already at the door. "It's your job to keep me alive. So you'd better come up with a good plan," he tossed over his shoulder.

In forty minutes Matthew was back with a briefcase full of money, which he placed on his desk. The sheriff and Beal tried to talk him out of negotiating with a known murderer, but eventually gave up.

When the phone finally rang, Matthew grabbed the receiver. "Sloan here."

"Worried about that little gal, Sloan?"

"I've got the money." Matthew came right to the point.

"Good. Wait for me at the bend on Hope Road. And, Sloan, if you bring the cops, I won't show—and I'll make sure your little gal dies."

Matthew hung up and told the sheriff and Beal about the meeting place.

"He chose a good spot," Watts said glumly. "No one ever travels that road anymore. It's isolated, with dense woods on both sides."

Matthew picked up the briefcase. "So what's the plan?"

"I know a back way into those woods." The sheriff got to his feet with a reluctant sigh. "My boys and me will cover you as best we can, but we'll need a good head start."

"Get going," Matthew said, feeling the adrenaline pumping through his veins.

"I'll come with you." Beal followed the sheriff. "I want this guy as bad as you do."

"Wait a minute." Matthew stopped them. "My truck is at the McIntosh place, and I don't have a vehicle."

Beal threw him a set of keys. "Blue Lumina out front."

"Thanks."

"Be careful," Beal said. "This guy is dangerous."

C.J. SAT ON THE STEP unbraiding her hair. Running her fingers through it, she tried to halt her troubled thoughts. She had to be sensible and calm, she told herself—but someone wanted her dead. Who?

To keep herself from screaming with frustration, she went into the house. The phone rang and she immediately picked it up. "Hello."

"C. J. Doe?" a woman's voice asked.

"Yes."

"This is Martha Cober. I want to talk to you."

C.J.'s breath lodged in her throat. Martha Cober! Was Matthew right? Could Martha be her mother?

At her silence Martha said, "It's about your birth."

C.J. swallowed hard. "You know my parents?"

"Come over here and I'll tell you all about them."

"Tell me over the phone," C.J. said. She didn't want to meet with this woman who seemed to hate her.

"I'll only tell you in person. It's not something I want to talk about on the phone."

C.J. hesitated, not trusting her, but the temptation was too great. "Okay."

"Don't tell anyone where you're going. This is just between you and me."

"I don't know if I can do that," she answered, thinking about Pete and Harry and the deputy outside.

"If you want to find out about your birth, you'll do as I ask or you'll never know the truth."

C.J. gripped the receiver. This was what she'd been waiting for all her life. She couldn't let it pass by. "Okay," she said once more, the word catching in her throat.

She hung up the phone. *Could* Martha Cober be her mother? Was that what she wanted to tell her? It did make sense. A lot of women had babies during menopause.

Shaking the thought from her mind, she tried to come up with a way to get to the ranch unseen. If she told any of the men, they'd refuse to let her go—or they'd accompany her, and then Martha wouldn't talk. Glancing outside, she saw the deputy sitting in a chair, reading a fishing magazine. Pete and Harry were working on Pete's truck, but she knew they were watching her closely.

She walked to the back of the house and saw Midnight grazing in the pasture. That was it. She hurried to her room, grabbed a scarf and tied back her hair. As she did, she saw the basket sitting on her dresser. Gently she touched the white lace. Would she finally know the name of the woman who'd bought these precious things?

No, she wouldn't think about it. She knew she couldn't

deal with all the conflicting emotions that churned through her when she looked at the basket. Right now she had to get to the Townsend ranch. She ran to Pete's room. Hanging on the wall she found what she wanted. A bridle.

Bridle in hand, she slipped quietly out the back door. She didn't have much time. She dashed across the yard and climbed over the fence. In one easy movement she slid the bridle over Midnight's head and swung onto his back.

"Easy, boy, easy," she coaxed until they were out of earshot. Then she dug her heels into his sides and set off at a gallop for the Townsend ranch.

MATTHEW THOUGHT about Beal's warning as he drove to Hope Road. It was crazy, he knew, but he had no choice. For C.J. he had to do this.

Hope Road was on the outskirts of town, but had been abandoned for the new blacktop not far away. The pavement was rough and full of holes, and trees grew thickly along both sides, creating a canopy that darkened the road.

Matthew saw a brown truck parked in the bend. Weeks was already here. Heart pounding, he stopped the Lumina and waited, but Weeks stayed in the cab. Matthew rubbed his sweaty palms on the steering wheel, wondering why the guy didn't get out or at least acknowledge his presence. Maybe he was making sure no one had followed him.

Rigid with tension, Matthew left the car and walked slowly to the back of the truck. "Weeks," he called. No answer. Just silence. Wind rustled the leaves and a crow landed in a nearby tree. "Weeks," he tried again, only to be met with the same eerie silence.

Taking a deep breath, he walked to the driver's door. He could see Weeks, head tilted slightly back. Frowning, Matthew moved closer.

"Damn!" He saw the bullet hole in Weeks's head and the blood matting his hair. Someone had gotten here first.

He kicked the truck in frustration, and the sheriff, two deputies and Beal appeared out of nowhere with guns drawn.

"What happened?" the sheriff demanded.

"He's been shot," Matthew muttered.

The guns were put away and they quickly searched the truck. They found nothing. Not Victoria Townsend's will or any evidence that would lead them to the person who'd hired Dale Weeks.

Before Matthew could marshal his thoughts, a patrol car pulled up and a deputy jumped out. "Mr. Sloan!" he shouted. "Pete Watson's been trying to find you. C. J. Doe has disappeared."

The blood drained from Matthew's face. Someone had gotten to her, too. He remembered the look in her eyes as she'd walked away. He shouldn't have left her.

He ran to the car and Beal got in beside him.

"I'll be right behind you," the sheriff called.

As C.J. RODE INTO THE YARD of Seven Trees, she saw no one. The place seemed deserted. She tied Midnight to a tree beside the mansion and followed the brick walk to the front of the house.

The place was so big and impressive with its white columns and mullioned windows that it snatched her breath away. She'd never been this close before and it felt a little nerve-racking. Should she even be here? Maybe this was a foolish risk; maybe she'd set herself up for disappointment or rejection—or worse. She should've talked to Matthew. And Pete. They were going to be so angry with her.

But she'd come this far and she wasn't backing down now. She took a calming breath and climbed the steps to

the front doors. Tapping the brass knocker, she waited.
Butterflies swarmed in her stomach and her nerve faltered,
but she knew that within minutes she could have the answers she'd yearned for all her life.

Martha opened the door, neatly dressed in brown slacks
and a white silk blouse. She eyed C.J.'s disheveled figure,
her muddy jeans and boots, with disdain. C.J. shifted uncomfortably. She'd lost her scarf and her black hair hung
all around her in long tatters, windswept from the ride. She
wished she'd left it in its braid.

With an obviously forced smile, Martha opened the door
wider. "I'm glad you made it," she said, and led C.J. into
a large room. C.J. surveyed the crystal chandeliers, marble
floors and magnificent staircases. *Wow!* was all she could
think. Inside the room, a sort of library, she spared the
antiques and books a quick glance, but what riveted her
attention were the portraits of Cobers. What did it feel like
to be part of a family that could trace its lineage back so
far?

Martha watched her with a scowl on her face. The scowl
unnerved C.J. and she blurted, "What do you know about
my birth?"

Looking around as if to make sure no one was listening,
Martha said, "We can't talk here. Follow me."

C.J. followed her without hesitation. They went down a
long hall, then descended a winding staircase to another
hall, where they came to a door.

Martha took out a key. "This is my private studio. We
won't be disturbed here."

C.J. stepped inside and felt a sudden sense of foreboding. There was nothing unusual about the room, except that
it had no windows, no outdoor light. Yet it was obviously
an artist's studio, filled with a confusion of canvases,
easels, still-life paintings and landscapes.

As she made her way farther into the studio, she noticed that all the paintings were stacked against the walls. Only two pictures hung in prominence—a painting of John Townsend and another of Clare. It was obvious how much Martha loved these people.

C.J. stared at the painting of Clare. In this portrait, she looked beautiful; her blue eyes sparkled and her light brown hair curled enchantingly around her face.

Seeing C.J.'s interest, Martha said, "She's going to take over the Cober and Townsend empires one day."

C.J. turned to Martha. "What about Rob?"

"He'll be busy in Washington, but it's *her* birthright," Martha snapped.

C.J. glanced back at the picture, wondering how Clare felt about this. She always seemed so quiet and meek, completely uninterested in business. "Does Clare agree with you?" she had to ask.

"She doesn't have to. She'll do as she's told," was the curt reply.

"I see."

"You see nothing."

At the unpleasant tone of Martha's voice, she replied, "I think I do. I know about Clare."

"And what do you think you know about Clare?"

Clearly Martha thought she was bluffing, and C.J. hated to say the words, to betray a trust, but she'd come too far and waited too long. "That you're her mother," she finally said.

Martha's face distorted with rage. "How did you find out, you little bitch?"

C.J. took a step backward, and she realized it was a big mistake to have come down here with this woman. Martha Cober hated her.

She swallowed and tried to pacify her. "Matthew's been

searching for my parents and he came across the information, but your secret is safe with us. We would never hurt Clare.''

''Interfering in things that don't concern him, just like his father,'' Martha muttered under her breath.

''As I said, your secret is safe.'' C.J. felt an intense urge to get away from Martha and that strange look in her eyes. But she'd come here for a reason and she wasn't leaving until she had her answer. ''You told me you knew about my birth,'' she said. ''Were you the one who left me on Pete and Maggie's doorstep?''

''Figured it out, have you?'' Martha laughed bitterly.

The sound made C.J.'s skin crawl. Oh, God, this terrible woman was her mother! *No!* her brain screamed, rejecting the thought. She'd wanted to know the truth, but she'd never dreamed it would hurt this much—or that her own mother would actually hate her.

She licked dry lips, forcing the words from a throat that felt like sandpaper, but she had to say them, to hear them out loud. ''You're my mother.''

''What?'' Martha's eyes grew wide with indignation.

''If you left me on the doorstep, you must be my mother,'' C.J. repeated.

''Your mother? Don't be stupid,'' Martha said with a sneer. ''Look at my Clare.'' She waved a hand at Clare's painting. ''She has class and breeding. Look at you. You're nothing but poor white trash.''

The cruel words pierced C.J.'s heart, but she stood her ground because one thing had become very clear. Martha Cober knew who her mother was.

''I thought you had it all figured out, but you haven't got a clue, have you?''

''No,'' C.J. admitted. ''But *you* know, so tell me who

she is. This…this woman who didn't want me, who threw me away like a piece of garbage.''

''Oh, she *wanted* you,'' Martha said, her voice full of scorn. ''You should've seen the way she cried and fussed over you, telling you how much she loved you.''

The words were said in a hateful way, but they warmed C.J.'s heart. *''Who is my mother?''* she asked again.

''After all these years I thought someone would've figured it out, especially after that ridiculous will.''

''The will?'' C.J. echoed.

''Do you think Victoria was so generous just out of the goodness of her heart?''

C.J. blinked, trying to assimilate what Martha was saying. ''But neither Rob nor John Townsend is my father,'' she said.

''Are you blind or merely stupid?'' Martha scoffed. ''Victoria Townsend is your mother.''

CHAPTER SEVENTEEN

THE WORDS FELL like bricks into the silence, and for a moment C.J. was stunned, caught completely off guard. It didn't make sense. "No." She shook her head. "That's not true. You're lying. Victoria Townsend couldn't have any more children after Clare. She risked her life to have her. Everyone…" She stopped as she realized Victoria hadn't given birth to Clare.

"The doctor never said she couldn't. He only said she shouldn't because it might kill her."

"You're lying."

"Victoria is your mother," Martha said in an irate voice. "She called you her miracle child, her love baby. You were born right upstairs in her bedroom."

"I don't believe you," C.J. breathed weakly.

Martha turned around and rummaged through some paintings. She pulled one out and propped it against the others. "Meet your grandmother."

C.J. gasped, holding a hand to her mouth. The painting was of a woman with long black hair hanging over her shoulder. Her eyes were green, her cheekbones high. A smile curved her bow mouth. She looked happy.

It was like gazing into a mirror. The resemblance was uncanny. "This is my grandmother?" she asked in a faint voice.

"Yes, this is Victoria's mother."

C.J. shook her head again. "That can't be. I saw her mother's painting upstairs."

"That's my mother, you idiot. This is Dad's second wife and Victoria's mother. She was one-fourth Cherokee Indian."

"Why doesn't anyone remember her, the green eyes, the black hair? Surely someone saw a resemblance?"

"Because it was years ago and they were married only a short while. Few people saw her and there are no photographs of her. Dad talked her into this painting. He kept it over his bed. I hated the woman and the way my dad worshiped the painting. When I was about ten, I stole the picture and hid it down here. Dad was distraught for a while but he soon got over it. I should have destroyed it, but as a kid I was scared. Later I forgot about it." She paused for a moment. "Victoria knew there was a painting and she always hoped she could find it. She wanted to hang it in the gallery, but I could never allow that. This Indian will never hang beside my mother."

A multitude of feelings raced through C.J., but she didn't miss the contempt in Martha's voice. "Why do you hate Victoria so much?"

Her face creased into a hard mask. "*Hate* is too mild a word for what I felt. I was the eldest. I should have been my father's favorite, the one to take over from him. But he started grooming Will for that position because he was a man. I couldn't let that happen. So I began putting arsenic in Will's food. It gradually made him sick. One day I took him out riding and just pushed him from the saddle. His head hit a rock and he died." Her voice was matter-of-fact, without remorse.

"You killed your brother," C.J. breathed in horror.

"Yes, and my father turned to me, the way he should have in the first place. I began looking after the Cober business interests, but I made some…errors. My father became angry and he turned to Victoria. She took everything from me—my father, my inheritance, my child and the man I love.'' Martha twisted around to open a drawer and pulled something out. Facing C.J. again, she pointed a gun at her. ''Now I'm going to take the one thing she loved most on this earth.''

C.J. stepped backward. ''You're the person who hired someone to kill me?''

''Yes, and he botched it up. Now I'm going to finish the job.''

''Why? Victoria's dead,'' she said in a shaking voice. ''What good will it do to kill *me*?''

''As you grew, so did Victoria's guilty conscience. She made a second will, giving you one-fourth of everything and explaining the circumstances of your birth. She made the mistake of telling me about it. I couldn't let you take away from my Clare what is rightfully hers. I wasn't going to let you share in my child's inheritance. I had to have the lawyer killed to get the will, but I got it, and now no one will ever see it.''

''But if you have the will, why—''

''Oh, I would have killed you years ago, but Victoria always threatened that if anything happened to you, Clare wouldn't inherit a dime. Now Victoria's gone. This will be my last revenge.''

''You…you talk of killing as if it's normal.''

''You do what you have to in life. The man I hired didn't destroy the will as I'd ordered. Since he kept asking for more money, I assume he's tried to sell it to other people, but I fixed him. No one double-crosses me.''

''You're insane!''

''Don't call me insane!'' Martha yelled, the gun wavering in her hand.

"Okay," C.J. soothed, knowing she had pushed a lethal button. "Just answer one question. Do you know who my father is?"

"Yes. Victoria had loved him since she was a teenager, but he was dirt-poor and my father wouldn't tolerate it. He had to send her away for a while to break them up. The years passed and he married someone else. Then Victoria stole my John—but I got even. I always got even."

"What do you mean?"

A sinister smile crossed her face. "The poison worked so well on Will that I started putting small amounts in her food. I tried so many times to kill her, but she had nine lives. Like a cat. Like you."

C.J. was so shocked she couldn't speak. She could only listen to a story that chilled her to the bone.

"John really loved *me,* not Victoria. She was only a pretty thing to hang on his arm for political reasons. She didn't understand him like I do."

"John Townsend is Clare's father?" she guessed.

"Of course."

"Does he know about Clare?"

"Sure," was the surprising answer. "He was so happy, but any hint of scandal, any rumors, would have ruined his career. Though Victoria and John no longer shared a bed, she knew the scandal would have hurt the twins—her own children. She agreed to raise Clare as her own, but I could never stand for that. I started the poison again, and Victoria became so weak she couldn't get out of bed, much less look after Clare. But something or someone always intervened and kept me from finishing her off. Eventually, though, I succeeded."

Martha paused, taking a breath. "We had an argument the night she died. I threatened to kill you, and she got so angry she managed to get out of bed. I pushed her down the stairs and she died instantly. Now everything I've always planned is going to come true. No one's going to stop me, not even that stupid nurse, that Stephanie. She thought she could take John from me, but I showed her. Now John, Clare and I are going to be a family, the way things should have been years ago."

"*You* killed Stephanie Cox?"

"Yes, and it was a pleasure. She was filling John's head with nonsense."

This woman was evil. Insane. Jealousy, a quest for power and unrequited love had warped her mind. C.J. doubted if John Townsend felt anything for her. Yet she'd hurt so many people to be with him. Where would it all end?

She had to concentrate on her own problems, though. "You said you knew my father. Who is he?"

"Can't believe you haven't guessed. The answer's right under your nose."

"I know him?" C.J.'s heart raced as she waited.

"You've lived with him all your life."

"*What?*" The words rocked her to the core.

"Pete Watson is your father."

"Pete," she echoed numbly.

"As I said, they'd been in love all their lives. When Pete was through with the rodeo circuit, Victoria hired him to run the ranch. Even though she couldn't have him, she wanted him near. He and Maggie were always fighting. That February Maggie kicked him out and he stayed in the bunkhouse. John was in Washington at the time. I was so close to finishing Victoria off, but Pete noticed how weak she was. He sat by her bed at nights holding her hand. I couldn't manage to put the poison in her food again, and she started to get better. They'd go for long walks and soon he wasn't sleeping in the bunkhouse anymore. Of course they were discreet because Clare was still at home, but it was disgusting. For a month they were like teen- agers—and then it was over. Maggie wanted him back and John was due to come home. I was hoping she'd run off with Pete, but Victoria always did the proper thing. Their parting was so touching. They both cried. I wanted to laugh.''

"Does Pete know about me?" She held her breath.

"No, she never told him. Clare had some…problems that spring and I took her to Switzerland to rest. When I got back in the early fall, I knew Victoria was pregnant. She hid it from everyone else, but I knew."

"Why?" C.J. cried. "Why didn't she tell him? Why did she let me go?"

"As I said, Victoria always did the proper thing. She loved Pete and wanted his child. Even though she could die giving birth, she wanted you. But telling Pete about the baby would have ruined his marriage and devastated her grown children."

"She was powerful and rich," C.J. replied sharply. "She could have done anything she wanted."

"It was different back then. It wasn't so easy for a woman. She was forty-eight years old with adult children. The scandal of her having a bastard child would have hurt a lot of people. She was torn between you and Pete and her family. Personally I thought she *would* die having you. It was Christmas Eve. The family wasn't expected home until Christmas Day. Victoria started having pains about eight o'clock and she had me dismiss all the servants. She yelled and screamed, and I sat and waited, waited for her to draw her last breath. Just like her mother, she would die in childbirth."

Wiping the sweat from her forehead, she continued, "But Victoria pulled through and you were born ten minutes past midnight on Christmas Day. I had to cut the cord and clean you up. I placed you in her arms and she nursed you. She held you, kissing you, telling you over and over how much she loved you. At five in the morning, she dressed you, wrapped you in a thick quilt and placed you in a basket. She had gone to Dallas to buy it. Plus the little gown. She'd also bought a boy's outfit. She was prepared, but it was almost her downfall. The sheriff was hot on the trail of those items, until she put a stop to his investigation.''

"*She* stopped the investigation?''

"Sure did. She had it all planned, and she didn't want the sheriff messing things up. I hoped he'd go against her wishes and expose her to the world for what she was, but he didn't have the guts.''

"Did the sheriff know Victoria was my mother?''

"If he did, he kept it to himself. He knew better than to question her.''

"I wasn't some toy to be given away,'' C.J. said, outraged. "I was a living breathing human being. How could she do that to me?''

"That was your loving mother,'' Martha said with a snort. "She didn't have to answer to anyone. She made decisions and expected everyone to follow them. Even I followed her orders, but I had no choice. She told me to put you on Pete's doorstep—the greatest gift she would ever give him, she said. I had no intention of doing it, but she must have read my mind, because she said if you didn't reach Pete's safely, she'd make sure Clare wouldn't inherit a dime. The same threat she always used. Personally I wanted to smother you and throw you away like the garbage you mentioned earlier. But I did as she instructed. I would do anything for my Clare. I removed the quilt, hoping you'd freeze to death before they found you, but as I got back on my horse, I saw Harry's headlights coming through the woods. He found you not five minutes after I left you there.''

"I can't believe all this!'' C.J. cried. "How could she hide a pregnancy?''

Martha shrugged indifferently. "She wore loose-fitting clothes and she stayed home, away from people. That Thanksgiving wasn't easy, though. I told everyone she was ill and she stayed in bed, but Joyce came home sick. I don't know what was wrong with her, but Victoria sent her off to Florida to recuperate before she could find out.''

"It's all so unbelievable!''

"But it's true. She watched over you for years. She was so angry when Social Services tried to take you away from Pete. She called the governor to make sure it wouldn't happen again.''

Oh, God, that was why no one had ever adopted her. Why every couple was found unsuitable.

She realized Martha was still speaking. "When Pete and Maggie were short of cash, she secretly put money in their account. She owned the bank, so no one ever found out. And, of course, with Matt Sloan's help she made sure you got an education, then she made sure you had a job at the bank. When you quit, she fired several people.''

"Unbelievable,'' C.J. breathed again, but it wasn't. Not anymore. Why hadn't she put it together before? No one in Coberville had that much power except Victoria Townsend—her mother.

"Now I'm going to get rid of you like I should have the day you were born.'' The gun raised a fraction, bringing C.J. back to her dire situation.

"If you shoot me, someone's bound to hear,'' she said, stalling, trying to think of a way to escape this crazy woman.

Martha's eyes narrowed. "I've dreamed of shooting you, watching you die. Nothing would give me more pleasure. But I have something else in mind."

C.J. frowned. "What?"

Martha walked over to a door and opened it. Behind was a large closet containing shelves with painting supplies. With her free hand she reached for a knife on the desk by the door. Martha bent down, keeping the gun on C.J., and jammed the knife into a crack in the hardwood floor. She applied pressure and to C.J.'s astonishment a door popped up.

Martha straightened. "Ingenious, don't you think? The door is installed in such a way that it's undetectable. My ancestors were brilliant. This was a hiding place to keep them safe from their enemies—Indians, Mexicans, Yankees or anyone else."

C.J. knew she wasn't just giving her a history lesson. "What's that got to do with me?"

A devious smile appeared on Martha's face. "This is your grave."

Fear darted up C.J.'s spine, stark and vivid. "You're crazy if you think I'm going down there!"

"Don't call me crazy!" Martha raised the gun and struck her on the side of the head.

The blow brought C.J. to her knees. The room spun and she had a sick dizzy feeling. Her face was hot and she reached up and felt the blood oozing through her fingers.

"Get up," Martha ordered.

C.J. stayed where she was, trying to breathe normally, trying to think.

"Look at it this way," Martha said. "In the hole you have a fighting chance. Someone could find you."

C.J. still didn't move. She didn't know what to do.

"Get up, or I'm going to shoot you and push you into the hole. It makes no difference to me. It's your choice."

C.J. got slowly to her feet. She couldn't let this woman shoot her. Not now. Could she overpower her and get away? The room swam around her and she saw two Marthas. She squeezed her eyes tight, realizing she wasn't in any condition to overpower anyone. She had to go down into the hole. It was her only hope. Matthew would find her, she kept saying to herself.

Dizzily she placed her foot on the ladder that led into the hole and started down into the dark void. When she reached the bottom, Martha began to pull up the ladder.

"No," C.J. screamed, and tried to catch the bottom rung. But it was useless; the ladder was gone.

She heard Martha's satisfied laugh. "Did I tell you the room is soundproof? So go ahead and scream your head off—no one'll ever hear you. You'll die a slow painful death and you'll never be able to hurt my Clare. She'll be the head of this family, just like I should have been years ago. Revenge is so sweet." On the last words she slammed the trapdoor shut.

C.J. trembled as the darkness engulfed her. *Don't panic, don't scream,* she repeated as she moved around with her hands in front of her. The blackness was total. The room was small with a dirt floor, and there didn't seem to be anything in it. She backed against a wall and sank to the ground. The place smelled damp and dusty.

The blood continued to drip down her neck. She needed something to stop the bleeding. Removing a boot and sock, she wadded the sock and held it against her face.

Was this how it was going to end? She would die in this tomb before she could savor the knowledge of her parents. *Oh, Matthew, find me. Please find me.*

AFTER HIDING THE LADDER, Martha hurriedly stacked paintings and canvases back in the closet, then closed the door. Seeing blood on the floor, she got some turpentine and paper towels and methodically cleaned it up. Then she studied the room, making sure there was no evidence left, and slipped on a painting smock, putting the gun in one pocket. From the desk she picked up Victoria's will and placed it in the other pocket. She grabbed the bloody paper towels and headed upstairs to the kitchen. She put them in a plastic bag and threw them in the trash compactor. After that she went out the back door. She had to get rid of that stupid girl's horse.

Martha found the horse and led him toward the stables. As she reached the double doors, she heard a car. She hurried inside. Looking out, she saw Rob, Francine and John pull up in front of the house. They'd gone into town to make funeral arrangements for that insipid Stephanie. She led the horse to a stall, deciding to deal with him later. Right now she had to talk to John.

She found him in the study, going through some papers. John glanced up and frowned. "What is it, Martha?"

"I want to talk to you."

"Not now."

"No. Now."

"Can't it wait? I'm not in the mood."

"You'll be in the mood for what I have to say." She smiled and stepped closer. "Remember when I tried to tell you about Pete and Victoria?"

"Don't start that again."

"I have proof I wasn't lying," she said, dropping the will in front of him.

He frowned at her suspiciously, then picked it up and began to read. "My God," he groaned. "The Doe girl is Victoria's child."

"You don't have to worry. I've taken care of everything."

His eyes narrowed. "What do you mean?"

"That's the original of the will. No one will ever see it but us. C. J. Doe won't get a dime from this family, and our Clare will have everything that's rightfully hers."

"What the hell are you talking about?"

"We can be together now. There's nothing standing in our way. I got rid of Stephanie, just like I got rid of Victoria. Now we can be a family—you, Clare and me."

John's eyes widened in horror. "What! You killed Stephanie...and Victoria?"

"I did it for us."

His features contorted with anger. "Are you insane?"

"Don't say that," she warned, clenching and unclenching her hands. "You love me. You always have."

"I loved Victoria."

"No," she denied vehemently. "You only married her for political reasons. You wanted *me*. I had the child you wanted."

"Your memory is very convenient. I wanted you to have an abortion, remember? It was Victoria who insisted you have the baby. She was so gracious, even after the way I'd hurt her."

"No!" Martha screamed. "You love me!"

He shook his head, his expression grim.

"You came to me when she wouldn't have you!" she went on.

"Once, Martha. I slept with you once, and I was drunk at the time. I wanted to hurt Victoria. That's all it was, nothing more."

Martha suddenly paled. "You're lying. Why are you lying?"

"Listen to me. We have to get you some help. I'll call Doc Haslow." His hand touched the phone.

"No." She reached into her pocket and pulled out the gun.

MATTHEW DROVE into the Watsons' yard at breakneck speed, the tires tearing up grass as he slammed on the brakes. Pete and Harry were hurriedly saddling horses. He rushed over to them.

"What happened?"

Without pausing as he tightened the girth of his saddle, Pete said, "She was in the house. When I went to check on her, she was gone. We looked everywhere. Midnight's gone, too. There's only one place she'd go on horseback."

"Seven Trees."

"Yep."

"Why? Why would she go there?"

"Deputy said he heard her talking on the phone."

"I'll meet you there," Matthew said, heading for his car. They were wasting valuable time.

"It's faster through the woods on horseback." Matthew glanced back as Pete swung into the saddle. "You're welcome to ride with me."

Matthew didn't need a second invitation. He ran back, put his foot in the stirrup and swung up behind Pete.

"Meet us at the Townsends'," Matthew shouted to Beal. "It's the big mansion down the road on the right."

With that Pete kicked the horse into a gallop; Harry was right behind. Matthew prayed they wouldn't be too late. They covered ground faster than he'd have believed possible on horseback, and fences were no obstacle. They galloped into the Townsends' yard, and Matthew jumped off the horse before it came to a complete stop. He raced up the steps and burst through the front door without knocking.

Rob and Francine were coming down the stairs, arm in arm. Matthew reached up and caught Rob by the collar, jerking him down and slamming him hard against the wall. "Where's C.J.?" he demanded.

"What the hell?" Rob spluttered.

"Where's C.J.?" Matthew asked again, his hold tightening.

"How the hell should I know?"

"She came over here. Now where is she?"

Harry whipped out his knife. Francine screamed and sagged onto the stairs. Pointing the knife at Rob's throat, Harry said, "Maybe he needs a little persuasion."

"You people are insane!" Rob cried.

"We can do this the easy way or the hard way," Matthew told him. "You can tell me where she is or I'm gonna let Harry cut it out of you."

Rob's face turned red. "I've told you I don't know! She's not here. For God's sake, man, why would I lie?"

The point of the knife touched Rob's throat. He swallowed. "Dad's in his study. Maybe he knows something."

Matthew pulled Rob by the collar down the hall and through the door into John's office. He was only vaguely aware of Beal and the sheriff coming up behind him, for his gaze was riveted on the gun in Martha Cober's hands. The gun pointed at John Townsend.

"Get out of here!" Martha shouted. The gun shook.

"Give me that," John coaxed, walking stiffly toward her with his hand outstretched. "Let's talk."

Martha eyes grew wild and a pitiful sob escaped her lips. "No, you hurt me. How can you hurt me like this? I did everything for you. That Doe girl was just in the way, like Stephanie and Victoria."

"What have you done to C.J.?" Matthew asked fiercely.

Martha didn't answer, her rabid eyes focused on John. "I love you," she wailed.

"I know. Just give me the gun and we'll talk."

"No." She shook her head. "I'm going to hurt you like you hurt me. You always ignored Clare because of Rob and Joyce. Now watch your son die." Without pausing she swung the gun to Rob and fired. The bullet sent him flying backward onto the floor.

So many things happened at once. Francine screamed. Beal and the sheriff drew their guns. Martha turned her gun back on John, but before she could pull the trigger a second time, the sheriff fired, slamming her against the wall.

Martha lay on the floor, blood oozing from her chest. John Townsend lumbered over to his son, tears rolling down his face.

With Beal's help Rob got to his feet. "It's only a shoulder wound," he said shakily, and sank into a chair. If Rob had ever doubted his father's love, he didn't anymore. He saw love in John's eyes for the first time in his life.

Francine ran to her husband and carefully placed her arms around him. Rob rested in the haven of her embrace, knowing he needed her, knowing that somehow he had to salvage the Cober-Townsend family.

Matthew rushed over to Martha. Blood trickled from the corner of her mouth, but she was still alive.

"Where's C.J.?"

"You'll never find her," she gasped.

"Please, don't do this," he begged. "Tell me."

"Never." Her bloodless lips curved into a sinister parody of a smile. "Never...find her." Martha's head fell sideways.

Matthew grabbed her, shook her. "Tell me, dammit, tell me."

Beal laid a hand on his shoulder. "She's dead."

CHAPTER EIGHTEEN

WHERE'S C.J.?

Through Matthew's tortured mind, he heard the voices in the room, but they meant nothing to him.

John ordered Henry to get Rob to the hospital and asked the maid to cover Martha with a sheet. The sheriff was making arrangements for someone to pick up Martha's body.

As people started to leave the room, Matthew stood and faced John. Pete, Harry, Beal and the sheriff stood by the door, but Matthew was only aware of John Townsend.

"Were you in on this with her? Did you hire Dale Weeks?" The words were spoken with force and without an ounce of mercy. Matthew was out for blood.

"Weeks?" John raised a startled eyebrow. "I haven't seen him in years, not since Victoria fired him for rustling cattle."

"If you know anything about this, you'd better tell me, and you'd better tell me now. Otherwise, when I get through with you, you won't know enough people to keep you out of prison."

John trudged heavily back to his desk. "I admit I hired someone to break into Ryder's lab, but everything else was Martha's doing. I knew she was slipping, but I hadn't realized she'd lost complete touch with reality."

John fingered the will. His first reaction was to shove it beneath some papers and destroy it later. After all, the Doe girl was probably dead and Victoria's secret would be safe forever. He stared across the room at Pete Watson and wondered why Victoria had never loved him the way she'd loved Pete. In a moment of bleak honesty he admitted that his selfish womanizing behavior had destroyed any chance of that happening.

The will. Victoria's last wishes. The Doe girl was Victoria's child. *Victoria's child.* The words kept running through his head. Against every instinct he picked up the will and handed it to Matthew. "This might answer some of your questions," he said hoarsely. It occurred to him that this was probably the most selfless thing he would ever do. He glanced at Martha's lifeless body and felt that somehow it would make up for the pain he had caused.

"Where did you get this?" Matthew asked suspiciously.

"Martha brought it in a little while ago. I promise you, Sloan, I didn't know what she was doing."

Matthew quickly read through the document. "My God," he murmured, hardly able to believe what he was reading.

He glanced at Pete and wondered if he knew. Judging by the blank look on Pete's face, Matthew figured he didn't. This was going to be a shock, but unsure of what else to do, he passed him the will. "You need to read this."

As Pete read, his body began to shake. "No, no, no," he moaned, sinking into a chair. Harry stood beside him.

Pete looked up, eyes dazed. "This *can't* be true. She would have told me."

"I don't want to believe it, either," John said, "but it's true."

Through all of this Matthew's mind was buzzing, going in circles. He wondered if C.J. knew the truth. God, C.J. They were missing the point. They had to find her.

"Where is C.J.?" he demanded of John.

"I honestly don't know, but given Martha's state of mind and how much she hated her, I'm afraid she's dead."

"No!" Matthew shouted. "I won't believe that. I'm going over this house inch by inch until I find her."

"You're welcome to search the house, the grounds, but be prepared for the worst."

"We'll start looking," the sheriff said. "Me and my boys will cover the grounds. Matthew, you and the rest comb the house. We're wasting time."

Matthew headed for the door. Pete sat in a state of shock, head lowered, hands dangling limply. Matthew paused for a moment, then said, "Pete, I need your help. C.J. needs us."

Slowly Pete stood up, and they began a diligent search of the house. Matthew could see that Pete's mind was years and years away, and he wondered if C.J. would ever see her father again. The pain was ripping him apart.

Beal came running down the hall. "The sheriff found her horse in the barn. She was here."

"Thank God," Matthew breathed. "That's the clue we're looking for."

"Harry," Beal said, "the sheriff wants you to do some tracking. Martha's horse has been ridden lately. The sheriff feels Martha might have taken C.J. somewhere in the hills and shot her. Let's go."

They all ran for the door. Matthew came to a standstill, looking down the hall. He felt an intuition, something in his gut he couldn't explain.

"Come on," Beal called from the doorway.

"Go ahead. I'll catch up."

Beal ran back to him. "What is it? Don't you want to find her?"

Matthew spared him a chilling glance and Beal immediately held up his hands. "Okay, bad question."

"There's someplace in this house we haven't searched, something we haven't found. I don't know where or what, but I can't leave. I'm going to check some more."

As Matthew walked down the hall, Beal shook his head and turned toward the door.

Matthew found Pete behind him. The man was drawn and haggard. He looked as if he'd aged ten years in the past ten minutes. "Aren't you going out to search?"

"I trust your instincts. If you feel there's something here, then I'm gonna help you."

"Okay."

Thirty minutes later Matthew and Pete met back in John's study. They'd found nothing in the house, no trace that C.J. had ever been there.

"Help us," Matthew appealed to John. "Tell us Martha's favorite places, where she liked to go."

John sat in his chair, staring at Martha's sheet-covered body. He looked like a man who'd finally had to pay the piper, and the price was more than he could bear.

He glanced at Matthew. "She has a studio in the basement. Did you check there?"

"No," Matthew answered. "How do we find it?"

"Follow the hall to the right until you come to a door. The stairs will lead you to the basement."

He raced down the steps with Pete following. He paused at an open door and then walked in. It was obviously a studio, littered with paintings and painting supplies.

One painting stood out among the rest and he walked over to it, staring at the dark-haired beauty. He caught his breath, knowing without being told that this was Victoria's mother. She looked just like C.J.

"My precious baby," Pete moaned, staring at the painting.

Matthew put an arm around his shoulder. "We'll find her."

"Yes," Pete agreed. "Yes."

"My guess is that Martha brought C.J. down here to tell her about her mother. C.J. probably didn't believe her and Martha showed her this painting. But what happened next?"

Neither spoke for a moment.

"We have to check every inch of this room," Matthew said, determined not to let his fears drag him down. They moved canvases and easels in their search. Matthew jerked open the closet door and went inside. Rummaging through the contents, he found nothing.

C.J. FELT WEAK, but she kept repeating the words to herself. *Victoria and Pete are my parents.* She should have guessed. The truth had been there, staring her in the face. She'd always felt so close to Pete. Even when she was little, he was the one she ran to when she was hurt. She could talk to him, tell him her feelings. There was a bond there, a bond neither of them had suspected.

And Victoria was always so nice to her, going out of her way to talk to her. Little memories surfaced in her mind—the way Victoria used to look at her, the way she'd touch her hair, her clothes, her face. The truth was there in Victoria's eyes, in her manner. Why hadn't she recognized it?

Her body stiffened. Was that a noise? She listened closely. She heard nothing.

MATTHEW THREW PAINTINGS, blank canvases and easels out into the hall. He kept searching, looking, until...

Behind some canvases stacked against one wall he found a wooden ladder. He knelt down, frowning at it. What use was a ladder in this room? He ran a finger along a rung and it came away with a coating of red dust. Where did it come from?

Matthew turned to Pete. "Look at this ladder. What's it doing here?"

Pete squatted down. "It's very old. You can tell by the wood, and it's homemade. See how the rungs are notched in?"

"Yes, but what's it for?"

"Don't know."

"Let's think about this," Matthew said. "There's nowhere to go below because this is the basement, so it has to go up, to a secret room maybe. Let's check out the ceiling."

The ceiling was made of ash paneling. Matthew found a hammer and pulled up a chair to stand on. He began to work at the panels until they came loose enough for him to look inside.

"Damn. There's nothing up here but rafters and wiring." As he drew his hand back, he noticed the dust on his hand. It was light brown, not reddish like that on the ladder.

He jumped down. "Look at this." He showed Pete his hands. "It's different from the dirt on the ladder. Where does that red dust come from?"

Pete shook his head.

"Martha said we'd never find her," Matthew said. "She was so sure, glad even." He wiped his hands down his jeans. "What did she know that no one else does?"

Pete shook his head again.

"Go upstairs and ask John about secret rooms and about

this ladder. Also ask the servants. I'm gonna check and see what's behind these walls.''

Pete quickly left and Matthew began to tear at the walls. Ten minutes later he stood frustrated. There was nothing but studs and wiring.

''Find anything?'' Pete asked when he returned.

''No,'' Matthew said. ''What did you learn?''

''John didn't know anything about a ladder. He said there once was a secret room in the master bedroom, but it was turned into a dressing room years ago. The servants didn't know anything. Said Martha never let anyone down here.''

''Dammit, Pete, what are we missing?'' He raked both hands through his hair in an impatient gesture and took a deep breath. ''Let's look at this another way. If the ladder doesn't go up, then it has to go down.''

''Down where?''

''I don't know, but this ladder was used for something in here.'' He picked up the hammer; kneeling, he began to pound on the hardwood floor, looking for hollow places. ''Get me a knife,'' he told Pete.

Pete handed him the knife from the desk. Matthew stuck it in the small cracks of the old hardwood floor and exerted pressure. He did this all over the room. Nothing happened. The floor was solid.

Matthew leaned back on his heels, feeling utterly defeated.

Beal appeared in the doorway and glanced around at the hanging ceiling panels and torn walls. ''My God, Matthew, what are you doing?''

Matthew didn't hear him. His thoughts were turned inward. ''Where are you, C.J.?'' he called. ''Help me. Please help me find you.''

Beal and Pete exchanged worried glances, then Beal

pulled something out of his pocket. A brightly colored scarf. "Is this C.J.'s?" he asked Pete.

Pete nodded, stroking the scarf. "Where was it?"

"Not far from the house, by a creek. The sheriff is centering the search around that area." He turned to Matthew. "We need your help."

Matthew glanced at him dazedly.

Beal showed him the scarf. "It belongs to C.J. Give it up, Matthew. There's nothing here. She's somewhere in the hills. The sheriff feels sure of it."

Matthew got slowly to his feet, wondering if he was losing his mind.

"Come on," Beal encouraged. "We're wasting precious time."

Matthew followed him to the door. Maybe Beal was right.

There was nothing here.

C.J. WAS FLOATING in and out of consciousness. She heard something again and fought to remain conscious. Was someone upstairs? Was Matthew searching for her? She could feel him so strongly. Was he calling to her? Or was she just hearing things?

She had to let him know where she was. She felt around on the cold dirt until she located the boot she'd taken off earlier. Then with every ounce of strength she had in her, she threw it toward the ceiling and screamed, "Matthew!" As the scream left her mouth, her head fell forward and the darkness engulfed her completely.

MATTHEW STOPPED in the doorway. "Did you hear that?" he asked, turning back into the room.

"I didn't hear anything," Beal said. "Did you, Pete?"

"No…"

"I heard something, I tell you."

Beal laid his hand on Matthew's arm. "I know you're worried, but please think rationally. There's—"

"Don't patronize me." Matthew shook off Beal's hand.

"Matthew," Beal pleaded, but Matthew wasn't listening. He was kneeling by the ladder, studying it again, trying to figure out logically what it was doing here. Then he saw it.

He whirled around and shouted, "Look at this!"

Both Beal and Pete crossed to his side.

Matthew pointed to red spots on the top three rungs. "This is blood. I didn't see it before because it looks so much like the dust, but it's blood." His finger touched one of the spots. "It's not completely dry."

Beal knelt down to investigate. "You're right! It is blood. And if you look at the ladder from this perspective, you can see the dust is disturbed all the way down."

"Someone used this ladder recently!" Matthew said excitedly.

"And that person was bleeding."

Matthew didn't want to consider what that meant. He just wanted to find C.J. and he felt he was close. "Help me, Beal. Help me figure this out. Where does the ladder go? It doesn't go up or down. I've checked the ceiling and the floor."

"Let's look for more blood. That might give us a clue," Beal suggested.

On hands and knees they examined the floor, the corners, the crevices. Matthew was the first to respond. "Here, I've found some," he exclaimed, kneeling by the closet door. "See." He pointed to faint splotches on the floor. "You can hardly see them. They're about the same color as the wood."

"Yeah," Beal said, "and there's several by this door. What's behind it?"

"A supply closet," Matthew replied, and yanked open the door. "Let's get these canvases out of here. I want to look at the floorboards."

Pete and Beal helped him remove every canvas. Matthew stared at the floor. "The blood ends here." He pointed to an area just inside the door.

Beal frowned. "What does it mean?"

"I'm betting there's something under this floor. Something the ladder goes to. It has to be. Pete, give me that knife."

Pete quickly got the knife and Matthew began to insert it in the cracks, hoping and praying the floor would give, but nothing happened.

"Damn," he muttered, leaning back on his heels. "Am I losing my mind? Am I just grasping at straws?"

"You've tried the boards sideways. Now try from the front of each board," Pete said. "If there's a trapdoor, it stands to reason it would open that way."

"You're right." Matthew began to do as Pete had suggested. The first time nothing, the second time nothing, the third time nothing. Frustration maddened him, but he had to keep trying. He took a deep breath and inserted the knife again, and finally he felt something. Then, as they all watched in shock, a door popped up.

"My God!" Matthew cried, peering down into the dark hole. "C.J.!" he shouted over and over. "C.J.!" But there was only a deadly silence.

"There're grooves here for the ladder. Bring it over. I'm going down." Matthew felt fear dig into his spine once again.

As he and Beal dealt with the ladder, Pete went to get a flashlight.

Matthew started down, but Beal stopped him. "Wait for the flashlight. You can't see a thing down there."

"I don't care, I'm going," he muttered. He'd taken one step on the ladder when Pete came back with a flashlight.

Matthew grabbed the light and shined it into the hole. He couldn't see anything but dirt. Then... The dim light pooled around something he recognized. "There's a boot! It's C.J.'s boot, and there's blood everywhere," he choked out. Hurriedly he began to back down the ladder.

Beal stopped him again. "Matthew, this doesn't look good. Be prepared."

Matthew didn't want to hear what the detective was saying, but he knew Beal thought she was dead. He wouldn't accept it, not now. She *had* to be alive.

As he reached the bottom of the ladder, he saw her, and all his fears became a reality. She sat against a wall, head tilted forward, her hair all around her, and she was covered in blood. He dropped down beside her, his breath in his throat. She was so still. With a shaky hand he touched her blood-soaked hair.

He fought the tears that stung his eyes. Her blouse was also blood-soaked, and her face was dead-white. Trembling, he reached for the pulse in her throat.

"Is she down there?" Beal shouted.

Matthew had to swallow twice before he could answer. "Yes. I'm bringing her up."

Scooping her into his arms, he felt her blood soak through his shirt. Almost paralyzed with fear and pain, he held her with one arm and carried her up the ladder.

He gently placed her on the floor.

Pete squatted beside her, tears streaming down his haggard face. "Is she...dead?"

Matthew had to swallow again. "I don't know. I couldn't feel a pulse, but I'm not sure I..."

His voice trailed off and he kissed her cheek.. "C.J., can you hear me? Please, can you hear me."

A sound, like a sob, left her throat.

"She's alive!" Matthew gasped, drawing air into his lungs. "Oh, God, she's still alive, but barely. We have to get her to a hospital."

C.J. AWOKE in a strange room. For a moment she was disoriented, her mind fuzzy, her body sore and aching. But then, through the haze, everything came flooding back. "Oh," she moaned. "Oh…"

The two men by her bedside were immediately alert. "C.J., are you okay?"

She knew that voice. Matthew. He'd found her. She gave him a tentative smile. "I knew you'd come for me," she said, her voice weak but filled with certainty. Looking into his eyes, she asked, "Is it true?"

He knew what she was asking and he nodded.

"Victoria Townsend is my mother." She had to say the words to make sure she wasn't dreaming. "And…" Suddenly a strong hand gripped hers.

"I'm so sorry, my precious girl. I had no idea."

She knew that voice, too. Pete. Her father. She managed another smile. "I know. It's okay." She wanted to reassure him.

Matthew watched as they embraced, trying to make up for missing a lifetime of father-daughter hugs. He went to get the doctor.

THE NEXT TIME C.J. awoke, the same two men were sitting by her bedside. Pete was slumped in his chair, head bobbing on his chest. Matthew's head was tilted to one side. He had a growth of beard and wore the same clothes she'd last seen him in. She knew without a doubt they'd been here the whole time. What stubborn men. Oh, but the thought gave her such a feeling of happiness.

She moved slightly and both men were instantly on their feet, gazing down at her with worried expressions. She smiled, and they both relaxed.

"How are you?" Pete asked.

"Better."

Matthew pushed the hair away from her bandage. "How's the head?"

"Still throbs a little."

A nurse poked her head around the door and said, "Mr. Sloan, you have a long-distance call from New York. If you like, I can have it transferred to this room."

New York, C.J. thought. Why would someone call him here? Unless…

"Yes, that'll be fine," Matthew replied.

As Matthew picked up the receiver, Pete squeezed her hand. C.J. turned toward him. "I want to hear all about my mother," she said.

Pete started to talk, but she was half listening to Matthew.

"Yes, Gail. It's okay. When? Can't you get another postponement? No. I guess the judge has been more than lenient…. I know I need to be there. It's just…okay. I'll catch the next flight out of Austin."

Those last words caught C.J.'s full attention. She shifted to look at Matthew, and she could see that a part of him was already back in New York.

"I guess you heard," he said tiredly, his eyes holding hers. "Jury selection starts day after tomorrow. I have to get back to New York. I need some time to prepare."

She'd known Matthew was going to leave someday, but she hadn't expected it to be this soon. Not when she was in the hospital. Not when she was so vulnerable. Not yet.

So many words hovered on her lips. "Yes, of course," were the ones that slipped out.

Matthew wanted to hold her, to touch her. He had to, or he wasn't going to be able to leave. He glanced at Pete.

Pete received the message loud and clear. "Think I'll stretch my legs," he said.

As the door closed, they gazed at each other.

Don't go, her heart cried.

She knew he had to. No commitments, she'd told him that night in Austin. And yet their relationship had gone way beyond that. Now they had to deal with their two different worlds. Matthew's career, his whole life, was in New York. Although she was too weak at the moment to contemplate living in the big city, she knew she'd live anywhere to be with him. But Matthew's roots were in Coberville, and C.J. was hoping she would be the catalyst that would pull him back. So she had to be strong. She had to let him go with dignity…without tears…without regrets.

She was the first to speak. "We knew this was going to happen. Your life is in New York."

"Yes…I have responsibilities, obligations."

"I know," she said quietly.

"I have to go."

"I know."

"I don't want to leave you like this."

"I'll be fine."

Why was she taking this so calmly? he wondered. Why wasn't she begging him to stay? But he knew that wasn't C.J. And he suddenly realized she was being strong for his sake.

Matthew leaned over and gently kissed her lips. No response. Except when he drew back, he saw that her bottom lip trembled and she caught it between her teeth.

The lady wasn't as strong as she appeared. He took a deep breath and wondered how to handle that stiff pride of hers. Then he asked himself what he'd do if she begged him to stay. He didn't know.

The thought of bringing her to New York drifted briefly through his mind. But he couldn't take her away from the one thing she'd waited so long to have—a father. He couldn't be that selfish. Besides, she'd hate New York and he'd be spending sixteen to eighteen hours a day on the Peterman case. Their two worlds had now collided, and he was feeling the force of the impact far more than he'd feared.

Taking another deep breath, he sat on the bed and gathered her into his arms, careful of the bandaged cut on her head. The smell of antiseptic mingling with the glorious scent of her wafted through his weary system. His lips met hers in a warm tender kiss.

C.J. hesitated for a moment, then eagerly kissed him back. She had to. Oh, she needed this!

His stubble against her sensitive skin was an erotic awakening. It reminded her of a morning in Austin when the two of them were alone, facing insurmountable odds. Now the odds of their ever being together were just as insurmountable.

She moaned and wrapped her arms around his neck, her hands smoothing and stroking his hair, his face. She wanted to remember every contour, every detail about him.

Matthew's hands found the opening in the hospital gown and he caressed her bare skin. Deep pleasure spiraled through him. Oh, yes, he needed this.

For a moment they were lost in the heady sensation of each other, making every touch, every kiss a fervent prayer.

Finally they drew apart. "I'd better go," he said in a raw voice, his hand stroking her hair.

"Yes." The back of her hand brushed against his cheek. *Don't cry.*

"I've got to get cleaned up and say goodbye to my mom."

"Yes," she said again.

He sighed heavily and got to his feet. So many times he had questioned his emotions for her. Staring at the sadness in her eyes and feeling the pain in his chest, he knew he loved her. And he knew she loved him, too. Now they'd put that love to the ultimate test. It would either thrive and find a way to survive between their two worlds, or it would die as they each went on with their separate lives. That thought intensified the pain he felt in his chest.

"If you need me, call."

"I will," she replied, fighting back tears.

"You sure you'll be okay?" he asked, unable to take the necessary steps away from her.

"Yes, I'll be fine."

He swallowed hard and headed for the door.

"Matthew…"

He glanced back.

"Thank you," she said. "Thank you for everything."

He nodded and opened the door. Pete walked in. Matthew looked back one more time. C.J. was gazing into Pete's eyes, her hand clutched tightly in his.

C.J. would be fine. She had her father.

Matthew walked out the door and down the hall and— maybe—out of her life.

THE NEXT DAY two dozen red roses arrived. Without reading the card C.J. knew who'd sent them. Matthew. She stared at the phone, remembering his words. "If you need me, call.'' She needed him, she needed him—more than her parents, more than the very air she breathed. But she couldn't call and tell him that. Matthew had to come back on his own. It had to be his decision.

THE NEXT FEW DAYS were overwhelming. The doctor said she was fine, but she was going to be weak for a while because she'd lost a lot of blood. So many people came to wish her well. The Townsends came, all of them, even John. It was hard to accept their smiles and apologies, but she knew she had to. They were her family.

For years she'd wanted only one thing—to find her parents. Now she had. All her life she'd felt so incomplete, so empty, because she didn't know who she was. Funny, she still had that same feeling, and she knew why. Matthew wasn't here. He wasn't here to share her life. Was she destined, like her mother, to love a man she could never have?

EPILOGUE

THE LAW OFFICES of Newman, Feldman, Smythe, Dickerson and Sloan occupied the forty-second floor of the Manhattan skyscraper. Matthew's office was decorated in a Southwestern motif, in tune with his Texas roots. Colorful area rugs enhanced the hardwood floor. Western paintings graced the walls. On the mantel over a stone fireplace a collection of horse sculptures was displayed. A wreath made of rope and barbed wire hung on the stone. The office and decor had been a gift from the firm when he'd become partner.

The room wasn't him, Matthew thought as he glanced around. It was too artificial. He shoved his hands in his pockets and stared out the floor-to-ceiling windows that looked onto the New York skyline. His gaze focused on the street, seething with activity. Yellow cabs jockeyed for position in the heavy five-o'clock traffic. People jostled shoulder to shoulder in their eagerness to get home. But in his mind's eye, Matthew saw only a beautiful woman with long black hair and sparkling green eyes.

"Matthew, come join the party," a cheerful voice called.

"In a minute," Matthew answered, and turned to see Gail Davis standing in the doorway. Tall and slim with dark hair and eyes, Gail was a woman any man would want. But not him.

Gail noticed his somber expression. "Aren't you happy? We won."

"Of course I'm happy about the win."

"Then what's wrong?" she asked. "You haven't been the same since you came back from Texas."

It was true. He hadn't been the same. A big empty space occupied his chest—the space where his heart used to be.

Realizing that Gail was waiting for a response, he said, "You're right. I've had to force my way through every second of this trial. My cases used to consume me, but this time I couldn't concentrate. My mind kept wandering and that frightened me, especially since I held a man's life in my hands. I don't have the same drive, the same goals, anymore."

"You're not thinking of quitting, are you?"

Matthew looked her in the eye. "I'm thinking about making some changes, yes. I'm not sure exactly what."

"You're experiencing burnout, that's all." She sent him a consoling smile. "Take some time off—take a vacation. That's probably all you need."

"It isn't," he said, and he shrugged wearily.

Gail studied him. "Does this discontent have something to do with that woman you helped in Coberville? The one who found her parents after so many years—and became a wealthy woman overnight?"

C.J. Every day he waited for her call, but the call never came. She was busy with her new life, her new family, and he was happy for her. But it hurt like hell that she'd forgotten him so easily.

His answer was sharper than he'd intended. "Why do females always assume that when a man's upset, it has something to do with a woman?"

"And why do males have such a hard time admitting it?" she countered.

"You're right." Matthew gave a lopsided grin. "C.J. has changed my life dramatically. I thought I had everything I ever wanted right here in New York, but she made me realize what's really important in life—home and family. I'd always taken those things for granted. She even made me realize that I'm a country boy at heart. There are so many other things that..." His voice trailed off. He knew he was rambling, showing Gail a side of his personality she'd never seen before—a vulnerable side.

"Sounds like a remarkable woman," Gail said.

Matthew didn't miss the envy in her voice. "Gail—"

She held up a hand. "Don't apologize. You can't make yourself feel something that's not there."

"Mr. Sloan, your mother's on line one." His secretary's voice cut through the conversation.

Gail forced a smile. "You'd better get that. Then come have a glass of champagne. It can work wonders."

"I will," Matthew answered, a slight smile curling the corners of his mouth.

Matthew scowled at the blinking red light on the telephone. Another call from his mother. Just what he needed, he thought sarcastically—more tidbits on C.J.'s new life. God, who was he trying to kid? He lived for these calls.

THE COBER RANCH buzzed with excitement. A victory barbecue for Rob Townsend was in full swing. People spilled from the house onto the patio, lawn and around the pool and garden.

C.J. stood with the Townsends, shaking hands and smiling until she thought her face would crack. Being part of such a prominent family was hard to get used to, but she was trying, and she had to admit the Townsends were, too—especially Rob. The family tragedy had had a profound effect on him. His whole personality seemed to have changed. The reckless philanderer had turned into a devoted father and loving husband. Francine was positively glowing by his side.

Rob had taken his place as head of the Cober-Townsend family with pride and determination. His first step had been to put his family back together, and that family now included C.J. These days C.J. was proud to call him her brother.

Two weeks before the election Rob had called a national press conference and told the world about his half sister and the circumstances of her birth. He welcomed her into the family and apologized for all the pain she'd suffered. The story touched the hearts of everyone, and he'd won the election in a landslide victory.

C.J. moved away from the crowd and noticed Pete and Harry talking to Miss Emma and Mrs. Sloan. She smiled, hardly recognizing the two men she loved so dearly.

They both wore new suits. Harry had cut his hair and beard into a short neat style. He reminded her of a college professor. The new look wasn't only for her sake, though. Miss Emma had a lot to do with it. When she'd come to visit C.J. in the hospital, Harry had been there. The moment had been tense, but eventually they'd started talking, and now it was as if the many years of estrangement had never been. Harry sometimes spent two or three nights in town. True love was amazing, C.J. thought.

True love. Everlasting love. She clenched her hands into fists and closed her eyes for a second. She wouldn't think of him. But his face swam before her, and she hated herself for that weakness.

Opening her eyes, she forced her thoughts in another direction. Pete. He was also sporting a new haircut, looking tall and dapper. C.J. could see what had attracted Victoria to her handsome father.

Father. At first the kinship name had rolled around in her head like a foreign word. She couldn't understand why, because Pete had always been her father. He'd raised her, taught her everything she knew and made her the strong independent woman she was today. For years she'd been searching for something she already had—a loving father. Her obsession with finding her parents had blinded her to the treasures in her life. She wouldn't make that mistake again.

Rob put an arm around her shoulder, bringing her attention back to the party. "Thanks for letting us have this event here," he said with a bright smile.

She frowned. "This house is much more yours than mine, and you can have a party here any time you want."

"That's not true, C.J.," he denied, "and you might as well get used to it. Mom left you the ranch."

He was right. Victoria had been exceptionally generous in her second will. C.J. had been left Seven Trees, the land surrounding it and controlling interest in the Cober bank. Rob, Joyce and Clare already had land and homes in their own names. All the other land, banks and newspapers she shared with the rest of the family. She'd expected that the Townsends would try to have the will broken, but they hadn't. This time they'd respected their mother's last wishes.

It hadn't been easy for anyone, but they were all adjusting. She and John Townsend would never be the best of friends, but at least he now treated her with courtesy. These days he was more interested in his twenty-five-year-old nurse than in causing problems.

C.J. worried about Clare, though. She was having a hard time accepting Martha Cober as her real mother, because of the evil Martha had wreaked on the family.

Some distance away C.J. saw Clare in the crowd, looking pensive but lovely in new clothes and hairdo. Joyce and Francine had taken Clare and C.J. in hand, spending a day in Austin and having them done over from head to toe. Clare looked enchanting, and the blue suit brought out the dazzling blue of her eyes.

C.J. crossed to her. "You'd better smile, or Joyce and Francine will be enrolling us in a self-esteem class," she teased.

"I'm so tired of smiling," Clare groaned, then glanced around to make sure Joyce and Francine weren't watching. "Do you think anyone would notice if I slipped away?"

"Yes, I'd notice," C.J. said, feeling closer to Clare than anyone else in the family. "And if I have to endure this, so do you."

"But you're so much better at it. You're so beautiful. Why Joyce and Francine thought you needed a makeover is beyond me."

"They wanted to take some of the rough edges off, I suppose," C.J. answered, and squinted down at herself. The slim emerald-green dress with matching jacket was an original, and every time she thought about the cost, she felt guilty and a little stupid, but it fit like a dream. Her long hair had been trimmed and now hung in a disarrayed style to the middle of her back. She wore a little makeup. That was as far as she'd go.

"I wish I had your rough edges." Clare laughed lightly, then her face became serious. "C.J., I—"

"If you apologize for Martha one more time, I'm going to get angry." C.J. knew exactly where Clare was headed. She carried the sins of her mother like a weight, a very heavy weight.

"I just feel—"

"Well, don't," C.J. said. "You are *nothing* like her. So stop blaming yourself and get on with your life." A band had begun to play in the background. "Go and kick up your heels. It's time to forget all the pain." And then, as if summoned, a man came up and asked Clare to dance. C.J. smiled at her as she moved away.

Then C.J. froze. She saw a tall man standing on the patio, looking out over the crowd. *Matthew*. What was he doing here? God, he looked handsome in his dark suit and white shirt! The city man was back. Her heart started to pound against her ribs, and she felt an excitement she hadn't felt in months.

Her first reaction was to run into his arms, but her courage wasn't that great.

She couldn't face him in front of all these people, she decided, and slipped quietly into the house. Luckily everyone was gathering on the patio for the dancing, and the living room was empty.

PETE NOTICED MATTHEW. He glanced suspiciously at Belle. "You called him, didn't you?"

Belle smiled at her son and waved. "Yes," she replied. "We talked about it, remember? We agreed they were both miserable, so I invited him to the party. I also mentioned a few things about C.J."

"You know I don't like interfering."

"It's not interfering," she told him. "It's a parent's right. You have to learn these things."

"I don't know, Belle. C.J. didn't look too happy when she went into the house. She's had enough pain. I want her to be happy."

"Trust me. Matthew will follow her in a few minutes." The words had barely left her mouth before Matthew walked into the house.

Belle winked at Pete.

He smiled. "Come on, Belle Sloan, let's dance. I can't

let my brother have more fun than me.'' Harry and Emma sailed by them in a waltz. ''Besides, our kids can sort out their own lives.''

C.J. STARED UP at the painting of Victoria Cober Townsend above the fireplace. In her early twenties, she was beautiful with her long blond hair and blue eyes. It was hard to believe this woman was her mother.

Matthew stood in the doorway. Just the sight of her sent a warm glow through his body. She looked different—sophisticated and elegant—and he wondered if the things his mother had said were true. Was she unhappy? She didn't look it. She was radiant and she had a right to be.

She finally knew who she was, and the whole town had embraced her. A regular Cinderella story, from rags to riches, and everyone wanted to talk to her, shake her hand, wish her well. She was no longer the town outcast. She was now the queen of Coberville.

''She's very beautiful.''

C.J. didn't turn around or she would have seen that Matthew wasn't looking at the painting, but at her.

''Yes, I can hardly believe she's my mother. I don't resemble her at all.''

''You're thinking about her coloring,'' he said. ''Look at the cheekbones, the shape of her eyes and face. They're the same, plus you have her gracefulness.''

C.J. took a deep breath and turned around, unprepared for the impact of seeing him face-to-face after so many months. Her pulse leaped, and her knees felt weak.

When she didn't say anything, he asked, ''How are you?''

''Fine.''

''You look wonderful.''

''Thank you.'' She hated that they were talking like polite strangers and not two people who had once shared something special.

"Is it everything you thought it would be?"

"What?" She frowned.

"Knowing who you are."

No, she wanted to say. *Without you it means nothing.* Instead, she said quietly, "Sometimes it's overwhelming."

"I can imagine," he said, studying the lovely lines of her face. "I have something for you," he added abruptly.

Until he gave it to her, she hadn't noticed the big manila envelope in his hand. All she could see was his face, his eyes...

Taking the envelope, she asked, "What is it?"

"Open it and find out."

She undid the clip and pulled out a document. A corrected birth certificate. Christina Jane Cober Watson, the name read. A lump formed in her throat and for a moment she couldn't speak. Looking at her name on a birth certificate suddenly made it all real. Up until that moment she'd felt as if she was living in a dream. but now she knew she wasn't. She was Christina Jane Cober Watson.

"Christina was the name Victoria wanted you to have. It was in her will," he told her.

"I know," she said, fighting back tears. "Thank you."

"You're welcome."

She turned to put the document in a desk drawer, knowing she had to get away from him or she was going to make a fool of herself.

"I'd better get back to the party," she said, walking past him.

"C.J.?"

"Yes?" She stopped, but didn't face him.

"Do you ever think about us? That night in Austin?"

She clasped her hands together. "No," she lied.

"I think about it all the time. It keeps me awake at night, and when I do sleep, I dream of you and me together, with nothing but your hair around us. But when I awake, you're not there."

She couldn't take it anymore. She couldn't keep pretending, lying. Whirling around, green eyes blazing, she said, "No, I'm here in Coberville, where you left me without a word for months."

"I had to go, C.J. I thought you understood that. We both needed time, but I told myself if you needed me, you'd call and ask me to come home. If you had, I would've been here in a heartbeat."

She fought her pride and admitted, "I wanted to, so many times."

A long silence. Then Matthew said, "There's a reason I came back."

Her eyes flew to his. "What?"

"You still haven't paid me for all the work I did in finding your parents."

For a moment she was completely disconcerted. He wanted money. "How much do I owe you?" she asked shortly.

"A lifetime of sweet passionate kisses," was the answer.

How could she have forgotten? The kisses. Suddenly all the doubts and fears disappeared. She smiled and walked closer to him, so close she could feel the heat from his body. "Never let it be said that I don't pay my debts." She stood on tiptoe and gently kissed his lips.

"That's only a start," he whispered, his dark eyes meeting hers. "Try again."

A wicked smile curved her lips, and she pressed her body against his, savoring the tensing of his muscles and the rapid beat of his heart. She wrapped her arms around his neck, and her lips teased, tasted, caressed until his control broke.

He groaned deep in his throat, and his arms tightened around her, his lips capturing hers in a heated kiss.

Love, too long denied, blazed through their veins, welding their hearts and bodies in sweet harmony. Matthew's mouth opened hungrily over hers, and she met it with a hunger of her own. The kiss went on and on, both needing, both giving, never wanting it to end.

Eventually Matthew rested his forehead against hers.

"Paid in full?" she asked, a humorous glimmer in her eyes.

"Never. I'm just catching my breath," he replied mischievously, then asked, "why did you cut your hair?"

"You said I looked wonderful," she reminded him.

"You do," he said, kissing her nose, her cheeks. "But I want my C.J. the way she was."

"She's still here."

"I know." His lips found hers again. "I want you so badly I can't stand it," he whispered against her mouth. "It's been too long."

She wanted him, too. That was the problem. Could she be an occasional lover?

C.J. pushed out of his arms. "I can't do this."

If she'd hit him, he wouldn't have looked more shocked, and she hastened to explain. "I don't want to be like my mother. Loving a man I can never have. I just can't make love with you and watch you go back to New York."

He breathed a deep sigh of relief. "You don't have to."

She frowned, not understanding.

"I've talked with my partners, and I'm going to cut back on my caseload, way back, until we can work things out. The rest of the time I'll be here in Coberville opening my dad's old office. Even a chicken thief needs a lawyer."

The blood started to pump through her veins with amazing speed, but she had to ask, "Are you sure?"

"Yes. It's simple. In searching for your identity, I realized I'd been running from mine. Living in Matt Sloan's shadow wasn't easy. I felt I had to leave Coberville to make my own way in life. I did, but that man in New York wasn't the real me, and I've been denying that for a long time."

C.J. listened with her heart full. She realized, for perhaps the first time, that having loving parents didn't guarantee a happy life. Matthew had been struggling with his own demons.

"My father knew what was important—home, family and love. The truth is, I want those things, too. It's taken me a long time to realize that. I've had my fifteen minutes of fame, and now I'm ready for a lifetime of happiness. That is—" he stopped, and looked deeply into her eyes "—if a certain black-haired green-eyed beauty will agree to add Sloan to that long list of names she's just acquired."

C.J. drew back, her eyes clouded with things Matthew didn't understand.

"Are you asking me to marry you?" Her voice was faint and puzzled.

"Yes," he answered slowly, wondering why they weren't halfway to heaven by now.

Her eyes narrowed. "Haven't you forgotten something?"

Matthew searched his brain, and for the life of him he couldn't find a thing he'd missed, but he was willing to go over the details. "I've told you how much I love—"

"No, you haven't."

He blinked in confusion, then it hit him. "C.J., surely you don't doubt that I love you!"

"I need to hear you say it," she replied, her voice full

of yearning. "I've never heard the words before, and it's very important to me."

Hearing the ache in her voice, it finally dawned on him that she'd never heard or spoken those three little words in her whole life. The thought tore at his heart. How could he be so stupid?

He cupped her face in his hands, staring into her beautiful eyes. "C.J., I love you. I love you more than life itself. You're the first thing I think of in the morning, the last thing I think of at night, and all the hours in between are filled with thoughts of you. I can't eat, I can't sleep, and if you don't kiss me soon, I'm going to explode."

She turned her face and kissed the palm of his hand. His hand closed into a fist, as if he needed to save that kiss for the rest of his life.

Her eyes melted into his. "I love you, too, Matthew Sloan, Jr.," she whispered, and began kissing his cheeks, his chin, the hollow of his neck.

Her gentle touch sent the blood rushing through his veins. "We're going to say those words every day for the rest of our lives," he told her. "That is, if *you* ever get around to saying yes to my proposal."

"Oh, Matthew, yes, yes!" she cried a moment before his lips took hers.

With each aching breath, each pleasurable moan, a tidal wave of passion and love flowed between them. Matthew's hands slid down her back to her bottom, pressing her hard against his hips. "Can you feel how much I want you?" he asked with a ragged sigh.

"I'd have to be numb not to." She laughed, then gasped.

"What are you going to do about it?"

C.J. took his hand and led him toward the stairs.

In the background the citizens of Coberville laughed, talked and danced. For the first time C.J. felt like one of them. Whole and complete. And loved. Very loved.

Coming in January 2000
Classics for two of your favorite series.

SECRET VOWS by **REBECCA YORK**
— & —
KELSEY ROBERTS

From the best of Rebecca York's

Till Death Us Do Part

Marissa Devereaux discovered that paradise wasn't all it was cracked up to be when she was abducted by extremists on the Caribbean island of Costa Verde.... But things only got worse when Jed Prentiss showed up, claiming to be her fiancé.

From the best of Kelsey Roberts's

Unlawfully Wedded

J.D. was used to getting what he wanted from people, and he swore he'd use that skill to hunt down Tory's father's killer. But J.D. wanted much more than gratitude from his sassy blond bride—and he wasn't going to clue her in. She'd find out soon enough...if she survived to hear about it.

Available January 2000 at your favorite retail outlet.

PSBR2200

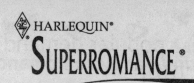

HARLEQUIN®
SUPERROMANCE®

Pregnant...and
on her own?

HER BEST FRIEND'S BABY by C.J. Carmichael
(Superromance #891)
Mallory and Drew are best friends—and then they share an
unexpected night of passion. Mallory's pregnant.... Being
"just friends" again is impossible. Which leaves being lovers—
or getting married.
On sale January 2000

EXPECTATIONS by Brenda Novak
(Superromance #899)
Jenna's pregnant by her abusive ex-husband. Her first love,
Adam, comes back on the scene, wanting to reconcile. Will he still
want her when he learns she's pregnant with another man's child?
On sale February 2000

BECAUSE OF THE BABY by Anne Haven
(Superromance #905)
They're friends and colleagues. One hot summer night, Melissa
and Kyle give in to the secret attraction they've never acknowledged.
It's changed their lives forever—because Melissa is pregnant.
On sale March 2000

Available at your favorite retail outlet.

HARLEQUIN®
Makes any time special ™

Visit us at www.romance.net

HSR9ML00